Encrypting My Heart

Copyright

Paperback ISBN: 978-1-961966-58-1

Published by: Carxander Publishing
Minnesota

Opening Quote

You got all of me. I belong to you. Yeah, you're my everything. In case you didn't know, I'm crazy 'bout you. I would be lyin' if I said that I could live this life without you. Even though I don't tell you all the time, you had my heart a long, long time ago. In case you didn't know.

In Case You Didn't Know by Brett Young

Chapter One

❦ Lance ❦

"So, you think you're coming home? I hate to pull you off Rosie's case, but if the trail has gone dead, I need you to help with this Ruthless Warriors bullshit. Maybe you and Robby together can pinpoint me a fucking location for this Gregory douchedick. Also, mom wants you home for Christmas. She won't forgive me if you aren't."

I chuckle at my boss' and friends' tone. Josh Lucinio, the leader of the Lucinio Mafia, is no one to be fucked with. When he's pissed, people tend to stay out of his way. Including me and the rest of those close to him. Today, though, his tone makes me laugh a little. Which is fine with me. I need it.

"Sometimes, I wonder why I didn't just quit when your ass took over. Alex is nicer. Less fucking demanding."

"The fuck he is," Josh growls with a touch of humor. "Where do you think I learned the ruthless asshole thing from?"

This time, I do laugh. "Uh. Let's see. Ryan Crane. He'd be my first guess. You know. Him being this big bad mafia boss of one of the two largest mafias in the world thing. My second? Definitely Gavin Vandenberg. Vandenberg has no fucking conscience."

Josh laughs. "Well, he does. It's just not as defined as some others. That's why he's my second in command. And why I like him so much."

I grin and laugh, pointing at my phone. "See? That's what I mean. You get it from him."

"Agree to disagree. My twin has just as much of a dark side as I do."

I laugh because he's right. Alex Lucinio, Josh's twin, really does have the same fucked up dangerous side my boss does. "Yes. We do plan on coming home. We'll be home for Christmas. But I need a couple extra guys. That's actually what I was calling you for."

"Right. Yeah. The new lead. Talk to me."

I lean forward on the couch in the living room of the penthouse I'm staying in. "Well, we sent Rosie to her grandparent's house in Huckleberry Grove, but we got word that the rogue Viper's Venom member has resurfaced."

"Let me guess. In Huckleberry Grove."

"Actually, no. A few hours away. He was seen with Rosie's mother."

"Where is he now?"

"We let Blade know, since it's his rogue, but when we got there..."

Josh sighs. "Fuck."

"Yep. Fucker was gone. Blade has been chasing him around the damn state of Texas for the past month, but I have a bad feeling." I pull up the map on my laptop that I've been using to keep track of where he's been spotted. "I've been staying out of this as much as I can per your orders, but instincts, Josh. You know we rely on them. I've still been looking into things and keeping track. Letting it go completely sends my techy senses tingling."

"Tell me what you sense."

I stare at my map for a few moments. To anyone else, it would look like a damn mess. Chaos. Nothing more. Nothing less. But to me, I see everything plain as day. I can't believe I didn't see it before. Not until one of our contacts down here saw the pattern that I didn't. Thank fuck for football Quarterbacks.

Now, I see the pattern. I see the taunt. And I certainly see the fucking name. I don't know what the fuck it means. Is he calling us out?

The Crane's? Is it a coincidence? Whatever is happening, I don't like that I don't know.

"Danger. That's what I sense. He's zig-zagging across the state. Or at least that's what I thought he was doing. The problem is it all leads to one area. One town. If my instincts are correct, we have a day at best, a few hours at worst, before he makes his move. Let me send you the map." A few clicks later, the map is on its way to Josh's phone via good ol' technology.

"It's a bunch of dots all over the state."

I chuckle. "Yes. That's exactly what it is." I click a few more keys. "Take a look at that." I send him another one.

He pauses. "Dates superimposed over the map with the dots. What are you getting at, Lance? I know you like your mysteries, but get to the point."

"I thought you might say that." I click a few more keys. "This next one is the dates over the dots. Except I've taken the liberty of connecting them." I send the final message.

"Ho…ly… shhhhh…it," Josh murmurs. "Are you fucking serious?"

"As a heart attack."

"If what you just showed me is right, then the last stop is -"

"Huckleberry Grove. The final letter of that name will be finished in Huckleberry Grove. And he has one stop before it. Which is where I think he is right now."

"What the fuck does Ethan have to do with this? Is this some kind of sick joke?"

I shrug. "Don't know, bro. But that's what it spells. Ethan."

"Ethan Crane? Is that what he's trying to say? Or is his name Ethan?"

"I don't know, Josh. I don't. What I do know is that is what this pattern spells. I don't think it's a coincidence. I don't know if he's playing with us, or if he's calling out Ryan. I don't know if it's just his name and he's taunting Blade, but I do know that it's intentional. And he's going for Rosie."

"I hate unanswered questions."

"You and me both, boss."

"Fuck. Stop calling me boss, you asshole."

I grin. "I do it to piss you off."

"You all do it to piss me off. Where's Damon?"

"Sleeping. But as soon as you get me backup, we're heading for Huckleberry Grove."

"You got the backup. I'll contact Blade. Grab some of the guys we left there for cleanup. Are we any closer to figuring out what they want with Rosie?"

"Nope. She doesn't know. She swears the only thing she saw was her mom and the shovel, but she did corroborate that she saw her mom with someone a lot."

"Just not that night."

"Nope. Just her mom."

"I think it's time we remove Rosie from the situation. I know she's happier in Huckleberry Grove, but she's not safe there."

I sit up a little straighter. "What are you thinking?"

"Time to move her. Put her under protection. Her being there is a danger to her grandparents and the entire town. We don't need a turf war in a small town. Especially one that the cartel runs. She needs to come here. There's no other option. Bring her grandparents with her."

I let out a breath. "Fuck me, I was hoping you'd say that. I don't like what's going on down here."

"Time to come home, Engle. We've done what we set out to do. The rest is up to the VV. Ace will let us know what he needs."

"Okay. Got it. I'll grab Damon now."

I hang up as I stand and stride towards the bedroom. It's barely five in the morning, but I haven't slept at all. I haven't slept well the past three months. Since I first stepped foot in Brystone Springs, Texas.

I quietly open the door to the bedroom and chuckle when I see Damon isn't in the bed. The shower is running. In true Damon fashion, his clothing is already lying out on the bed. He's a very organized person and a really early riser.

In every sense of the word.

I walk to the closet and start pulling out our suitcases while he showers. We're very efficient. We've been here for three months, except for a week when we went home after Gavin, Josh's second and one of our best friends; brothers, was shot. We barely unpack anything ever. No matter where we are. We're always ready in case we need to leave quickly.

I sigh. Brystone Springs, Texas. We were called down here by a detective who is way too smart for his own good. He saw things happening that he wasn't supposed to and put pieces together that he shouldn't have known about. When things didn't add up, he called us.

It was probably one of the smartest things Colton De Lise ever did. When we arrived, we quickly discovered a lot of corruption in this city. And it all circled back to a gambling ring that was tied to big name universities and their football teams. They would pay the teams to lose and shower them with a fuckton of gifts and incentives to do what they said to.

It trickled down all the way to small towns and large cities across the state. There would be bets on dog fights, chicken fights, bull fights, and snake fights. The bets didn't just stop there, though. They went from underground card games, to betting on high school sports events, all the way up to buying virginities and betting on how long the woman it was stolen from screamed. Sick and disgusting shit that made my blood boil even when I wanted to fucking puke.

Thankfully, we caught the leader and were able to stop the entire gambling ring. We even saved the wife of the leader and relocated her. The past couple months were spent overseeing the cleanup of the rest of the city, from cops all the way up to the Mayor.

Though it should have been calming down, that's not how it seems to be going. Things in Brystone Springs have, but other things we found ourselves involved in have ramped up.

Rosie Haven.

The girl is just sixteen-years-old and already she's led a fucked up life. Her father was killed not too long ago. She saw her mother with a shovel and told the police exactly that. Despite a lot of testimony from other people about her mother and another person her mother was seen with, including on the night of the murder, her mother was never convicted of any wrongdoing.

As soon as she was cleared, she took Rosie and moved the two of them to Brystone Springs. She enrolled Rosie at the high school. Rosie was immediately taken under the wing of some of the most popular kids at the school. She even became a cheerleader.

But it didn't last long.

Rosie got caught up in a scandal in the school that led to us finding out about her past. The man her mother was seen with was a rogue member of the Viper's Venom. Which meant things got very dangerous for her. Especially since it became known very quickly that we were involved in not only helping our allies find their wayward member, but also finding the truth behind Rosie's father's murder. We knew she was a target and put immediate protection on her.

It didn't take long for us to decide she'd be safer with us than she would be staying with her friend, even if her friend did have a lot of security at her house, given her father is a Senator. Rosie was staying there because her mother had gotten fed up with her and more or less kicked her out.

Her friend's mother, however, decided Rosie being there was a burden on their family. Damon and I had her move in with us in our secured penthouse. Safety and protection for her, and peace of mind for us. Besides, we'd become pretty close to her by that time anyway.

After a while, though, we couldn't justify keeping her, even though we really wanted to. Rosie is a delight to have around, and we adore her. She became a little like a daughter to us. We hated the idea of her going back to Huckleberry Grove, but we couldn't keep her. And by that time, her mother disappeared anyway. Technically, her grandparents have more claim than us.

The positive is that she forged solid relationships with the group at school who had taken her under their protection, so-to-speak. They're all still very close. And she has us.

I look up as I put my laptop in my bag and smile when Damon comes out of the bathroom with nothing but a towel wrapped around his waist. Damon is tall, dark, and handsome. He's every man's and woman's fantasy. Hell, he's everyone's wet dream in the flesh. His muscles are well-defined. He's graceful and confident. His abs are just as lickable as the length that dangles between his legs. It's just as big as the rest of him, and it's all mine.

As I'm staring at the water droplets making their way beneath the towel that's hiding his nine inch cock, he's raising an eyebrow. "What the hell is all of this? Did we get move out orders?"

I snap myself out of my thoughts and look down at the already packed suitcases. "Sort of. We're getting our girl and bringing her home."

Damon gives me a hopeful grin. "Yeah?"

I nod with a grin of my own. "Yeah. I showed Josh the map. He agrees Rosie is a target and said exactly what you did."

Damon nods and tosses the towel aside. He quickly gets dressed, and I have to tear my eyes away so I don't maul him. "Ready to go get our daughter, husband?"

It's a running joke between me, Damon, and Rosie, but we've been talking more and more about it. We want to officially adopt her. As we've gotten to know her, she was very open to it becoming a reality. She even liked the idea of moving with us to Chicago. But her grandparents wanted her with them. I think they feel better knowing she's close in case anything happens. I suppose I can't blame them. Not after losing their only son.

"Ready as ever, husband," I say with a smile as we both start grabbing our stuff.

I follow Damon out of the penthouse and help him load our SUV. Just as we're finishing, our backup starts arriving. Damon tells them our plan as I get in the passenger seat of the SUV. I flip down the mirror and rub my eyes. Besides brushing my teeth and putting on deodorant, I didn't do much grooming this morning. I just want to get out as quickly as possible.

Even still, I don't look too bad. My dark blond, almost brown hair is messy, but it's the hot kind of messy that makes people swoon. I have a bit more scruff than I usually do, but at least I don't look unkempt. I yawn and flip the visor back up as Damon jumps in the driver's seat.

Damon Knight.

He's everything I've ever wanted ever since I first laid eyes on him. But at that point in our lives, while I knew I was gay and had accepted it, though I didn't really date, Damon was in complete denial. We became close, though, because while I've always been comfortable with who I am, Damon was struggling. He dated women and hated that he had to think of men to get off. Not that he didn't keep trying to be straight. It took him time to come to terms with his sexuality, but I think he did it because he was mostly tired of fighting it so hard.

About a year ago, though, Damon and I were in Las Vegas on an assignment. When we caught the guy we were after, we decided to spend an extra day in the city and let loose. At least as much as we dared. We are part of the mafia. We'd never do anything to draw attention to ourselves or make our family look bad.

When we woke up the next morning, we were both naked, smelled of alcohol and sex, and were wearing rings. Damon freaked out. I panicked. But after we talked about it, we realized one thing. It happened for a reason. I'd fallen more and more in love with him over the numerous years I've known him, and so had he, though he'd refused to admit it.

Instead of getting an annulment, we'd decided to stay married and see how it worked. We haven't said anything to anyone, though, because we weren't sure we'd stay together. We wear our rings on chains around our necks and portray that we're just friends and roommates. I'm pretty sure everyone knows the truth. At least the part about us being a couple. I'm pretty sure when we finally tell them we're married, they'll all try to kill us.

It's going to have to happen soon, though. Damon and I are very much in love and in this forever. When we first got home after Vegas, things were awkward and a little tense as we found our footing. As time went on, and the more time I spent with him, the more I fell for him, and the more he fell for me. He opens himself up further. Eventually, he accepted himself for who he truly is. As soon as that happened, our relationship grew stronger and intensified. Now, we're truly happy and in love.

A couple of hours later, the sun is rising and we're a few miles out of Huckleberry Grove. I yawn as my phone rings and smile when I see it's Rosie. I answer it, and since I'm connected to the Bluetooth in the SUV, Damon can hear her, too.

"Hey, honey. What's -"

"Please get here," she whispers as she sniffles.

Damon and I look at each other. He steps on the gas and speeds up. "What's happening?" he asks.

"Aaaaaaahhhh!" someone screams in the background.

My heart leaps into my throat. "Rosie? What the fuck is happening?"

"They're here," she whispers. "I'm hiding, but they have my grandparents."

"Stay hidden. We were on our way to you anyway," Damon says.

"Who is it? Who's there?"

"They all have Viper's Venom patches." Her voice is so quiet that I can barely hear her.

Damon takes out his phone and dials a number. I don't need to see it or hear the person on the other line to know who it is. He's calling Blade, the leader of Texas' chapter of the Viper's Venom. Which means I can focus completely on keeping Rosie calm.

"Where is she?" a deep male voice asks. Far too close to Rosie for my liking.

"She's not here!" the person I assume is her grandfather says. "Let my wife go! Please! You can take me!"

"Oh, I'll be taking you both," the man says.

"Rosie," I say quietly. "Stay calm. Don't move. Don't breathe. Don't speak. But don't you dare close your eyes. You have to be vigilant. You can't do that with your eyes closed. If he sees you, you run. Don't you fucking hesitate. Just run."

"Aaaaaaahhhh!" Rosie's grandmother screams right before I hear gurgling. The first sign of someone who just had their throat slit. I can hear Rosie inhale sharply but quietly.

"Nooooooo!" her grandfather screams.

"Ssh… Stay quiet, honey. We're close," I whisper.

A gunshot.

Thank Hell Rosie doesn't scream. I can still hear her shallow breaths, so I know it wasn't her who was just shot.

"Torch it. Search the town for the little bitch," the man says. My heart stops. I look at Damon with wide eyes. She's in that house.

"She doesn't have many friends," a female voice says. "She won't be hard to find."

Damon glances at me as he hangs up his phone. "Her mother?" he asks as we fly into town.

I hear fluid being poured near Rosie. She lets out a near silent whimper but says nothing. I glance behind us and see all of our backup is having no issues keeping up with the over hundred and twenty miles and hour that Damon is driving. Thankfully, it's still early. There aren't any cars on the road in this sleepy town.

"Stay calm, sweetheart. We're almost there," I whisper.

"They're outside," she whispers. "They poured something all over.

It smells like gasoline. What do I do?"

My heart is racing. "We're almost there, Rosie. Where are you?" I hear the roar of motorcycles starting up just as Rosie starts whimpering.

"They lit it on fire!"

The motorcycles are growing more distant, but I don't give a fuck that they won't be there when we get there. Let Blade take care of them. He's in one of the SUVs behind us.

"Rosie! Where are you!" I ask as calmly but commandingly as I can.

She screams and coughs. "In a closet!"

"Get out of the closet! Can you get out of the house?"

"I'm out of the closet. The fire is everywhere!" She starts coughing again and screams when something pops close to her. "I can't get out! It's too hot!" She screams again at another pop.

"Is there an upstairs?" *Please say there's a fucking upstairs.*

"Yes!" She coughs more. "It's s-so hot!"

"Rosie crouch down as low to the ground as you can. Cover your mouth and nose with your shirt. Smoke rises. Get upstairs. There won't be flames up there yet, but there will be smoke. They didn't have time to douse the upstairs. You have time, but stay low and keep your nose and mouth covered as best you can. I'll get you out. Okay? I promise."

Damon speeds past a group of bikers, neither of us giving a fuck who they are. Several of the SUVs follow us, but some give chase to the bikers.

"Keep going!" Blade commands over our earpieces. "They won't be leaving Texas alive."

"Like there was ever a chance we'd be turning around," I say.

"Aaaahhh!" Rosie screams again as she cries and coughs.

"Rosie, go to your bedroom. Close the door and open your window. In that order. Get a t-shirt or anything you can, wet it down, and tie it over your mouth and nose," I say as calmly as I can as we approach a house on the outskirts of town that's already fully engulfed. "Fuck."

"Holy shit, Rosie. Talk to us!" Damon yells.

"I…" Cough. "I… am in…" Cough. "In my room…"

"Close the door!" Damon commands as he skids to a stop. "Where's your room?"

"B-back…" Cough. More coughing. "Please… Hurry…" A fit of

coughing.

Silence.

"Rosie!" I yell as we both jump out of the SUV. "Rosie! Fuck!"

More silence.

The SUVs that followed us all skid to a stop behind us. Everyone jumps out of the vehicles and scatters to look for anything that can help us get to her. Any possible way in.

As the seconds pass, our chances look more and more bleak.

Damon and I keep yelling for Rosie but are met with nothing but deathly silence…

Chapter Two

🍎 Damon 🍎

"Fuck!" I yell. "A ladder! Find me a ladder!" I bark as I run to the back of the house. Lance is on my heels. There are flames shooting out the windows of several of the rooms.

Lance looks up in horror. "How is that possible? They had no time to get an accelerant up there!"

"The house is old!" I yell over the roar of the flames. And they had a lot of people there, judging by the bikers that passed us. Who the fuck knows what they did? They could have been dousing the house after they searched it.

"Which window?" Lance asks me when we reach the back of the house.

I look between the two upstairs windows. Flames are streaking out one of them. Smoke is billowing out of the other, but I can see the orange glow of flames. My heart is pounding. There are a couple of other windows. The rooms behind them are all fully engulfed. I look around for anything I can use to scale the house. I don't give a shit that flames are licking the bedrooms. I'm saving our little girl.

"I don't know, baby," I rumble.

"Knight!" one of our guards yells. I turn. He and another guy are carrying a ladder.

"Thank fuck," I whisper as Lance and I help them set it up under the window the smoke is coming out of. "She said back of the house. I'm truly hoping she meant the far back of the house. That would be this room."

"Jesus," Lance growls as he starts climbing the ladder.

I stop him. "What are you doing?"

"Getting our little girl!" he says, panicked.

"Lance, no. I'll go." I physically push him back and hold up a hand when he starts to protest. "I'm faster. You can't argue that."

Lance looks up as he nods. "Just get her, baby." It doesn't get past me that he called me 'baby' in front of a lot of people or that he called Rosie our little girl, but it's the last thing on my mind. Something to deal with later.

I start to climb the ladder, but the heat from the fire is making the metal rungs hot. "Fuck," I rumble.

"Damon! Attic!" someone yells.

I duck as I glance up, not sure what to expect, but thinking fire is about to rain over me. The attic has three windows that let a lot of light in, but each window looks dark. My eyes widen when I see an arm. "Oh fuck!"

I quickly climb down the ladder so we can reposition it. We work quickly to extend it as far as it will go, which isn't quite high enough, but it's one more thing I don't give a shit about. Lance's gorgeous hazel eyes meet mine.

"How are you going to get to her?" he asks worriedly.

I take the gloves someone hands me and quickly put them on. "I'll get to her." I waste no time in scaling the ladder, completely ignoring the heat radiating off the house.

The higher I get, the more in the smoke I'm in. I cough and keep my eyes on the arm in the window. I can hear coughing. It's weak, but it's persistent. It sounds like she's going to throw up or already has. Good. If she can get anything she's breathed in out of her, I'll take it.

I keep my focus on the window and ignore the sting in my eyes and burn in my lungs from the smoke. Rosie is pulling herself up, though slowly. I can see her shoulder and some of her head. She's coughing harder.

"I'm coming, sweetheart!" I yell.

"Da…" Coughing. Hard coughing that makes my heart hurt for her.

I'm a good six feet below her and as far up on the ladder as I should safely go. Trusting my guys, I let go of the ladder and step up a couple more rungs. With nothing but the house to hold onto, I know damn well I'm in dangerous fucking territory.

I let out a breath and steady myself the best I can. "Rosie, you need to help me, honey," I say. I reach for her hand. I can't reach her. Flames are shooting out from both windows underneath us now. We don't have a lot of time. The house is already snapping. Things are popping and cracking. I can hear the roar of the flames inside the walls.

"Help…," she croaks before she starts coughing again.

"I will. I'm here. I'll get you out, but I need your help, honey. You need to be strong. Climb out to me. I'll catch you."

Something loud cracks behind her. "Ah!" she squeak-screams. She clings to the window with wide eyes. More smoke starts snaking out the window.

It's dark.

Black.

"Rosie, we need to move! I need you to move! You have to trust me! I'll catch you!" Black smoke like that means one thing. We're about to have a huge problem. The fire may not have reached her room, but it's about to. And it's gonna come fast and fucking hard.

She pulls herself up more. Tears are streaming down her face. My heart feels like it's about to beat out of my chest. All I want to do is save our little girl. And I damn well mean ours. She was ours a long time ago. The connection we all felt almost instantly was nothing less than the hand of fate.

"What do I…" More coughing. "What do I do?" Cough.

"Trust me. Trust that I'll catch you, Rosie."

She nods. "O-" More coughing. I need to get her out before she passes out on me again.

Before the flames reach us.

17

"Just a second, sweetie." Using the house for my anchor, I step down a couple of rungs and let out a breath. I look up again, refusing to let her see the fear I'm feeling. This needs to happen right. We're only getting one chance. If we do it wrong, we're both falling.

Rosie looks over her shoulder. "Ah!" she screams, though quietly. "Fire! In here! Dad!"

"Fuck," I rumble, swallowing hard. Her calling me dad has my heart flipping. It's unexpected but puts a word on the tumultuous feelings I have going on right now. Feelings I need to figure out later. We're out of time. "Rosie, listen. Swing your legs out of the window like you're sitting on it," I say as calmly but dominantly and fatherly as I can.

She cries but shakily does what I say. "Ah!" she screams again. I can't see much of what's going on behind her, but I don't doubt the flames are getting closer.

"Rosie, sweetheart. Eyes on me. Don't jump. Fall. Just slide out. I *will* catch you. I promise." I focus completely on her, keeping my eyes trained on hers.

She nods and closes her eyes as she sobs and coughs from the smoke. She slides her body out of the window, but doesn't let go. Using my legs and trusting those holding the ladder, I brace myself the best I can.

"Damon! Hurry up! You're out of time!" one of the guys yells. Rosie's eyes snap open.

"No, no, no! Rosie, don't listen to them!" I command. "Close your eyes. Slide out the window. I got you, honey. I won't let you fall."

Rosie closes her eyes. I can see the flames behind her now. They're close enough that she has to feel them. She whimpers and slides further out of the window, bringing her close enough to me that I can reach her legs.

"D-dad," she cries.

"I got you, baby. I'm right here. Let go."

"Ah!" She lets go and falls into my arms just as flames start licking along the window frame.

"I got you," I whisper in her ear as I wrap her in my arms, steadying us both, and covering her from the flames shooting out the window above us. "We need to get down. Can you climb? Are you too weak from the smoke?"

She keeps her face buried in my neck as she clings to me. She's still coughing. It's weak. I just nod. The house could go at any minute. The fire is poking through different parts of the wall and snaking across the house. The structure could collapse any time.

"Damon! Get the fuck down here!" Lance yells.

I don't look around. I don't question. "You need to hold on, Rosie. I have to get us down. Can you get on my back?"

She nods, and I quickly help her maneuver to my back. She wraps her arms around my shoulders and legs around my waist, freeing me to climb down a lot faster. She's still coughing quietly as she cries. I take each rung one step at a time, but as quickly as possible until I reach the ground.

Lance and a few others pull us back. "We need to get the hell out of here," Lance says. "The house is going to collapse."

With Rosie still clinging to me, I take off running with everyone else. The SUVs have been moved. We run towards them. We need to get Rosie to a hospital. Smoke inhalation is never good. Just as we reach the SUV, I hear a whirring noise, something that can only be described as a helicopter.

I look up. Dirt kicks up around us as a sleek black helicopter starts to land in the open field. "No fucking way," I say.

Lance grins. "Fuck yes. Yes fucking way." He takes my arm and pushes me towards the chopper as it touches down.

Ducking down, we both run for the chopper just as a couple of fire trucks speed down the long driveway to the farmhouse. Why they took so long or how is something I don't understand. Then again, I really don't know how long it's actually been. Seconds. Minutes. Maybe fucking hours.

"Someone call for a ride?" Cole Westwood, one of our close and trusted friends, asks with a huge grin as he slides the door of the chopper open. The engine hasn't been cut, so the blades are still going. Cole is yelling over the noise.

"Man, am I glad to see you!" Lance says as he jumps in. He turns to me and helps Rosie into the chopper.

I turn to the team and move my hand in a circle. It's the signal for roll out. I jump into the chopper as Cole and Lance settle Rosie. Cole is a cop. He's got a lot of first responder experience. Even though I don't want to, I climb into the co-pilot seat of the chopper and let Cole help our girl.

I strap in before I even glance at who's piloting.

Alex.

"Fuck, you don't know how happy I am to see you, bro."

Alex grins. "Josh sent us out as soon as he got Lance's text this morning about calling him when he woke up. He mobilized us before calling him back. We were in the air already. He let us know what was happening as you guys were rolling out. We changed our flight plan in the air and flew into East Texas Regional instead of Brystone Springs."

"How did you just know to grab a chopper?" I ask.

"Instinct. The airport isn't far from here. We landed about fifteen minutes ago. We were loading up when Josh called and said there was a fire. Someone called him. There was a guy who looked like he was getting ready to take off from their private hangers. I bought the chopper."

I laugh. "Of course. Of course you bought the fucking chopper. Thank fuck, bro. I'm constantly grateful everyday that we met when we did all those years ago."

He grins as he pilots the chopper through the sky. "As soon as we got in the air, we saw the smoke. I didn't see a hospital on the way in. I'm hoping there's one in town."

I nod and glance back at Lance and Rosie. Lance is hugging her. Cole is having her sip water. Her coughing is lessening. I turn back towards the windshield as the town approaches. Alex is calling out some kind of a mayday call over the radio. I tune out everything as I close my eyes and allow myself to breathe. It feels like the last fifteen or so minutes have been days.

I slide a hand over my face and run the conversation I need to have with Josh through my head. Everyone really. Lance and I haven't told anyone that we're married. It's completely on me. I'm the one who wanted to hold back because I didn't know how to deal with my own fucking sexuality.

I'm gay.

I've been in love with Lance for longer than I even really know. I've been married to him for nearly a year, and it's been the best year of my life. But I held back telling anyone because I'm a damn idiot. How the hell does an experience like this suddenly put a person's entire life into perspective?

Well, no more.

Everything changes today.

I reach up and clutch my wedding ring. It's under my shirt so no one can see it, but that needs to change. It's time for everyone to know. Especially since Lance and I want to adopt Rosie. We're going to need help from Josh and our family to make it happen. I don't know the first fucking thing about adoption, but Josh has ways of making shit happen.

I open my eyes as Alex nears a building and prepares to land. Luckily, there's just enough space behind the small building for the chopper. I'm not sure the town would like Alex dropping the thing in the middle of the street but I have to chuckle because he would if he had to.

After he lands and a doctor helps get Rosie out and on a stretcher, I climb out with Alex. We watch as Lance and Cole make their way in with her. I hang back only because I need to compose myself.

"She's gonna be okay, Damon," Alex says next to me. "You can't beat yourself up for this. You did all you could, and she technically wasn't under our protection. We didn't have a reason for her to be until we saw that map Lance sent."

I shake my head. "It's not just that."

"Hey! That's a nice chopper! How much did it run you?" a guy with a heavy Southern accent asks as he approaches us. I take a breath. I hate interruptions, but this one is welcome. It gives me more time to compose my thoughts.

"Keep it. Merry Christmas," Alex says, tossing him the keys with a wink. "I'll have my guys get you the paperwork." He nods towards a black SUV turning into the parking lot with a convoy of black SUVs, all Ford Escapes, behind it.

"No shit?" The guy looks at him wide-eyed and in disbelief. I chuckle. It's not the first time Alex has given some random person something extravagant. He already has a chopper at home. He doesn't need another one.

Alex nods at one of the guards getting out of the SUV. "Help this guy out with the paperwork for the chopper. It's his now."

The guard grins as he shakes his head. "Got it, boss."

"Must be nice being a billionaire CEO of the largest tech company in the damn world," I tease.

Alex laughs. "It has its perks."

I shake my head as we walk together into the hospital. Lance is pacing in the small waiting room. Cole is sitting in a chair rubbing his head. I pick up my pace and wrap my arms around Lance when he walks right into me. He stiffens slightly, but then hugs me as tightly as I'm holding him.

"She'll be okay," I murmur in his ear as I sway with him. "She'll be okay. Everything will."

I know Cole and Alex can't hear me. Alex sits down next to Cole on the other side of the room. It's not the first time Lance and I have hugged. We've all hugged each other several times over the years. I'm sure they think nothing of it.

But as I stand here with my husband, I want them to know. I want them all to know. I don't want to hide anymore. I don't want to wait to get back home for everyone to find out at the same time. I've been putting off admitting the truth, my truth, *our* truth, for long enough.

We almost lost Rosie today. Our daughter. The girl no one knows we've been discussing our future with. I know how close I was to losing my own life. The flames were already eating the frame of the house. It wouldn't have been much longer before they reached us.

I pull away from Lance slowly and look deep into his eyes. I reach for the chain around my neck and pull it off. Lance watches me curiously, but when he sees me removing the ring from the chain, his eyes snap to mine. They're filled with so much hope that I'm both elated and heartbroken that I made him wait this long for me to get my head out of my ass.

I put the chain in my pocket and slide the ring on my finger. Lance quickly does the same. Gripping the back of his neck, I lean in and kiss him long and deeply. My tongue twines with his and ignites the sparks low in my stomach. Kissing him always does that. Lance's arms wrap around my waist as we sink into each other, not giving a single fuck what anyone might think.

We're close enough to Louisiana that I'm pretty sure this part of Texas is probably included in the infamous Bible Belt. The thought makes me roll my eyes. I can't understand for the life of me how so many people are still ignorant to sexuality and other differences in human beings as a whole. How can they still try to fit them in a box and say it's wrong for them to love who they do all because of an admitted mistake in the Bible's translation?

"About damn time you two out yourselves," Alex says. Lance and I break away from our kiss, but stay wrapped in each other's arms.

"What the fuck?" I ask, shocked at his words.

"You can't think you've been very good at hiding it," Cole says. "We've all known for years you two have a thing for each other."

Lance and I glance at each other before looking back at them. "I thought we'd hid it pretty well," Lance says as we turn towards them.

Alex shrugs. "Maybe to those who don't know you." His eyes fall to our hands. "Can't say we guessed that, though." He nods to our rings.

Cole grins. "How long?"

"Uh…" I look at the simple gunmetal band on my left ring finger. It matches Lance's. "Almost a year."

Alex nods. "You'll have an easy time with us guys, but you two are going to have to face the girls for keeping it from them. Lyric is gonna be pissed. Jessa might cry. And I think Dallas might slap you both. You know she adores the fuck out of you."

I take Lance's hand with a grin and sit down next to them. Lance sits next to me with his fingers still entwined with mine. Lyric Sharpe is Josh's ex-girlfriend but we all still love her like a little sister. She's happily married now, but we still see and talk to her regularly. Jessa Crane is Alex's ex-girlfriend. She's married now, too, but she's still just as much like a little sister to us.

And then there's Dallas Cassidy. She has become family. She's Josh's best friend's sister. We saved her life not long ago when she fell into the clutches of Josh's and Alex's father, Matthew. He's dead and gone now, but Dallas has become close to us all. We aren't sure what exactly to think of her, though, because she's very young and seems infatuated with our boss and brother. Josh, however, seems to be drawn to her in a way that even he can't explain.

I'll happily face them, though, because it's time. It's time to announce us and our intentions of adopting Rosie.

It's time to finally show our love.

Chapter Three

☙ Lance ❧

For the first time in who the fuck knows how long, I feel whole. Having intense feelings for a man, my best friend, for as long as I have without being able to truly express them has been hard. It got even harder after we were married because even though we were free with our feelings behind closed doors, we weren't being honest with everyone else.

I'll never forget a few months ago when Damon found out that Raleigh, Alex's fiance, was his sister. He broke down in my arms. At that time, we were still trying to piece together Raleigh's history. All we really knew at that time was Matthew Lucinio had his hooks in her when she was just an infant and raised her as his own.

Only Josh, Alex, and their mother, Rebekkah, had no clue. Matthew lived an entirely separate life. He used business and mafia trips as his cover to be with Raleigh. When he wasn't with her, he called her each night. She was raised by nannies, but Matthew was still very present in her life. She thought he was a successful accountant with his own business who traveled a lot. She led a decent life and felt very loved by the man she knew as her father.

Only all of that was a lie. It turned out that Damon's parents gave her to Matthew. They were high on drugs most of the time. They were clean for a while but relapsed a lot. They knew Damon was close to Alex and Josh. They went to Matthew for help. They believed he'd provide her a better life than they could.

Damon was devastated. He never knew Raleigh existed, but he did know how evil Matthew Lucinio was. When his parents died a few months ago, he got a few things they wanted him to have. One of them was a baby blanket they had made for Raleigh.

It had her initials on it. He also got a letter pleading with him to find her. They figured out that Matthew wasn't who he portrayed himself to be. It hit Damon hard. Knowing he had a sister and not being able to be a part of her life took its toll on him. When we told Raleigh and the rest of the family what we'd learned, though, one of the things that hurt me the most was not being able to comfort him the way I wanted to. The way I knew he needed to be in that moment. Behind closed doors was one thing. In front of everyone was something else entirely.

I never said anything, though, because I love my husband. I've loved Damon for many years. Way back when we first met, I was still in college when I was recruited by Gavin to be Alex's tech person. I didn't bat an eye when he told me what I'd be doing. I'd heard of Alex. I knew he was good friends with the leader of the Crane Mafia, Ryan Crane. After I'd met him and learned of his plans to help his brother turn the mafia into a legit operation, I was even more on board.

Not long after that, I met Damon. He was dating a woman at the time, but I had a feeling there was a lot more to him. We hit it off very quickly and became really good friends. It didn't take long for him to open up to me about his struggles, but I was already in love with him by then.

I let out a long breath and rub my eyes before letting my head fall back against the seat of the plane again. The hours are blurring together. I don't know how long we were in that hospital in Huckleberry Grove before the doctor let us see Rosie. It was even longer after that while he ran tests. At least what he could at his small facility.

By the time it was all said and done, Alex made the decision to have her released. The doctor couldn't do much there anyway. X-Rays looked good. A few other tests he ran looked okay. The doctor believed she could make the trip, so we packed everything up and left. We have a lot better facilities in Chicago.

We're in the air now. Hopefully, the flight won't take too much longer because I'm tired. We all are. Even Alex, who I swear never fucking sleeps, passed out not long ago after answering a few emails. Damon fell asleep almost as soon as we hit cruising altitude. Rosie has been in the bedroom since we took off. Even Cole has dozed.

I've been sitting here going over everything that's happened in my head. And then replaying it all over again. I can't figure out why the fuck the last stop in the sick and twisted game being played in Texas was Huckleberry Grove. As soon as we heard Rosie's mother's voice, though, that was it. It all clicked.

Rosie knows too much, even though what she knows isn't a lot. She saw her mother with the shovel. She told the truth to the police and caused them to actually open an investigation. From there, I think there were a lot of people paid off. It's something I've been looking into, but my attention has been pulled in different directions.

Specifically to the rogue VV member.

I didn't think it was all connected to us at all, but after seeing Ethan's name spelled out in the chaos, I don't know what to think. It's way too much of a coincidence for my liking, but I have absolutely no real proof that the shit going on in Texas with Blade's rogue has anything to do with us.

I let out a long sigh and glance up when I see Rosie slowly walking towards me. She's rubbing her eyes. She's wearing one of Alex's hoodies that he keeps on his jet and a pair of Raleigh's slacks, which are too big for her. Thankfully, the flight attendant is well prepared for any emergency, fashion or otherwise. I suppose she has to be, considering who she works for. Alex isn't just a CEO and billionaire. His company provides technological security from the normal household with the internet to Governments around the world.

Rosie sits next to me, still rubbing her eyes. "At the risk of sounding like a child, are we there yet?"

I chuckle. "Shouldn't be too much longer. I think I felt the pilot start descending."

She hugs herself and leans against the wall of the plane as she closes her eyes. "Why is this happening?"

"I wish I knew, cub. I'm working on it."

She smiles softly but keeps her eyes closed; her head on the plane's wall. We started calling her 'cub' because of the tattoo of a wolf cub on her ankle that's howling at the moon. She got it on her sixteenth birthday with her father because she loves wolves. He told her that day that they were going to have a new beginning. Apparently, over that previous year, Rosie's mother had become distant and turned into quite the bitch. It was only about a week after Rosie's birthday when her father died. It's another mystery to add to the list of things needing to be solved.

"How is this going to work?" she asks. "I called Damon dad. I feel you both are in my heart." She looks at me sadly. "I don't know if it's right to even feel. Am I betraying the memory of my father?"

I bite my lip. I want to say no. I'd like to reassure her, but I know that isn't what she needs. The question is one she needs to answer for herself. "Well, how do you feel about that? Do you feel you are?"

She purses her lips as she thinks. Finally, after a few moments, she shakes her head. "No... I feel like... well, like he'd want this. I feel like he'd want me to be taken care of and provided for. And safe, above all else."

I nod. "Me too. Is it what you want? We've talked about it when you were staying with us, but maybe it's time to really have this conversation in more than just a hypothetical sense."

I look up at Damon as he yawns. He's sitting across from us. He stretches and yawns again. He looks at his watch as he groans. The plane descends a little more. Rosie puts her seatbelt on as Damon and I do the same. It's probably not necessary. I can't begin to even say how many times we've touched down with people not wearing seatbelts, myself included.

"I do want you to adopt me," Rosie says after a few moments. "I feel safe with you. I..." She trails off and wipes a tear falling down her face. I put an arm around her as Damon reaches over and squeezes her knee. She sniffles. "I love my grandparents, and I'll always miss them, but... I... just don't... really think they wanted me. I feel like they just..." She shrugs. "I guess I just think maybe they wanted to hold onto their son through me."

"We talked about that," Damon says, patting her knee before he sits back. "Nothing to feel bad about. Huckleberry Grove felt like home, too, for you. At least those first couple days."

"I still feel bad about it, but I guess I feel like I need to be away from all of that. Away from the people looking at me with pity. Even my friends just felt bad. Everyone heard about what happened in Brystone Springs with that teacher. Some of the people I thought were friends thought I asked for it and helped the other cheerleaders get him in trouble when we got caught."

I hug her. "We know that isn't true. We saw the video. And you know the truth. You were there."

She rests her head on my shoulder. "It's more than that, though. I want to go to Chicago to start over, but I do honestly feel safe with you. I think of you both as dads. I know we joked about it some, but when everything was happening, all I could think of was the both of you. Not even because I knew you'd help or because I trust you. I was thinking how sometimes even my dad didn't treat me like you both do. Sometimes, I felt like he was too busy for me. I've never felt such a strong... parental connection, I guess would be how to describe it, with even my parents. I really look up to you both and feel like I can count on you in all aspects like a kid should be able to do with a parent."

"Well, you can," Damon tells her with a soft smile.

"I know it's something we talked about before, too, but I think it's just more serious now. It's real. It's happening."

"It's more than just a 'wouldn't it be cool' kind of conversation," I say with a half-smile.

"Yeah," she says as she looks down.

My heart plummets at her devastated expression. "I know this isn't exactly what we planned..."

She smiles softly. "No... I wanted to talk it over more with my grandparents. Their initial reaction wasn't exactly positive, but I hoped they would at least hear me out. If they didn't agree to let me go, I kept telling myself it was only two years before I could leave. It gave us all time. I hoped that they would see that I was making the right decision for me. I know they didn't want to let go of their connection through me to their son, but even the short time I was there, I was already miserable. I really didn't think I would be. That in itself was hard on me. I felt awful for it. And they just kept telling me that I should be ashamed for trying to replace my dad. I would never try and do that."

Damon smiles. "There's a difference between replacing your father and opening your heart to the embrace of another paternal love. It's no different, really, than if you had a good relationship with your mom and she remarried. There's nothing wrong with considering that man your father, too. Provided you get along with him, of course."

"That's what I said," Rosie says. "I just wish they could have heard me. We were fighting when those men came. I saw my mom get off the back of the bike of one of the bikers. I hid because I didn't want to go with her. I thought she was coming to take me back." She turns her face into my shoulder and shivers.

"First of all, I know they know you loved them. I heard them on the phone. I'm sure they knew you were there," I tell her.

She nods. "They knew. They saw me hide."

I kiss her head as the plane touches down with barely a bump. "And second, even if you were fighting, it changes nothing. They felt your love for them. Just as you felt it from them. That love is something you need to hold onto. Not what happened. Not the fight. The love. They're looking down on you, cub. And they're proud of you for surviving. Just as they'll continue to be proud of you in all you accomplish."

We all fall silent as the plane taxis to a gate. Damon and I help Rosie off. As I expected, she's shivering instantly, even with Alex's hoodie. Damon leads us both to the waiting SUVs. I help Rosie into the back seat as Damon starts it and turns on the heat. I turn just as Josh arrives.

"Thank God," I say loud enough for only Damon to hear me when he reaches my side.

He turns as Josh climbs out of his SUV. "Man, am I glad to see him."

We both step aside as the staff continues loading our stuff into the SUV. We meet Josh by his vehicle. I run my hands over my face with a low groan.

Josh raises an eyebrow as his gaze falls to my hand. "Uh... you two get hitched in Texas? Couldn't take the lonely nights anymore?" he teases.

I groan under my breath. "Um… fuck." I look at Damon. This has always been his show on when we come out to people. If it were up to me, everyone would have known already, but I love and respect him. I'd never do it if he wasn't ready.

"We got married a year ago," Damon says, pride lacing his words. It makes my heart flip. My breath hitches.

"A year ago," Josh says low and rumbly. After a few moments of looking between us and making me uncomfortable as fuck, he finally nods. "I wish you would have let us know. We wouldn't have missed it. We would have been on the first flight out to be there. You know we're not judgemental." He looks directly at Damon as he continues. "And you know damn well I've known for a long time about your sexuality."

Damon groans. "Seriously? Do all of you fucking know? I thought I was good about hiding it."

Josh barks out a laugh. "Dude. First thing Lyric said to me when she met you both was 'are they together? If they ain't, they should be. Because the way they look at each other is anything but platonic.' I told her she was a hopeless romantic, but then I saw exactly what she was talking about and stopped mid-sentence. You two have always had a thing. I just never really noticed it until she said something. She's gonna be pissed, by the way." He points between the two of us with narrowed eyes. "I'm not gonna be the buffer. You two can deal with her on this one."

I just grin like a fool because I'm fucking looking forward to it. I want everyone to know. I'd shout it for all to hear if I could. Maybe I'll hack into the media outlets and broadcast it all over the fucking world.

Damon laughs. I love his laugh. "Tell her to line up. She'll be right behind Jessa and Dallas on this one."

"Fuck that," Josh says with a wicked grin. "She'll be leading the pack. All of the girls are going to want a piece of you two on this one. And all of your brothers are going to be sitting back watching the whole show."

It's my turn to laugh because I can see them doing it. "Hey, as long as I get to actually be out in the open with him, I'll take whatever they give."

Damon grins but sobers quickly. "That was a good lead in because we need your help. Brother to brother."

Josh leans against the hood of his SUV and folds his arms over his broad chest. "This why you called me out here in the middle of the night?"

I glance at Damon. "Well, kind of. Yeah. I guess it could have waited, but we need to get on this. Fast. It has to do with Rosie."

Josh glances at our SUV. "She doing okay?"

Damon nods. "She is, considering what she's been through." He pauses and runs his fingers through his already messy hair. "We got really close to her down there." He looks back at Josh.

"We want to adopt her," I blurt out.

Josh whistles through his teeth and chuckles. "I'm just finding out you're married. And now you want to start a family?" He gives us a half-smile. I should have known he'd make us explain ourselves.

"She's a good girl, Josh," Damon says. "You know all about her mom. She verified to us that her mom was there. Her mother watched them kill her grandparents. She knew they torched the house. We heard her on the phone. She said they'd find her. She didn't have many friends. We left some guys there. Blade went after them. We don't know if he caught them or not. I haven't talked to him."

"He didn't. They got away," Josh confirms. It's what Damon and I already suspected.

"I was hoping they'd catch a few," I grumble. I shake my head. "Listen. Josh, we were talking to her before all of this happened. She's the one who brought it up. She told us she wished we could adopt her. After that, we really started to think about it. Then we started talking about it, but we knew her grandparents wanted her with them. So, she said she'd talk to them and tell them what she wanted, which was a new life somewhere where no one knew her. They weren't receptive to the idea at all. I can't blame them. They didn't know us, and she was all they had left. But things changed. We can't let her mother get to her."

Josh is quiet as he thinks. Finally, he drops his arms and looks at us both. "You're asking me to pull a lot of strings, do things behind the scenes, and pay people off to keep quiet and do this without her mother knowing until it's all said and done."

Damon nods. "Yes."

Josh looks at me. "You're gonna have to find me her signature and forge a lot of documents."

"Aren't marriage certificates digitized nowadays? Her signature would be on that, wouldn't it?" Damon asks, offering an easy solution to the signature issue.

"Done. I'll do what I need to. But this adoption needs to be legal binding. Ironclad. And fast."

Josh looks at his watch then back at us. He nods to the SUV. "Get her home. You said she was smaller than Raleigh and Harleigh, so I asked Dallas to help me out. She grabbed some stuff of hers and raided the clothes Lyric keeps here for when she visits just in case Rosie is a little bigger than her. We left them in the guest bedroom near the stairs at your house. They'll last a little while until you two can get her her own things. As for the adoption, it's Christmas Eve. I'll do all I can, but you'll have to get me the paperwork tied in a nice big red ribbon." He grins.

"I'll make it happen," I say. I've already started. It's what I was doing on the plane when everyone was asleep.

Josh nods and pats us both on the back. "Get that girl home. We need to figure out school, too."

Damon sighs. "Yeah. I don't know how this is gonna happen, but please, bro. We need to make it quick."

"We got this." Josh winks as he heads back to his vehicle and climbs in.

I shiver as Damon and I walk back to our SUV. Damon climbs in the driver seat as I get in the passenger one. Rosie's window is down. Her eyes are wide, and her hand is sticking out the window. It takes me a second to figure out what she's doing. When I do, I laugh. She's shivering, but it has started to snow.

"I've never seen real snow before!" she exclaims as she sticks her head out the window and tries to catch a flake on her tongue. I grin. I bet she's happy about the hoodie because the temperature in Chicago is about fifty degrees less than it was in Texas when we left.

"You'll see plenty of it, cub," Damon says with a grin. "Put your window up. We're going home."

She does as he says, but a huge smile is plastered all over her face. As we start driving, her eyes are fixated on the snow and everything we pass on the way. The lights. Buildings. It's obvious that she's fascinated by all of it.

Home.

My home has been wherever Damon is ever since I met him. As soon as we met Rosie, we both discussed something we hadn't before.

Kids.

Neither of us ever thought we'd have the option to have them. It's why we both got vasectomies when Alex and Gavin got theirs. We never wanted them.

Then she came along, and all we could talk about was how we may not want kids, but we want her. It was that connection. Strong and something we'd never felt before. She's about the same age as Dallas, yet we never felt this type of parental bond to her. It was like our life didn't feel quite right without her. As if there was a Rosie shaped hole just waiting to be filled.

Now, we have her.

And we're going *home*.

Chapter Four

🍎 Damon 🍎

"Holy shitting ninja turtles," Rosie mumbles under her breath as we walk into the house.

I can't help but crack up. "What did you just say?"

She giggles. "Sorry. It just… popped out." She turns in a slow circle. "Dylan's house was huge, but this…" She blinks a few times before stopping in front of us with wide eyes. Dylan might be one of the only people she misses anywhere in Texas. Her and the other few people she met in Brystone Springs. Dylan became her best friend. "How did you find time to get it decorated for Christmas? It's beautiful."

I smile as Lance stands next to me while we all take in the decorations. "This would be the girls of the family. If we're all sent on a mission, they all get together before we get back and make sure we have fresh food in the fridge. They make sure the housekeeper is in and has everything cleaned up. And if it's a holiday, they'll come over and decorate." I gesture around the house.

Lance grins. "They really outdid themselves. That tree is huge."

We all smile. The tree is tall. It has to be a ten foot Kennedy Fir. No one in our family likes real Christmas trees because they make a mess, so the tree is fake. It's decorated elegantly in silver, gold, and red, our favorite colors. Lance's is silver and gold. Mine is red. The rest of the house is decorated just as elegantly and matches the tree.

If I didn't know better, I'd think a decorator was hired, but I know this family. Between Raleigh, Harleigh, Dallas, and the Crane wives, no one needs an interior designer. They've even got garland that looks like tree branches wrapped around the banister of the stairs and on the mantle of the fireplace. Like the tree, they are pre-lit with clear lights.

"It looks so real and smells like a real tree," Rosie says as she touches a branch and closes her eyes. She inhales deeply with a soft smile.

I glance at Lance. He has a huge smile on his face as he watches her. I take his hand and squeeze it. In true family fashion, we didn't walk into a dark house. The Christmas lights, both on the inside and outside of the house, are shining brightly, and I realize that this is all something I've taken advantage of for a long time. Having the house ready for us when we walk in is what I've come to expect. But seeing this all through her eyes makes me grateful I'm part of a family who loves as fiercely as they do. A family who truly cares.

"She's going to be okay here," Lance says as he squeezes my hand. "We have a hell of a family. She's going to truly thrive."

I smile at my husband. "I was just thinking that."

He leans in and gives me a soft kiss that still has the power to make me weak in the knees. I squeeze his hand again and head for the kitchen to grab some bottled waters for us all. I take a second once again to appreciate the clean house, full refrigerator, and decorations. I don't think I've ever actually thanked anyone for this, but I need to start.

I smile as Rosie turns to me when I walk back into the living room. "Who is this?" she asks curiously, pointing to a picture on the mantle.

"That's me and my little sister a little while ago. We were out sailing on Lake Michigan. Raleigh. You'll meet her tomorrow. She's Alex's fiance. You'll meet Harleigh, too, I'm sure. She's Gavin's fiance."

Her eyes widen. "Oh! I like Gavin. He's really nice."

Lance laughs. "It's all an act. He's really an asshole," Lance teases.

We all laugh because Gavin really is an asshole. Unless he's around people he actually cares about. Not many people get to see that side of him though. It's honestly how most of us are. We all have a dark side. Even our saint cops, Dane and Cole.

I turn at a knock on the door. I look at my watch. A knock at this hour is never a good thing in my line of work. I sigh because I'm too fucking tired to deal with anyone or the shit they usually bring with them. I want to get Rosie cleaned up and in bed. Then I want to fuck my husband. In that order.

I check the peephole in my door and see Josh with our family's personal doctor. "Fuck." I open the door quickly. "I'm already turning out to be a horrible father. I completely forgot that she still needs to be looked over."

Josh chuckles. "That's what you have me for. You both need to be checked out."

I shoot him a grateful smile and step back, opening the door. "Doctor Freeman," I say to the tall, silver fox smiling at me. He's in sixties now, but I swear he doesn't look any different than he did when I first met him years ago.

"Damon. Nice to see you again." Doctor Freeman shakes my hand. "You, too."

"So, it's my understanding you had some smoke inhalation issues." He steps inside. Josh follows.

I close the door. "Yeah. We all did, honestly. Lance wasn't directly in it like I was. I'm feeling okay. My chest was hurting on the plane but it's not anymore. Throat's a little scratchy, but I was tested in Texas. Everything looked alright."

Doctor Freeman nods. "Well, I'm going to run my own tests. I have some portable things here with me. If I feel like we need more, I'll ask you to accompany me to my office." He smiles.

I laugh. His office is in our compound. He doesn't need to take appointments for anyone else. We all pay him plenty to keep him exclusive and always on call to us. If we need him quickly, he's available. He still has hospital access just in case he needs more equipment or something he doesn't have here in our compound.

"Rosie, this is Doctor Freeman," I tell Rosie with a smile as she yawns. "He's our family doctor and lives on the compound. You'll see him around a lot. Him and Doctor Chantau. He's the Crane family doctor, but he also lives on the compound so he's available if he's needed."

"Compound?" Rosie blinks a few times as she stares at us in wonder.

"Yes, ma'am," Doctor Freeman says with a grin. "It's a huge area. All gated and swarming with the mafia." He gestures to the couch. "How about we have a seat? I'd like to see how you're doing after that scare earlier."

The wonder on her face falls away as she nods. I feel like my heart is being squeezed. I hate that she went through it and has to live with memories of that. Her own mother not caring at all about her well-being is insanity to me. With the sudden obsession with finding her, I'd think her mother did something stupid and sold her to a fucking trafficking ring or something.

But the more and more I've run that over in my mind, the more I feel it's completely unlikely. Why the fuck would they burn the house down before searching it for her? The only logical explanation I can come up with is they want her dead because she saw something she shouldn't have. They're playing some fucking game I don't understand. We need to figure it out because the longer they're out there, the higher the risk to Rosie is.

I watch as Lance sits down on the other side of Rosie to help and comfort her if she needs him. I let out a tired sigh and take a drink of my water from the bottle I'm holding. I glance out the window at the snow falling faster and harder.

"I'm expecting Raleigh to show up any second," I say with a soft smile.

Josh chuckles. "I told her I know she wants to see you but to let me get Doc to check you both out first. You and Lance would be able to handle it, but a lot of people might overwhelm her." He nods to Rosie. "Raleigh understood."

"She's pretty easygoing. I didn't think she wouldn't."

"Listen, uh… The Ruthless Warriors."

I sigh and rub my head. "I thought we eradicated them." I hold up a hand and shake my head when Josh opens his mouth. "Let me rephrase. I hoped."

"We pissed them off. Remember what Gregory's son said?"

I let out a low growl. While interrogating Gregory Franklin's son, one of our guards shot Gavin. We found out the guard was part of the

Ruthless Warriors. He knew he was on a suicide mission. If he'd had a little better aim, Gavin wouldn't be with us today. Thankfully, he sucked at aiming, Gavin is fully healed and still with us, and that motherfucker met a hail of bullets that added several holes to his miserable body.

"He kept saying they'd be coming for us," I mumble a lot more aggressively than necessary.

"He wasn't kidding. His father has been making a lot of moves all over the fucking place. He was in Italy. We knew that. But he must have been studying us for a long time because he pulled a move right out of Ryan's playbook."

This throws me. I raise an eyebrow. "Alex has been working with Ryan for years. Hell, Lance and I have, too. And Gavin. You didn't start until a few years ago when you took over Lucinio Mafia. How the hell long has he been watching us? Because we just learned about him."

"I'm glad you asked such a sarcastic and fucked up question," he says with a grin. I laugh because I'm glad he caught onto the humor I had laced into my miniscule soliloquy. "The answer is more complicated than I care to admit."

I grin. "You know how much I love complicated."

He laughs. "I know I've said it before, but fuck, I'm glad I know you. You've always fit right into my life."

I pat his back. "Might not have come from the same mother or father, but we're close because of how alike we are. And we compliment each other's differences. At least that's what I've always thought about being a part of your family. Me, you, Alex, and Gavin have been through a lot together. Even before Lance, Cole, and Dane came into the picture."

"Honestly, I don't think I would have come out of how fucked up I was without you." He gives me a pained smile. I give him a side hug before dropping my arm. Josh always ends up feeling guilty and beating himself up when he thinks of everything his father put him through. And everything he did because of it. He shakes his head. "Anyway, we've been chasing him, but the fucker is a ghost. It's like we get near him, and he vanishes. I don't know how he has the money to do it, but he's been all over the fucking world."

"There has to be a money trail," I say as I watch the doctor check Rosie's throat.

"That's the thing. I pulled Robby. He can't find anything. I've had Lance working on it while you both were in Texas. He couldn't find anything."

I scrub my hands over my face. "It's not possible. It has to be in the deep dark parts of whatever interweb bullshit those two work with." I look over at Josh. "Even if he's using cash, there has to be a cashflow.

He shrugs. "It would stand to reason, but we can't find it." He rubs the back of his neck. "I just got back a couple days ago. I've been chasing him, but he keeps moving before we find him. It's like he's dropping his location but not until after he's gone."

I chuckle. "And that would be the page out of Ryan's playbook."

"You got it. It's not just that, though." He drops his hand back to his side. I fold my arms across my chest and lean against the wall. Josh mimics my position, standing against the wall across from me by the door, and looks at me. "It's his connection Matthew."

I watch him, unsure what to say. Matthew Lucinio is Josh's and Alex's father. We killed him nearly a year ago, but he keeps popping up all over the fucking place. He had his damn fingers in everything, including Alex's company. He's just as big of a pain in our ass as he was when he was still breathing.

The connection Gregory Franklin has to Matthew that Josh speaks of is through Gregory's brother, Edward. Edward was Matthew's business partner in some kind of accounting firm he had. Raleigh, my sister, had been promised to him when she was just a kid. Edward was killed trying to kidnap Raleigh.

Charles, Gregory's stupid as fuck son, went after Harleigh, Gavin's fiance. He had been promised Harleigh's hand in marriage through a deal between his father and Harleigh's. What none of them knew was Harleigh already had a connection to us through a one-night-stand with Gavin. She ran to Lucinio Tech after watching them kill her father when he went back on his promise of giving them her. They also didn't know that her father knew who we were and had been trying to contact us.

When all the bullshit was over, Charles was tortured to death, his inside man was killed, and we've been chasing his fucking ghost of a father since. I shake my head. No paper trail. No cashflow. We have nothing.

"He has to have known about us for a long time. I'm sure they've been keeping an eye on us ever since I took over," Josh says. "Which means, they've been around longer than we thought."

"We have to find that cashflow." I rub the palms of my hands against my eyes. "This is fucking bullshit. He can't be a ghost. We're better than that."

"I'm open to suggestions."

"Ryan had the media dropping hints where we were on his and Arianna's honeymoon. He had them releasing videos and pictures of them in locations after we left them. He used cash. Didn't make any withdrawals during the time we were gone. Lance spent a lot of time masking all of us and making sure our flight information wasn't leaked. Between him and Robby, we were well hidden."

"Lance checked. No accounts. The only accounts they have are what we already know about. No money has been removed from any of them."

"Then they have an account we don't know about. We have to find every connection they have. What about the NSA? Or Homeland Security? Or the DEA? Luke used to be DEA. Does he still have contacts now that Shane is retired?"

He tilts his head. "I didn't think about Luke. But Ry has been on this, too. I'll double check and see if he pulled any of our contacts. I haven't had much time to sit down and discuss anything with him."

"We need some kind of lead. If Robby and Lance hit a dead end, we need something else for them to go on. I don't know if Lance or Robby has gone as far as hacking into their servers or not, but maybe the Government can give us something." I chuckle. "I wouldn't put it past either one of them to have done it, though."

"Me either."

"Damon," Doctor Freeman calls.

I look over at him. "Yeah, Doc?"

"Rosie looks good. Lance checks out. Your turn."

I chuckle and walk over to the couch where Doctor Freeman is set up. Lance kisses me. Rosie hugs me. Just the two sweet gestures calm the thoughts whirling through my mind. There are so many, I don't even know where to begin so I can sort them.

"We're going to head upstairs. I'll get her settled and let her pick her room. We can run through all the security features of the house and compound tomorrow. We'll get her all scanned in with security and get her codes and everything. And give her the tour. Right now, she's exhausted."

I nod as I settle on the couch. "Good idea. I'll be up shortly."

They both hug me again before Lance leads her up the stairs. A few moments later, there is a quiet knock on the door. While Doctor Freeman is examining me, Josh lets a distraught Raleigh into the house. She takes one look at me, and her lip starts quivering. I do nothing but hold out my arm. My sister rushes to me.

I hug her the best I can while the doctor does his thing. She cries into my shoulder. "I'm okay, Ral," I whisper into her hair. "Really."

She clings to me and nods, but I know her well enough to know words will never convince her. She'll be around as much as possible until she's convinced I really am alright. Over her shoulder, I meet Alex's eyes. He smiles and gives me a slight nod. It's his way of thanking me for helping his girl calm. Not like he'd have to ask me even one time. She's my sister. I'd do whatever it took to help her.

Just as I would anyone in this family.

My family.

I know them all well enough to know that news we have to share with them isn't something they'd ever judge us about or look down at us for. My heart knows they'll be very accepting of both me and Lance and our relationship as well as Rosie and our decision to adopt her.

My head, though, is taking its sweet ass time catching up.

As Raleigh hugs me, I have to wonder if she'll still feel the same about me after we tell her what we've been hiding. If everyone will.

Or if they'll be hurt we've been lying to them all.

If they'll hate me for not being truthful with them about myself...

Chapter Five

❦ Lance ❦

"You know when you feel like you've jumped and hit the ground landing flat on your face?" I ask Damon as I flop on the bed, still fully clothed. I'm too tired to strip. I just want to sleep.

Damon chuckles low and deep. He's not even near, but the sound reverberates through my body. He's the only one who has ever been able to do that. Just his eyes on me sends shivers down my spine.

"Are you saying you've finally reached your limit and are about to crash?" He grins as he crosses his arms and pulls his shirt over his head. He tosses it into a corner of our bedroom.

"Well, that's what I was saying. But then you had to go and take your shirt off."

He laughs and starts undoing the button on his jeans. "So, if I take these off, will I get you conscious for long enough to get my dick wet?"

I groan at the sexy grin. He slides his jeans down with his boxers, freeing his long, thick, and irresistible cock. "You're the fucking definition of temptation."

"It's your fault. You're the one who introduced me to fifth base."

It's my turn to laugh as I sit up. Fifth base. Anal sex. He'd never done it with any of the girls he pretended with because it reminded him too much of being gay. Which he refused any admission of and wouldn't do anything that made him think of it until he had to think of me in order to come. His journey has been painful.

For both of us.

"Imagine how pleasurable it could have been for you if you hadn't been a dickhead all of those years," I tease as I take off my own shirt. He knows I'm joking. It's been a thing between us for a little while now.

I strip my pants and grin when his eyes drop to my dick. I'm close to him in size. Far larger than average. Thick. Damon and I compliment each other well. I knew as soon as I met him that I would never find another like him.

I was right. Damon is unlike anyone I've ever been with. I don't ever want another.

"Damn, how did I live without you for all these years?" His eyes slowly travel up my body until he reaches mine.

I shiver. "Thankfully, you finally came to your senses," I say, my voice thick with desire.

He stalks towards me, growling low in his throat. I wouldn't be able to hear it if I wasn't listening for it. But I was because I love when he does it. My dick gets harder and harder as I watch him get closer.

"Thankfully," he rumbles when he reaches me.

His lips are on mine less than a second later. Before I know what's happening, we're a tangle of naked limbs in the bed. I have no idea how we got here, but I don't care. I'll take being pinned underneath Damon over sleeping any day of the week. Especially when his hard dick is against mine. I don't care how tired I am.

Our tongues clash in a war of dominance that I don't want to win. Damon has always been top in this relationship, and he knows it very well. I've followed his orders for my entire mafia career. We're thirty-six now. Damon is a few months older than I am.

Since we've known each other, Damon always thought me following his orders was because of his mafia seniority. That had a lot to do with it, but it was mostly because it's just who I am. Something he's found out since we've been married. I'll be the top sometimes, but only when I really need to be.

Damon always knows when that is. Sometimes even before I do. This is not one of those times. I just want him. I want to hang onto him and feel him just to remind myself that he's still here. That the fire didn't take him from me.

My fingers inadvertently grip him tighter as I kiss him deeper. Damon, reading me just as well as he always does, holds me closer and slows everything down. The bed wrestling and bucking into each other fades gradually into soft touches and caresses. The hard and punishing kisses become lighter and far more loving.

I let out a quiet sigh and low moan. My eyes slowly close, and I let myself sink into Damon. My husband. The love of my life. I wrap around him as tightly as I can.

He's here.

Alive.

I just went through these same feelings with Rosie. Granted, it was paternal feelings rather than romantic. After she picked her bedroom, I started the water for her in the bath. Then, I hugged her for several moments. It must have been something she needed just as much because she held on tight. Much like right now, the closeness went a long way in making me feel better.

Damon leaves light kisses along my slightly stubbled jaw and down my neck, making me groan low and tilt my head to the side, giving him more access. His arms wrap tightly around me, making me sigh.

"How do you do that? Know just what I need?"

He smiles against my neck. "I know you, baby." He trails searing but gentle kisses across my throat. "I know you need to feel me." His deep voice vibrates against my skin.

I open my eyes and guide his lips back to mine, kissing him softly. "I need you."

"You have me. You always have me." Damon shifts, and I feel his tip pressing against me.

My stomach clenches in anticipation, but I hold him closer to me because I don't want to let him go. Maybe that fire scared me more than I thought. There was a brief period of time I couldn't see him. The smoke was too thick. Then when we saw the flames licking into the room, I'm pretty sure my panic level reached heights I've never dreamed of. The thought of losing him was beyond my comprehension, but it didn't make me any less terrified.

Damon pushes himself into me, and I moan, gripping him even tighter. The deeper he goes, the more and more I allow myself to really believe he's still with me. Real. In the flesh. Everything that happened feels like more of a dream to me. What's real is him.

"There was a period of time I couldn't see you or Rosie. The smoke was too thick." My voice cracks. I tremble, but only slightly. If Damon weren't holding me so tightly, if his dick weren't buried in my ass, he'd never feel it.

But he does.

His arms wrap around me tighter. He sinks deeper, making me jerk into him as I pulse around him. "Lance. I'm here. We both are. We made it. We brought our girl home." He kisses my neck and up my jaw to my lips. He smiles as he looks reassuringly into my eyes. "You're never losing me." He kisses me softly when I open my mouth to protest; to tell him we can never be sure of the future. "Never, baby. I'm always going to be by your side. Always."

His lips land on mine again as he starts thrusting slowly and deeply, allowing me to feel all of him. Every single inch. Every ridge. His tongue slips between my lips. His kiss is loving and reassuring, yet firm and demanding. He steals my breath and swallows my moans.

I know he wants to quicken the pace; to take me in a fast, punishing manner, but he knows it's not what I need. One thing I've learned about him over the years is he always makes sure I have what I need before he even thinks about taking what he does.

Even when we were only friends, Damon had that way about him. He'd let me in line first at a buffet, movie, or concert that we attended together. He always made sure I got a drink before him. After missions, even though I'm rarely ever on the battlefield, Damon always made sure I was settled in my hotel room before he ever went to his. If we shared a room, which was more often than not, I was always the one who showered first.

I always thought it was his protective side; that he'd do the same for everyone. The longer I got to be in his life, though, the more I realized it was just me. There were so many things he did for me that he never did for others. I believe now that he was doing those things to show me how he felt about me without actually saying the words he couldn't bring himself to.

I arch into Damon and clench around, squeezing his dick. He moans into my mouth and nips my tongue before sucking it lightly. One of his hands spears my hair. The other snakes its way down to my waist and pulls me into his thrusts.

I let my head fall back. "Fuck, Damon." My hard cock jerks against my stomach and his.

Damon's lips sear their way down my jaw and to my neck once more as he groans. "I've missed this," he rumbles. His deep voice makes me shiver and jerk over his dick as I buck into his thrusts, silently begging for more.

Damon doesn't miss the cue. He never misses any signals in any area of his life, but he's learned mine like no other. His kiss becomes deeper; more dominant. He shifts and rolls his hips against me. My legs wrap tighter around him all on their own. He slams into me, and I meet each of his thrusts, moaning at how good he feels buried inside me; stretching me.

"Damon," I moan against his neck. I can't even be sure what it is I need, but I know he does. He always does.

Keeping one hand tangled in my hair, Damon kisses me again. My lips mold to his while his other hand reaches between us. Still thrusting into me, he grips my dick and strokes me. I immediately thicken for him as my ass clenches tight around him.

"Fuck, baby," he whispers against my lips with a cocky smile. He knows exactly how to make me lose control, and he loves doing it.

He trusts harder, as deep as he can, and faster until he's pounding into my ass. He strokes my dick at the same pace of his thrusts. He squeezes it and twists his wrist as he strokes. I'm so close to coming, but I don't want him to stop. He feels too good.

Damon is way too talented at this, though. While he's slamming his dick deep into me and stroking my cock, he starts fucking my mouth with his tongue. The possessive groans that rumble from his throat crash over me like a tidal wave letting me know I'm his. The dominance in each thrust of his tongue, stroke of his hand, and thrust of his dick makes me feel safe and brings me more and more contentment.

Reassurance.

"Fuck me, Damon," I moan. I can't think of anything but his tongue, strokes, and thrusts. My brain is swimming in him. Just him. Precome beads from my tip. He catches it and uses it to coat my dick.

"And here I thought I was fucking you," he teases just before he shifts his hips, slamming into me again and again, sending me straight to my peak.

"Oh shit, baby, I'm gonna come!" I gasp out. Jolt after jolt of pleasure shoot down my spine and straight through my dick.

He grins. "Come, baby. You know I love you making a mess of me." He doesn't stop jerking me or thrusting. His hips continue shifting back and forth as he rolls his hips against mine. His cock keeps pounding into my ass.

I pulse and clench tight around him. I use my legs to hold him still inside me. I want him to come at the same time. I need to feel him fill me as I make a mess of us both just the way he likes so much.

I throw my head back. "Oh fuck yes, Damon!" I shout, throwing my head back. I come hard for him. Come streams from my dick and shoots over my stomach. Damon keeps stroking me through it all. Come slides down his hand. Since we're so close, it hits his stomach just as it does mine.

And still he doesn't stop. He slows his strokes but thrusts inside me one last time. "Holy shit. Lance! Yes! Oh yes!" he yells against my neck. He buries his cock deep in my ass and comes so hard, I swear to fuck I feel him in my stomach.

We both pant against each other for several moments before Damon pulls slowly out of me. He leaves a soft kiss against my lips as he stands and walks to the bathroom. I don't miss him licking my come off his fingers. It makes me groan. I'd follow him, but that's not how it works with him. He likes taking care of both of us. I'd never take that from him.

I smile when he comes out a few moments later cleaned up. With a level of love I've come to crave from him, he uses a warm washcloth to clean me up. His touch is light. The sparkle in his eyes as he looks at me makes me melt. I may look tough on the outside, but Damon will always have the power to turn me into mush.

He kisses me softly again before he gets back up and walks back to the bathroom. I hear him rinsing out the cloth. Seconds later, he's shutting off the lights and crawling into bed next to me. He wraps me in his arms and pulls me against his body. We're close to the same size in all senses of the word, but he seems so much bigger than me. Like he can engulf me.

"How's Rosie?" he rumbles against the back of my neck as he hugs me. My back is against his chest. My ass is against his dick. It's my favorite way to fall asleep. "She was fast asleep when I came up."

I smile. "She's okay. She's a tough girl. She passed out just after her bath. I put her clothes in piles though. I'm not certain Dallas' will fit her. They look really small. There's some of Lyric's there, though. Hopefully, something will work."

"Well, before we head over to Rebekkah's and Kent's we'll need to spend some time online getting her things she needs. She'll need a phone, too. I'm sure she's going insane without one. Being a teenager and all." He smiles against my neck.

I laugh. "I always thought it was a complete anomaly that I didn't see her with her phone attached to her hand. That girl is content with a book or movie or just spending time with those close to her."

"We might have lucked out with her."

I smile. "We did luck out with her. I still can't believe she chose us."

"Even knowing all the shit we're into. It takes a special kind of person to willingly choose this life. But I think she'll fit right in. She didn't bat an eye when we told her everything that was happening with her mother."

"She's a very open-minded and honest young woman." I wince. "Yeah, I'm gonna keep calling her our little girl. Not ready for a young woman yet."

Damon chuckles and snuggles me closer. "I'm with you. But she's almost eighteen. Pretty sure we already need to think about college."

"Good thing we're in the mafia. We can scare all the boys she dates away. What's that song called? Something about cleaning a gun when her date is around? Have her back at a decent hour."

Damon grins. "*Cleaning This Gun* by Rodney Atkins. I live for the day I can say the words y'all have some fun. Bet I'll be up all night just cleaning this gun."

I laugh. "The really great part of that is I can actually see that happening. He comes to pick her up. Goes through security. Finally gets to the house. There you are sitting on the couch with a loaded gun next to you and your rifle torn apart next to you just casually being cleaned." I let my eyes fall closed, a smile on my face.

"He'd run away screaming."

I yawn as exhaustion overtakes me once more. I press myself closer to my husband. "Or be too terrified to disobey and stay a good ten feet from her."

Damon wraps his arms around me tighter, locking them around me. "I'd be okay with either option." He kisses the back of my head.

As I drift off in the arms of the man I love, our daughter sleeping peacefully just down the hall, I can't help but wonder...

If life is this perfect right now, not considering the threat of Rosie's mother and her allies, what does the future have in store for us?

Chapter Six

❦ Damon ❦

I yawn as I slowly open my eyes, then instantly groan. My head is pounding, and the bed is cold. Which means my husband woke up before me after a long as fuck night. We didn't close our eyes until just before the sun started brightening the sky. I glance at the clock on the nightstand as I roll onto my back. That was only five hours ago. It's barely noon.

"Fuck," I mumble as I rub the grit from my eyes.

I sit up and catch a whiff of smoke from that fire and realize that neither of us took a shower last night. We were both too tired. We used our second wind convincing each other we were still breathing. Lance may not have been on that ladder, but that didn't stop visions of the house collapsing and killing all of us in the burning rubble from invading my mind.

The thought has me quickly jumping out of the bed and stripping the sheets and blankets. It's all going into the wash. No fucking way I'm letting either of us be reminded of how close death was. I felt the heat from the flames shooting out over our heads after Rosie dropped into my arms. How close the flames licking across the outside of the house was.

I put everything by the door and head straight for the shower. I scrub myself down until I can't smell yesterday's reminder of death on my skin anymore. I've been shot at. I've even been injured during some of our wars against our enemies. Nothing, and I mean that, has ever scared me as much as yesterday.

Maybe it's because this time I have people I care about with everything I am. Not that I didn't have that before, but it's far different when love is involved. When a child is. It's not the same for me anymore. I didn't give as much of a shit about my own well-being. My job was to protect everyone else. If I didn't make it home, at least they did. Now, I have people in my life that I want to make it home to. People waiting for me.

I get it now. All of it. I understand now why the guys who have families or significant others light up when their phones ring. I get why they're so relieved when we all walk away without any injuries or losses. But what hits me hardest is why they all seem to feel worse when we do lose someone out there. They feel it on a different level. They understand that there are people who are going to desperately miss that person. I can't believe it's taken me this long to finally understand it all.

I don't know how long I'm in the shower lost in my own thoughts, but when I come back to myself, the water is lukewarm. I shut it off and step out. I grab a towel and quickly dry off. I go through my morning routine, then quickly get dressed. It's after I have my jeans and black long-sleeve shirt on that I realize the sheets and blankets are gone, and the bed is made.

I smile and shake my head. It's a very Lance thing to do. He probably came up to check on me, heard me in the shower, and decided to pick up everything. Which means he probably had the same thoughts I did when he woke up. Even our clothing from yesterday is gone. He even sprayed something that smells fresh and calming.

My husband.

I'm learning very quickly that he just knows. He knows how to make me better. How to make everything right again. I smile as I make my way downstairs. The smell of bacon eases the rest of the tension I had been feeling. I groan and follow my nose to the kitchen.

When I get there, I have to stop and grin. I quietly lean against the wall and fold my arms over my chest as I watch Lance and Rosie cooking.

Rosie is laughing and mixing some kind of batter. "You're just not allowed to make Eggos. Not when you can make real waffles. It's, like, illegal or something."

Lance laughs as he flips bacon. "I'll have to have Dane or Cole arrest me because I haven't used that thing at all since I bought it." He nods to the waffle maker sitting on the counter. "Too much work."

Rosie giggles. "I'm throwing away all the Eggos."

Lance feigns horror as he clutches his chest. "Not the Eggos! What will I eat when I'm working at three in the morning?"

"How about real waffles?"

"How about leave my Eggos alone or I throw you in a snowbank?" He says with a grin as he reaches for her like he's going to do just that.

She squeaks and holds up the spoon she's mixing with in front of her like a weapon. "I am not afraid to batter you."

I can't help but crack up. "That was a good one. Batter." I laugh.

Lance laughs. "This isn't over, cub. We'll be going over to Rebekkah's and Kent's house later. There's plenty of snow on the ground." He grins and winks mock threateningly.

She giggles again as she starts pouring batter in the waffle maker. "I can't believe it snowed so much in just a few hours." Her eyes are sparkling when she turns to me. "Is this an every winter thing? I've only seen real snow once in my whole life."

"Uh, well, we get snow." I make my way to the back door. "I haven't seen how much has come down yet."

"A lot," Lance says. "Rebekkah called a little bit ago and said we should think about getting over there soon. The storm is going to get worse. She wants us all under one roof before it hits as hard as it's supposed to tonight. I guess Ryan told her we should go to his or Josh's house, but she's insistent we all go there. She's prepared with blankets and everything, but asked us all to bring our own. Just in case."

I chuckle. Rebekkah is like a mom to all of us. She's Ryan's aunt by blood. She's his late father's sister. For his entire life, he and his brother's believed she was dead. No one knew she'd been sold by her father to the Lucinio Mafia as part of a business deal. Her brother, Ryan's father, was told she'd been killed in a car accident. They had a funeral for her and everything.

No one knew she'd been promised to Matthew Lucinio. For years, Rebekkah thought she'd been abandoned by her family. Her calls to her brother were blocked. Eventually, she believed everything she was told. They didn't want her. Matthew even had her believing Ethan, her brother, was dead. She was isolated from everyone and everything. All she had were her sons, Alex and Josh. Well, them and me and Gavin.

Little did anyone know that Rebekkah also had another son. She'd returned home from college the day she was sold to tell her family that she'd planned to marry and had just delivered a son that she kept hidden from them. During her pregnancy, she made herself scarce to them. She knew her parents wouldn't approve of the man she planned to marry or the child she'd had with him out of wedlock. She knew the only one who'd be on her side was Ethan.

Only, Ethan wasn't there when she arrived. She was sold and forced against her will to go with Matthew's father. No one knew the truth of what happened until around a year or so ago. Maybe a little longer. The amount of truth that came out still makes my head spin just thinking about it all.

I open the back door that leads to our backyard, complete with a pool that currently doesn't have water in it and is covered because of the winter. It's snowing heavily enough that I can't see the other end of the pool.

"Holy fuck," I say. "There has to be a good foot on the ground right now. It's coming down hard."

"Yeah, it's going to let up in a little while," Lance says as I close the door. "We all agreed we'd head to Rebekkah's then. Josh already came by and collected the blankets requested."

I lock the door. "Do we need to grab anything?"

"Nope," Rosie says with a smile as she works on the waffles. "We gave everything to Josh and Gavin. Gavin came for the gifts."

"Shit. Gifts. How did we get gifts?" I ask Lance, slightly panicked.

He grins. "Thank God for online shopping, huh?" He winks at me. "I had everything sent to Raleigh for us. She had a big wrapping party with Harleigh and Dallas. I was even under orders to get things for a five-year-old boy and five-year-old girl."

I sit down at the high chairs we have around the kitchen island. "The fuck?"

"Yeah, I didn't question. Just did what Rebekkah said."

I just laugh. "Probably a wise decision." My heart suddenly clenches tight in my chest. I get up quickly and head for the fridge to grab orange juice. I clear my throat quietly as I open it. Lance looks at me and takes my hint. He walks to me and stands close. "What about Rosie?" I whisper.

Lance grins. "Ryan has it covered," he whispers back and gives me a quick peck before he goes back to the bacon.

I've never been so grateful for this family. We've all pulled together and rallied around members of our family in the past. It's what we do. It feels a lot different when the person on the other end of the support is us, though. It's an overwhelming feeling. Especially since Lance and I have always been the people on the giving end, not the receiving end.

I set out the orange juice and milk, then grab the whipped cream and syrup for the waffles before cutting up fresh strawberries. All things I find myself once again beyond grateful to our family for. Something I need to express my gratitude for. The food in the fridge and so much more.

After we're settled, and begin eating, Lance takes out his tablet and gives it to Rosie. "You'll need clothes. Don't worry about electronics or anything. I'll get you that. Just grab whatever you'll need for clothes and school. Backpacks and whatever."

She nods as she eats. "What's my limit?" She licks a finger and takes the tablet.

"You don't have one," I tell her.

She blinks and looks at me. "That's not fair. I have to have a limit."

"Rosie." I shake my head. "You have nothing. You're completely starting over. You need things. I don't care what you get. I don't care how many different stores you go to. I don't care if the grand total is five-thousand. You need to replace things and get what you need."

She chews her lip as she turns back to the tablet. "I... don't want to be that spoiled rich girl...," she whispers before looking back at me.

"Then I'll happily give you an allowance and make you budget things." I nod to the tablet. "After you buy the things you need. I'm not limiting that because I know what things cost. And I know you need things for school, for yourself, and things to make you feel at home. If you really want a limit on that, we'll say ten-thousand."

Lance grins. "You're not winning this one, cub. Damon is the type of man who will make sure everyone around him has what they need before he'll even consider anything else. I'd argue with him, but he's right. You do need to get things you need and replace things. This is a new beginning for you. It's a beginning for all of us. It might just be things, but sometimes things are important. Sometimes, things help us to reacclimate to new surroundings."

"Couldn't agree more," I say. "Don't worry about a limit on this. If you weren't old enough to shop for yourself, you know we'd be doing it. And we wouldn't give a shit about a limit. I do promise not to turn you into a spoiled rich kid, though." I grin and teasingly bump her shoulder.

"Good. Fair deal." She pulls up a website for a store and starts scrolling through things as she eats.

Lance and I finish eating and start cleaning up. When we're finished, several minutes later, I'm pretty sure she's just getting started. I grin as Lance leads me into the living room. We're out of earshot of her, but we can still see her. All of our houses are open floor plans. It's what we're comfortable with. I'd feel strange sitting in a kitchen that's closed off to everything. It makes me feel isolated. Mostly, that I could be ambushed. Price of being in the mafia, I guess.

"Ryan went out a little while ago to shop for Rosie, but this storm is getting bad," Lance says low enough so only I can hear him. I'm not sure Rosie would be able to anyway. We're far enough away.

"Has anyone had phone contact with him?"

"Arianna did. But she called Josh because that was over an hour ago. No one has heard from him or the guards he has with him. Josh just texted while we were cleaning up. He asked me to track him because Robby is already with Luke at Rebekkah's. He left his laptop home. Visibility is so bad out there, he can't see more than a foot in front of him. He tried to walk to the house, but he got completely turned around and had to actually call out for help to get back to Rebekkah's. He was down by the lake."

I cough in surprise as my eyebrows shoot up to the ceiling. "That's the complete opposite direction of his and Luke's house." I shake my head. "Why didn't he just use the underground system? Ours might not be ready but the Crane family's is."

Lance shakes his head. "When we were in Texas, they started connecting the tunnels underground so we're all connected to each other and the bunker and can travel underground, if needed, between houses. Some of the tunnels are closed off right now."

"Fuck. I forgot about that. Track him. Let me know. Taylor and Dane are the best drivers in snow. I can contact one of them. Actually. Switch Taylor for Alex. He's second to Taylor when it comes to driving. With the storm this bad, you know Tait won't let his dad out of his sight. Taylor would go, but he'd be thinking of Tait. It would put him in danger. The road wouldn't have his full attention."

Lance just nods as he sits down and types something on his phone. He opens his laptop as I sit down next to him. One thing I've always admired about him is his ability to figure shit out and fast. I love watching his fingers fly across the keys of his laptop or computer. But watching him decipher code as easily and quickly as he does is on another level of talent. Lines of jumbled letters and numbers show up on a black screen that make no sense to me.

But Lance understands everything.

Seconds later the screen switches from complete nonsense to a map of Chicago. After a few taps of keys, Lance has a dot on the screen. And just a couple more strokes later, the map is zoomed in on the dot.

"Well, that's… fucking odd," Lance says.

"That's just a block from the gate," I say.

Lance picks up his phone and puts it on speaker. "I'm calling the gate."

"How can I help you, Mr. Engle?" a deep voice answers after just one ring. Our team is efficient.

"We've been looking for Mr. Crane. I have him a block away from the gate."

"Yes, sir. Mr. Crane just arrived a few minutes ago. He had to walk the last block because the SUV got stuck. He used the gate to help him get here. We have a few guards getting the SUV. The storm has let up just a little. Mr. Crane is being escorted to his estate right now."

"Thank God. Why the hell didn't he have his phone in weather like this?" Lance asks.

"He said he dropped it outside the door of his SUV when he got out to investigate. He knew where he was because he was using GPS to navigate and was going really slow. But he hit a huge drift just up the block. He was hoping he could get out. When he realized he couldn't, he went to call us but dropped it when a gust of wind hit him unexpectedly."

"As long as he's safe," I say, relieved.

"Yes, sir. I just got word he's home. The guards also radioed in and said they got the SUV free."

"Good," Lance says. He says his goodbye and hangs up.

I look down at my phone when it buzzes and smile. "Arianna just sent us a group text saying he's home." I lean over and kiss him. "Good job on finding him so fast. I'm surprised Robby couldn't just do that from his phone." I grin.

Lance laughs. "You know we have a program specially designed for us. Though, remind me to work with Robby to make it work on a phone. I can't believe we haven't done that yet."

I chuckle. "If the storm is letting up, we should get over there." I look up at Rosie as she stands, her eyes still glued to the tablet.

After a few moments, she looks up at us. "I'm not really sure what to take. Lance said before we went to bed that we'd probably be staying the night because of the expected blizzard. The clothes that are smallest fit best, but there isn't anything I can use to sleep in. There are jeans and some slacks. There's a hoodie or two and some shirts, but nothing is really long enough or comfortable enough." She bites her lip and folds her hands in front of her, still holding the tablet.

"No worries," I say with a smile. "I have a hoodie I'm sure is big enough. And some sleep pants. They'll be big on you, but they'll keep you warm in the event we lose power. I'm not sure if the generators have been hooked up or not to the house because we've been gone. There's been a lot going on here. Better safe than sorry, though."

"I don't think they have been, considering we were all asked to bring extra blankets," Lance says. "Unless the fireplaces work. I still don't know if they're gas or electric, since we've never used it."

"Guess we'll find out," I grin as I stand. "I'll grab our stuff. You two get ready too. I'll be down in a minute."

I jog up the stairs with a huge grin on my face. We haven't had a big family holiday celebration in longer than I can remember. I think the last one was way back in college, and it can't be considered a celebration. It was put on by Josh's and Alex's father on one of the many days he was trying to woo Alex back into the folds of the mafia Alex so desperately wanted to leave behind.

I throw everything in a duffle bag, barely containing my excitement. Not only because this will be our first real Christmas where all of us are together, but also because this is the night. We're telling everyone we're married and are adopting Rosie. I'm sure we'll get a few death stares, but I know our family. They'll support us just as much as Alex and Josh do.

I can't wait to open up and share us with them.

Chapter Seven

❦ Lance ❦

"Okay, everyone. Rebekkah and I have an announcement," Kent Michaels says.

We're all gathered in the giant area Rebekkah calls a family room. It's larger than any of the family rooms anyone else has in any of their houses, but I think it was intentional. Rebekkah loves hosting our combined families for holidays, so this room was specifically designed to hold all of us comfortably.

It takes up most of the bottom floor. There are two fireplaces at opposite ends of the room. It's warm and inviting. The furniture is a deep, rich brown. The plush carpet is a lighter tan. The light in the room is dimmed to give it a more cozy feeling.

Near the large, floor-to-ceiling front window, is a tree as tall as the one the family put up in our house. Where ours is elegantly decorated, Rebekkah's and Kent's is bursting with colored lights, colored balls, popcorn strands, and garland. I'm pretty sure a tinsel monster came by and threw up on it. Yet somehow, the tree looks fantastic. It makes everything feel more homey.

"Now that everyone is here and settled," Rebekkah says with a smile. She puts one last gift underneath the tree. It's overflowing with presents as it is and that doesn't count the ones from the almighty Santa Claus. "Kent and I have made a decision."

"Uh oh," Alex rumbles teasingly.

"Hush," Rebekkah says with a laugh and sweet smile as she bustles out of the room quickly. Kent smiles adoringly.

I glance at Damon. "Ideas?"

"Well, I'd say they're getting married, but they already did that. I got nothing."

I grin and wait for her to come back. Moments later, she comes back with two kids. Both are holding one of her hands and are clinging to her. When she stops, they both turn and bury their heads in her thigh.

One is a boy. The other is a girl. The boy has brunette hair that's scruffy, but not in a deliberately messy kind of way. The girl's hair is shoulder length and the same color. The boy is dressed in adorable dress pants with a button-down white shirt. It's tucked into the pants. He's wearing suspenders and black socks. The girl is wearing a cute black dress with a pink sash around her waist that's tied in a bow in the back. Her tights are pink and the socks she has on are pink and fuzzy.

Both keep themselves tucked into Rebekkah's side, but I can see the boy has a very pretty set of gray eyes. I raise an eyebrow as we wait for an explanation. Glancing around the room, I know I'm definitely not the only one confused and wondering where they're going with this. The only thing that makes sense right now is why we were asked to get gifts for a five-year-old boy and girl.

Rebekkah leads them both to Kent's side. Kent puts an arm around his wife with the little girl between them. "Everyone. We'd like you to meet Jordan," Kent says, nodding to the boy. "And Harper." He puts his hand on top of the girl's head. "Our adopted son and daughter."

I lean into Damon in shock. "Damn," I whisper.

"Well, holy shit," Damon whispers back. Ryan whistles. Dane grins like an idiot. Alex and Josh look at each other with open mouths. Everyone else starts murmuring.

Rebekkah clears her throat, and silence falls over everyone once more. "A couple of months ago, DJ and Matt were on a SWAT call. It wasn't good. It was a domestic that didn't end well for Harper and Jordan's parents. Drugs were involved. These two were starving." She tears up. "They were malnourished and had definitely been abused." She gives us all a watery smile as she turns on the big screen TV. Kent quickly taps a few keys on his phone and looks up at the screen as three faces we all have come to know very well appear on the screen.

"Hey, everyone! Merry Christmas!" Lyric's English accent fills the room. The kids light up as their heads whip to the TV.

"Auntie Lyric!" Harper squawks.

"Uncle DJ and Matt!" Jordan yells, waving like a madman.

"Hey, munchkins! Having fun?" DJ's deep Southern accented voice asks.

"Yep!" the two kids say in unison.

"Mom and Daddy say Santa is coming tonight!" Harper says excitedly.

"I hear he has a whole sleigh full of goodies for you," Lyric says with a grin. "Candies and presents, but you have to be good and go to sleep on time."

"We will!" they both say in unison again.

"Okay! Kids, come with me," Rebekkah says. "Time to get the cookies and hot chocolate!"

Kent picks up Ryan's and Arianna's three-year-old son, Christopher. Jackson, Jason's and Jessa's three-year-old runs as fast as he can after Tait, Taylor's and Nicole's five-year-old. Everyone follows Rebekkah to the kitchen leaving all of us with Lyric, Matt, and DJ.

"First of all," Matt begins. He and DJ married Lyric a few years ago and made our little sister the happiest she's ever been. "We're sorry we missed out this year. Chicago's airport closed this morning just after the first wave of your storm hit. Our flight was canceled, so we're doing the next best thing and Skyping in."

"We'll take it. At least we get to say hi!" Nicole Reddick, Taylor's wife says. "We miss you guys!"

"Can't wait to see you!" Raleigh chips in as she waves at the screen.

Lyric giggles and waves back, smiling happily. "We miss you guys, too! We'll be there soon!"

Dane clears his throat. "Not to be a dick, but what's going on? Mom and Dad just told us they adopted two kids. Which means, Alex,

Josh, and I have a new little brother and sister. Which isn't a big deal. They're fucking adorable. Just… what the fuck is happening? What went on down there?"

DJ rubs his head. "We got a SWAT call in the middle of the night. Fucked up shit. A guy was holding his wife at gunpoint. We got there. It was a small house. I'm talking really small. One bedroom. A kitchen. Bathroom. A small living room. All on one floor. When we got there, things had escalated pretty hardcore. They were screaming at each other. There was a shot. More screaming at each other. We saw smoke coming out of one of the rooms. Turns out it was the bedroom. We had to act fast."

"We called in fire and had them on standby a block away," Matt continues. "We had to go in. We didn't have a lot of time to formulate a plan. We tried yelling to get them to come out, but the dude started shooting at us. That's when the woman started screaming for help. We found out she was in the bedroom. He was lighting shit on fire around the bed and had her tied to it. He was shooting at her at first. He'd shoot the bed or the wall behind her. A few minutes after we got there, she started screaming that she was burning. That's when we went in. We didn't have a choice."

"As soon as the door busted open, he started shooting." DJ hugs Lyric when she shivers. "We couldn't throw any tear gas or smoke bombs because of the fire. It could have ignited the gasses. Not a chance we wanted to take. We shot him and went for her. She was screaming in agony. Horrifying screams. The kind you'll never get out of your mind. We went for the bedroom as some of the others cleared the house. Another went for a fire extinguisher. Of course, there wasn't one. There was nothing we could do for her."

"They burned her alive," Lyric whispers. She burrows into Matt.

I shiver. "That's fucked up."

"Gross," Rosie says as she cuddles into me. "So cruel. Why are people so cruel?"

"That's disgusting," Dallas says, shaking her head. Josh hugs her.

"Very," DJ says. "One of the officers saw a door in the kitchen. It led to a basement. Imagine our surprise when we saw two kids down there."

"Christ," Damon growls. The protectiveness makes me jump slightly and swallow hard. I fight the shiver that runs down my spine. His tone is sexy as hell.

Matt hugs Lyric tighter. "The kids were malnourished. They'd both been beaten. We feared they'd been sexually assaulted. After a complete checkup, we were very happy to know they hadn't been. Those two kids were beyond neglected. It's the worst case I've ever seen. We couldn't get them into a temporary shelter or a temporary home. Things were just not available. But they'd taken a liking to us while we were trying to find them a place. We took them home with us after calling Lyric and talking to her."

Lyric smiles softly. "When they got them home, I helped them clean up. We got them fed. The little their tummies could manage, anyway. And then they slept for the entire rest of the day, through the night, and half the next day. We called Kent and Rebekkah because we knew they'd been thinking about fostering and possibly adopting. They decided almost right away to take them."

"You little sneak," Josh says to Lyric with a grin. "And you didn't tell us?"

"Cause it was a secret," Lyric singsongs with a cheeky smile.

"How did all of this get done with none of us knowing?" I ask, smiling.

DJ laughs. "We did it all the legal way. You know. The non-hacking way. Though, they'll probably have to finalize a few things."

I grin. "I'll take care of it."

"The hacking way!" Robby says from where he's sitting in his husband's, Luke's, lap. We all laugh.

Lyric smiles and leans forward. "Are the little ones back yet?"

I look up and see Kent poking his head around the corner. I wave him into the room. "Coming now, Lyric."

Lyric's face lights up when the kids come back into the room. She engages them in a conversation all about the Christmas dinner we just had. The three of them stay on Skype all throughout the family gift giving portion of the night. They even open a few gifts themselves to make everyone feel like they're right here with us.

After all the chaos has come to an end, I have to smile even wider than I already am. Over the years, our family has grown a lot. We've had to split the gift giving portion of our time together into two parts. Family is Christmas Eve. The kids and Santa are Christmas morning, but to keep up the Santa narrative, we always make sure each of the adults has one gift from Santa as well. This is the first year we've done this as a huge family with both the Crane's and the Lucinio's. I have to say it's perfect.

"I think it's time," I say to Damon, a little hesitantly. I don't want him to feel like I'm pushing him.

My tight chest settles instantly when he smiles and squeezes my hand. He clears his throat. "Everyone? Lance and I also have an announcement."

As the kids play, all other eyes turn to us. We even have Lyric's, DJ's, and Matt's attention. I'm not one for attention. This time is no exception, even though these are all people we love and trust. I'm definitely feeling like we're under a microscope and being studied.

"We're married," I blurt. "And adopting Rosie." I choke back sudden rising panic. I've never been ashamed of who I am, but I'm terrified everyone in this room is going to be pissed off at this news.

Damon's thumb soothingly rubs the back of my hand. I glance at him, confused at how he can possibly be so calm in this situation. This entire time, it's been Damon who was nervous about this moment. Maybe he's finally just come to terms with everything. Or maybe he's passed all of his nervous energy to me. While he's smiling softly at me, I'm fighting to breathe. Not because I'm afraid of their reaction to us being gay. It's because we kept this from them.

"We were married last year in Las Vegas after a mission," Damon starts. "We didn't say anything because I wasn't sure we were going to stay married. As you all know, I've never admitted my sexuality. I've dated women. I've only ever been with women." He looks at me. His deep brown eyes soothe the war going on in my lungs. "What I never admitted is that it was Lance's image that got me there with them. For years." He leans in and kisses me. It's our first kiss in front of our entire family and sends butterflies flying through my entire being.

"Well, you all owe me. I'll take my winnings in the form of my own private jet," Lyric says.

I jerk my head over to her as several people in the room crack up. "What the crap are you talking about, girl?"

She giggles. "We all had a bet going. Everyone was taking down dates of when Damon was going to come out and tell you that he was in love with you. I said I bet that you're already married. Looks like I was right. Though, I was just kidding." She blinks. "I didn't think I'd actually win." She laughs.

"Such a fucking brat," Damon grumbles through his huge smile.

"Ugh! I'm so mad at you." Jessa throws a throw pillow at both of us. Damon catches it with a laugh. "You know how much me and Dallas love planning parties! And you've known me forever! How could you keep it from me?" She pouts, but she's laughing.

"Hey! I've known both of them longer than you," Alex says. "And I just found out yesterday!" He smiles at us both. "Well kept secret. Don't ever do it again."

"Never." I hold up the one hand Damon isn't holding in a show of surrender.

"And about Rosie," Josh says with a grin. "Welcome to the family, honey. It's big. Sometimes loud." He points to the screen. "We have a sassy as hell brat in the family that her husbands are barely able to contain. But we're lovable. For the most part."

"Hey! I resemble that remark!" Lyric protests.

Matt laughs. "Damn right you resemble it. Your face is next to the word brat in the dictionary!"

Rosie giggles as Lyric pouts but laughs along with everyone else. Rosie leans into me. "Everyone is really nice."

I wrap an arm around her and hug her tight to my side. "I may have been a little nervous about how they'd take me and Damon being married already without telling them, but I never doubted their acceptance of you."

Rosie melts into the both of us as we all say goodbye to Lyric, Matt, and DJ. It's getting late. The blizzard is blowing full force outside. The lights have flickered more than a few times. We'd rather say our goodbyes now then be cut off and have her worry. Not like she won't be anyway.

"Okay, everyone! Time for Christmas movies!" Rebekkah announces just after we hang up with our extended Florida family. The kids excitedly cheer. "Let's get everyone in their jammies!" The kids and everyone else scurry off to rooms to change.

Rosie smiles softly but bites her lip. She hugs herself and looks at me and Damon nervously as she sits up slowly. "Everyone is going to look so cute," she whispers.

"So are you," Damon says with a grin.

I know he's trying to make her feel better, but I get where she's coming from. Everyone in our family is well to do and will be in their own clothing. I'm sure some of the girls will be in their husband's clothing. Rosie has hand-me-downs and pajamas from her dad who towers over her. She'll not only be self-conscious, but uncomfortable. Even if she tries to convince us both that she's okay with it.

"Hey," Dallas says softly and shyly. "I know it's probably not exactly what you want, but I did bring an extra pair of some warm jammies when Alec, he's my brother, and I came today. Just in case. I wasn't sure if you had anything."

Rosie looks up at her with tears in her eyes and a soft smile. "Da…" She trails off and looks at Damon, unsure if she should call him dad as she started to or not.

Dallas, though, doesn't miss a beat. She's quiet but intuitive as hell. "Your dad let you use some of his stuff?"

Rosie nods, her soft smile turning grateful. "It's… probably super big, but I don't mind wearing it."

Dallas takes her hand and pulls her up. "It's up to you, but check out what I brought first. You can choose." Without releasing her hand, Dallas leads her away from us. I just grin when Rosie looks over her shoulder in shock and wonder.

Damon stands, pulling me with him. He leads me to one of the bedrooms that we left our bag in with our change of clothes. He made sure Rosie got her own bag so she felt special and like she had something that belonged to her.

We know she's grateful she has her life and us, but we also know it's difficult for anyone to have no possessions. Especially possessions that mean the world to them, such as the locket her father gave her. We're hoping it will be found in the rubble of her grandparents' home, but none of us are holding out hope.

A few moments later, we're all snuggled and ready to start Christmas movies. Dallas has taken an immediate liking to Rosie and has her cuddled with her. When Rosie looks at us, her smile tells us all we need to know.

She's going to be okay.

We're all going to be just fine.

Chapter Eight

☙ Damon ☙

(One Week Later)

"Motherfucker," I grumble for the millionth time in the past five minutes. I shuck another shovel full of snow into the already growing pile of it.

They called the blizzard we just had the storm of the century. And it really fucking was. It broke all kinds of records. The one day snow total was something like two feet. Just when we got cleaned up, we got another foot. And last night, because it wasn't enough, Mother Nature decided it would be fun to throw another foot on the ground.

As Rebekkah predicted, the power did go out. It was the middle of the night. Their generator was working. We were very lucky in that because hauling all the kids to another house in the amount of snow we had would have sucked a giant set of sweaty balls. None of us looked forward to that. We probably wouldn't have had to unless it got too cold. With the amount of blankets we had, that would have been unlikely.

One good thing that came out of the storm, though, was that we'd all decided to invest in some kind of green energy. That way, if something like this happens again, we don't need to rely on a generator and pray we have enough gas.

We didn't, by the way. Thankfully, the first wave had ended, though, and we were able to move to Ryan's house. We decided that the best option for us was to all stay with each other. If the power didn't get fixed before the gas in the generator ran out, we'd move to someone else's house.

The power just came back on today. An entire week later. I'd be pissed off, but I can't be. The lines in our area were severely damaged. One of our guard's quarters was almost damaged by a power line that went down near the house. And it didn't help that it got frigidly cold right after. Water pipes are freezing all over the city. Cole's house had a pipe burst.

"Motherfucking fuckity fuck," I grumble.

"Why don't you just hire a kid to do this like all of us have been doing? Give them some money in their pocket."

I chuckle at Gavin. "I have. But I have a teenager who needs to get to school. I don't need her trudging through a foot of snow just to get to the damn SUV."

"Or you could, you know, park in the fucking heated garage like a normal person." Gavin grins as he takes another shovel and starts to help.

"I'd love to do that. But the door is messed up since the outage. Or frozen. Haven't figured it out yet."

"How is Rosie? Settling?"

"She settled in quickly. She already feels at home. We're all used to each other from the time spent in Texas. She was hoping that she'd have her clothes and other things she ordered here before school started today. And none of us believe Christmas was just a week ago and kids are back in school already. I thought they went back a week after New Year's."

Gavin chuckles. "No clue, bro. I haven't paid that much attention. Don't see a need since we don't have kids."

I stop shoveling to take a break and turn to Gavin with a smile. "It's a change."

He smiles and stops as he turns to me. "I came over here to let you know I think we found someone who can lead us to that Gregory fucker. Thought you might like to come with me to grab him."

I glance towards the house. "I'm sure I could. Taylor is going to come by and grab Rosie to drop her off at school since he needs to take

Tait. Lance slept like shit. He's up for Rosie, but he'll be going back to bed."

"Good. Because Josh is chasing another lead and took Dane with him. Cole is working on a case with Taylor. We think it might be connected to VV's rebel."

I shake my head and start shoveling again. Gavin follows and helps as I talk. "Dude. Don't tell me that. If the VV motherfucker is here, it means -"

"It means things got fucked up. We have guards all over the school. It's a private school, so they do have some tight security measures, but we have guards acting as more security. They won't have contact with her. They're acting as if they work for the school. The only people allowed on campus are those on a very specific list. Parents or people authorized by the parents to pick them up. Teachers. Faculty. Any new faculty has to be vetted by us. Josh told them it's because we're looking for someone who has ties to one or more of their students and/or staff members."

I laugh. "Leave it to Josh to throw everyone into a damn panic by being fucking vague as hell."

"I know. I agree with him this time, though. The least amount of information we give, the less likely anyone will be able to give out any to the wrong people."

"And the least likely we'll have an issue with Rosie. I'm hopeful for that, anyway. That girl has been through enough."

"Fuck, I'm with you on that."

I look up as Taylor pulls into the driveway with his blue Ford F-150. I smile at Tait waving from the backseat. Gavin and I both wave back as we stop shoveling.

Taylor rolls down his window. "She ready for her first day?" he calls out to me.

"Uh. Well, as ready as she can be. None of her shit showed up yet because of the storm. She's trying to be positive, but it's pretty hard for her having to keep borrowing things from Dallas. We did get her some clothing, at least, but the third wave of that storm hit, and we had to get home before it stranded us. We didn't get much. She's borrowing some more stuff from Dallas for school. We did get her uniform, though."

"Nikki is still on a rampage about how they only give the women skirts and not pants," Taylor says. "I fucking swear she's going to take on the entire system before it's over."

I nod as I hear the door to the house close. "Hell, I'd let her."

Rosie makes her way carefully down the sidewalk. She looks so uncomfortable in the uniform, I honestly feel like I might cry for her. It's not just that, though. She tries to hide it, but I know she really wanted the things she picked out for school. She feels bad that Dallas gave her the extra backpack she keeps at Josh's. And she feels even worse that everything she's bringing to school is used.

It's not even because she's stuck up. As soon as she learned the school we planned on sending her to, she was incredibly excited. It's a private school, and she even already has a friend who is going there. Dallas may be a little younger, but she's in the same grade because she skipped a grade when she was younger. Both her and Rosie are Sophomores.

"Ready for the big first day, honey?" I ask, trying to cheer her up slightly.

She shrugs and keeps her head down. "I guess." Her voice is soft and low.

I wrap her in my arms and hug her tight, kissing her head. "I know this isn't what you envisioned, but I promise you tomorrow will be different. Your stuff comes in today. If it doesn't show, I'll go down there myself."

"Maybe I could just miss today?" She looks up hopefully. "Kids at private school can be so mean. I've never been to one, but I've heard about them. I don't want to get bullied over not having new things." She sniffles and breaks me more. "I'd be just fine going to public school! You don't have to spend money on me for a private school."

"Rosie, you know the reason we're sending you to a private school," I say, my voice dropping an octave to a more dominant level. "You know this has nothing to do with money or clout and everything to do with you, your intelligence, and your protection. We talked about this." I pull away slightly so I can look at her. "The biggest reason is public school isn't challenging for you. We're hoping this will be better for you. Right?"

"I know. It's just -"

I shake my head. "Sweetheart, I get it. I completely understand, but I also know how tough and resilient you are. Walk in there with your head held high. Like you don't give a fuck what they think about you. Be confident. Focus on your work. You have a lot of classes with Dallas. And they were even nice enough to make her your welcome guide." I grin.

She smiles and giggles softly. "I'm positive that's because you pulled strings."

I shrug, grinning wider. "That's what father's do, right?"

She nods. "I'm happy you and Lance chose me."

I kiss her head again and guide her to Taylor's truck. I open the door and help her in. "We're happy you chose us. You're the best gift we could've asked for."

She smiles as she settles. I start closing the door, but she stops me. "Wait! What about… the name? My last name."

I smile reassuringly. "Lance and Josh got all the paperwork dealt with. We're just waiting on your new documentation, but as far as the world knows, your name is Rosie Knight. Lance and I are your official parents."

Her smile brightens as I close the door. "Bye, dad. I'll text you."

"You do that." I wink and wave as Taylor puts the window up. Tait and Rosie wave to both me and Gavin as Taylor pulls away.

"I've never seen that much relief wash over anyone at the mention of a last name," Gavin says.

"Yeah, we talked a lot over the last week. She wants a whole new life. Brand new start. Away from everything and everyone. Well, except for the friends she made in Brystone Springs. Other than that, she just wants the chance to be a normal teenage girl." We start shoveling again.

"I don't blame her."

"You know, I didn't know this, but part of the reason her grandparents wouldn't allow her to be with us and were pushing so hard to get her back was because of our sexuality. I don't know why the fuck that hit me so hard."

"Because you're afraid of judgment, and they gave it. Even though they aren't here anymore. There's a difference when you come out to your family. Being a couple in front of everyone else is a step neither of you have taken. I mean Lance has been out for a long time, but he hasn't had anyone special in his life, so really, not even he has really experienced that judgment as part of a couple."

"You're probably right. It's all still pretty new to me. Both of us, I guess." We finish shoveling and put the shovels inside the garage. Thankfully, I have a door I can get into, at least. Even if I can't get my vehicle into it. "I should've parked in the garage before that fucking storm," I grumble.

Gavin laughs. "Don't worry about it. Things are coming back up. We'll have everything fixed soon. Power crews and everyone have been out."

"Here's to no more snow. I'm just going to head in and tell Lance I'm helping you out."

"I'll meet you back here with my new truck."

I smile as we part ways. Gavin just bought a black Dodge Ram. Most of us have Ford's. Gavin had to be different. It's typical of him. He and Alex both have to be sure they stand out from everyone else.

I chuckle as I walk into the house. I leave my boots by the door and smile when I see Lance on the couch already asleep. He really needs it. He hasn't slept well in a couple of days. Tossing and turning. Sweating.

I hurry upstairs to grab my second gun. Even shoveling, I was armed, but whenever I go out, especially on a mission, no matter how big or small, I always have a second. After strapping it on, I hurry downstairs and quickly write Lance a note. I put it on the table where he'll see it and lean down over him. I kiss him softly, making him smile in his sleep.

As I stand, something on his arm catches my eye. I furrow my eyebrows and tilt my head. A bruise? I don't remember him running into anything. Having a bruise on his upper arm of all places seems strange. I make a mental note to ask him about it as I head back to the door. I quickly put my boots back on and meet Gavin outside.

I jump in his truck and shut my mind off as I turn to him. "So, where is this guy?"

"He works at the docks. I've had someone on him all day. He's still there." Gavin pulls out of the driveway and navigates the snow covered streets.

"Docks are gonna be busy as fuck right now."

Gavin just grins darkly. I laugh. I should have known he didn't give a shit about that. He's well-known for being the demon to Josh's

Satan. There's a reason Gavin fucking Vandenberg is Josh's second-in-command. A reason I'm third. It's because I have a little more of a conscience than the asshole next to me does. I'll still do what needs to be done when it needs doing, but I usually end up living with it in my mind for longer than Gavin does.

Unless, of course, it has something to do with my family being fucked with. Then, whoever the culprit is usually wishes he had died by Josh's or Gavin's hands over mine. Josh and Gavin exude complete control. I do, too. But put my family in harm's way, and the end is going to be gruesome.

Several minutes later, we arrive at the docks. It's a place we, unfortunately, know far too well. A lot of Chicago's underbelly dwells at the docks. Illegal shipments. Drugs. Guns. Bullshit scams. Gangs. The people here trying to make an honest living are caught in the middle of good and fucked up.

As we both get out, a few people see us and give us a small smile before scurrying away and pretending we don't exist. A lot of people here know exactly what we do and are capable of. They won't call the police when we're taking care of our business because they know we're dealing with Chicago's scum, but they also have no desire to go out to dinner with us. They might give a small smile and wave, but no more.

I follow Gavin as he leads the way to an older, fairly rundown, small building in the middle of a lot of activity. I glance at Gavin, but his confident as fuck exterior doesn't waiver. The closer he gets to the building, the wider his cocky as hell smile gets.

When we're a few feet away, some middle-aged man with hair I'm pretty sure might be blond comes out of the building. As soon as his eyes fall on us, they widen. I chuckle because it's obvious we've found our new source of information. Before the buckets even hit the ground after he drops them, Gavin and I already have him in our grasp. We're good at what we do. He has no chance to run.

"Let go! Help!" he screams at the top of his lungs. Not a single person looks his way.

I let out a howl of laughter as we drag him into the building he just exited. A couple of people look at us in surprise, but not a single person says a word. A few people go about whatever their business is, which appears to be weighing fish.

"Out," Gavin growls dangerously. "Now."

We both hold our terrified and still screaming prize between us. Everyone drops what they're doing and quickly exits the building. No one makes eye contact. I can't imagine for a second they would. Many of them know us as coldblooded murderers. The others just don't want to fuck with us.

"Alright," I start, raising my voice against his screaming one. "I'm not about to fuck around. Either tell us everything we want to know…" I keep my grip tight on him as I take my gun out of my shoulder holster. I squeeze his arm tighter as I turn to him. I put my gun right underneath his chin. He shuts his mouth instantly. "Or I blow your brains out right after I gut you like a fish. Got me?"

He squeaks out a reply that sounds a little like 'yes, sir.' I can see his Adam's apple bobbing with each hard swallow. He's trembling so much, I'm starting to think he might actually be a pissed off tree from the *Wizard of Oz*.

And then I smell something that overpowers the stench of the fish.

Gavin wrinkles his nose as he looks down. "Motherfucker. You did not just piss your damn pants."

I chuckle. "I don't think that's all he did."

Gavin looks behind our guy. "Fucking hell. You shit yourself, too?" He grins demonically as his eyes flash. "I think that might be a new record for us, Mr. Knight."

I keep my gun tucked underneath the guy's chin as his eyes roll back in his head. "I swear to hell, if you pass out on us, I'm shooting off your dick first."

His knees buckle, but he somehow snaps to. Gavin and I hold him up. "Y-yes, sir."

"You're gonna be a good boy and answer all of Mr. Vandenberg's questions. Do that, I let you live. Fuck around, you're dead. Which means I'll need to call someone to clean up the mess you'll make me make. And that means all of your buddies will lose time and money. You don't want that, do you?"

He vigorously shakes his head. "N-no, s-sir."

"I didn't think so." I turn him towards Gavin, not moving my gun.

"Mr. Emilio Roberto. Father of an eleven-year-old baby girl. Divorced. Wife couldn't handle your drug addiction. Took the baby with her when she left your ass. You fell in love with the wrong woman after that. She fucked you up even more with drugs and got you arrested for weapons trafficking. Only, you were able to prove in court that it wasn't you. You got released. Hired here. You're paid a pretty penny. Much more than you've ever been before at all of your shitty restaurant jobs. You've even managed to get back into the good graces of your pretty little ex. Got some visitations going with your little girl. How 'm I doing so far?"

He swallows hard and nods. "R-r-right."

Gavin grins. "Good boy. You have two choices. You tell me what I want to know, and I'll be your fucking best friend. I'll even offer you protection from the assholes threatening you and your family. You know damn well I can make you disappear and give you a new life with your ex and baby girl. Piss me off, though, and Mr. Knight here puts a bullet through your brain. What's the choice? Option A or B?"

"A!" he says with no hesitation at all.

"I thought so. Tell me the name of the Ruthless Warriors member who has a stronghold on you, and tell me why."

"I only know him as Abyss. I th-think he's the l-leader. He's older. Um… gr-gray hair, but darker. Salt and p-pepper beard. Neat. Trimmed. H-he dresses more business-like. N-not jeans and leather. Suits."

I raise an eyebrow at Gavin. Sounds a lot like Gregory Franklin. Gavin's slight nod tells me he's thinking the same thing. "Where do you find him?" I ask, looking down at him.

He swallows. Gavin and I both tighten our grip. "I'm not supposed to know," he whispers. "I followed him one day b-because I th-thought m-maybe I could get leverage against him."

"I'm sure that didn't go over well," Gavin says.

"He never knew. I was a-afraid to do anything. He th-threatened my girls. To their faces." He looks between us both. I don't know if the fear is for us or this Abyss fucker. "They were so s-scared they moved in with me. Th-things have been going well."

"And they'll continue to. As long as you play ball with me," Gavin says. "Tell me where he is."

"He has a house on South La Selle Street and West 57th Street. It's a house on its own. There's a dry cleaners behind it, but it's abandoned. Big white house. Don't look like anyone lives there, but it's alone for a block. There are a couple on the other side of 57th."

I drop my gun from his jaw. "Good boy," I say as I put my gun away.

Gavin takes out his phone as he looks at our guy. "Go clean up. I'm not taking your ass anywhere like that."

He scurries away as I shake my head. "You're gonna make me follow him, aren't you?"

"I have calls to make." He waves his phone with a wicked grin. I laugh as I walk after the guy. I might not have learned his name, but I don't give fuck. "Burn those fucking clothes! Parade him naked for all I care."

"Asshole!" I call over my shoulder.

But I'm not above doing it. As he goes into the bathroom, I make sure the door stays open. I narrow my eyes. "Where's the office? Should have a first aid kid or some shit."

He points to a closed room next to us. "Door's probably locked."

"This door stays open. You try to run, I shoot first and ask questions later."

"If you help my family, you have nothing to worry about from me."

I nod and keep one eye on the bathroom as he strips and cleans up. The door to the office is locked. I shoot the lock as I roll my eyes. After a few seconds of rummaging around and keeping my eyes and ears open for him, I finally find a first aid kit. As I was hoping, there's an emergency thermal blanket that would be used in case someone falls in the water or something. It would be used to keep them from getting hypothermia.

I grab it and step the two steps back to the bathroom. I don't feel like he'll attack, but I'm always ready for one. When I see he's finishing cleaning up, I breathe a sigh of relief at not getting into a fight he won't win.

When he's done, I hand him the blanket. He wraps it around himself. He's wearing nothing but that and boots. We leave his clothes right where they are and lead him outside. He keeps his head down. I'm sure he expects curious eyes, but no one dares do something so stupid.

As we get him into the SUV, we already have a place for him and his family to go that's a long way away from here. A team is being sent after his family. By the time we get him to the airport, his family is already onboard. New clothes and a new life await him. When they land in

England, he and his family will have all new identities, a place to live, and a large sum of money to start them off while they settle into their new life.

As for Gregory fucking Franklin, he doesn't know it, but his days are numbered. We're getting closer. Soon, his sick game will end. The last thought that will cross his mind is how Lucinio Mafia bested him once and for all.

I can't wait to be there when the smug smirk I'm sure he wears is slapped right off his face.

Chapter Nine

🍎 Lance 🍎

I stretch as I slowly open my eyes and yawn. After a few moments, I realize I'm on the couch in my living room. I blink a few times and sit up, reaching for my phone.

"Christ," I grumble. "How is it after noon already?"

"You were still out when I got back. I left you a note," Damon says as he comes into the room with a cup of something that's steaming and smells delicious.

"Please tell me that's tea."

"Green tea. Just like you like it." He sits down next to me as I rub my head.

"Man. I was out like a light. I don't even remember Rosie leaving." I take the tea and let it warm my frozen hands. I close my eyes as I take a sip. "That's really good tea." I smile over the rim of the cup as I open my eyes.

"Lance, I know you're not going to want to hear this, but…" Damon trails off and starts rubbing my back.

"Don't." I shake my head. "Don't. That's not what's going on. I'm just tired." I feel my husband's eyes on me as tears sting my eyes. I'm not going down that path again. I won't. I refuse to.

"Baby, I know it's scary, but your symptoms -"

"Damon!" I turn and glare at him as I stand, nearly sloshing my tea over the rim of my cup and all over my hand. "I probably have the flu! I'm not fucking..." I trail off and swallow. I can't even say the words. "I don't have it. I don't."

Damon gets up slowly, keeping his concerned and loving eyes on me. He reaches for me, but I back away. The tears break free and stream down my face, but I'm silent. I don't make a sound. Instead, I turn and quickly walk away from him. I hurry to our bedroom and close myself in. I sit on the bed and set my tea on the nightstand before covering my face in my hands and sobbing.

It's been years, so many years, since I went through what I did. The single worst event of my life that happened again years later. Something that almost killed me once, then came back to haunt me a second time. I've done everything, everything in my power, to keep the beast at bay. I've never told a single soul about it.

The only reason Damon knows what happened to me is because about five years ago, I had a scare. Damon knew me so well by then that he could tell something wasn't right. He refused to let me push him away. He obliterated the walls I had tried to keep between us. He showed me that no matter what he would be by my side. When I finished telling him everything, he didn't hesitate. We were driving to the hospital so fast that it almost gave me whiplash.

It was then I knew beyond a shadow of a doubt that I was screwed. It wasn't just some crush. Not a wish that we could be together. I was in love with him. Head over fucking heels. The feelings I had when we first met hit me full force once more.

But the most important thing was I realized that I wasn't alone anymore.

The first two times, I had my parents to help me through it. But they both passed away peacefully in their sleep a few years ago. They were older when they adopted me. They were both very busy people. By the time they wanted to have kids, it was too late for them to have kids of their own without severe complications. My mom was nearly fifty-five. My dad was almost sixty and didn't want to lose his wife in childbirth. She was his whole word.

When I entered their life, the three of us were each other's universe. I was just six-years-old and in the hospital. My parents abandoned me there after they got my diagnosis. They couldn't take care of a kid who would be going through the expensive treatment I would be forced to endure to survive.

Only, I didn't know that then. The hospital staff basically became my family. The nice lady who visited me every single day I found out later was my social worker. I asked her every single day where my parents were. Why I didn't see them. If I was bad. And every day she told me that I wasn't bad. That my parents just weren't able to see me. That she was going to help me find new parents.

"Lance," Damon says quietly as he sits down next to me. His warm hand finds my back. He rubs soothingly as I cry.

New parents.

Those words stuck with me for so long afterwards. How could my mother carry me, birth me, then abandon me when I got sick? Was it really something so easy for her? Did she cry? Feel pain? Did my father?

I never got answers to those questions because years later, when I was barely fifteen and in the hospital again with a second wave of my curse, my biological parents were killed in a drive-by shooting. They lived in downtown L.A. the entire time, my whole life, and never once cared enough to see how I was doing. If I'd lived or died. It was like a sucker punch to my already sick and pained stomach.

I'd never have known if the children's hospital my adopted parents took me to hadn't been searching for records that the hospital I'd been in as a child apparently lost. They were looking for family history. Anything that could help them save my life. I'd never been so angry at anyone as I was with my biological parents. Not only had they abandoned me, but they left me with questions that I'd never get answers to.

Damon wraps me in his arms and says nothing as he hugs me. It's comforting. Warm. Loving. Protective. It's everything I need in this moment to calm my tumultuous feelings. The anxiety of having a relapse courses through my veins, but Damon is right here helping me battle my war. A war he never asked for but accepts because he loves me.

Hours go by with him hugging me and me clinging to him before the alarm on my phone goes off. It makes me jump a little because it would mean that Damon has been silently holding me while I fall apart in his arms for just over two hours.

I pull away slowly and wipe my eyes. Damon doesn't let go of me. I reach for my phone. He loosens his grip so I can move, but he keeps me close to him. I love that I don't need to tell him that I need exactly what he's giving me. Damon always knows.

"Rosie should be getting home soon. Alec is picking her and Dallas up. They have what they're calling a First Day of School Decompression date." I smile at the thought of Rosie.

Our daughter.

"Then we have a little time to talk," he says softly.

I sigh. "I don't want to." I look down.

"Baby, just because you don't want to doesn't mean it's all going to go away. It won't. We won't know if it's come back unless we get you checked out."

I shake my head adamantly. "When I got it back the second time, I knew. I knew it. When you brought me in after I told you what had happened and how I was scared because the pain was similar to then, I honestly thought I had it. I believed I did because the pain was the same. The nausea. Everything. I'm just tired. I feel like I have a cold coming on. Really."

"Lance, I think -"

I shake my head and cut him off with a kiss. I pull away slowly and give him a brave smile. "Baby, please. If I get checked every time I feel sick, everyone is going to start thinking I'm a hypochondriac or a druggy. I promise that if I feel like I did before, I'll talk to you. We'll discuss it then. Right now? I have a cold coming. I feel stuffy and congested. My throat hurts. I'm tired."

Damon watches me for a few moments. His eyes are filled to the brim with worry. The love he has for me slams into me in waves. Finally, he pulls me close to hug me once more. He kisses my neck and squeezes a little tighter.

Keeping his lips against my neck, he whispers, "I love you, Lance. Please, please don't hide it from me if it gets worse. You won't be alone. You'll never scare me away. I may have taken vows, but it wouldn't matter. I'll always be here for you. With or without the words we spoke to each other when you took my name, baby."

I smile and let him hug me, knowing he needs it. He spent hours giving me all I needed. It's my turn to do the same for him. "We really should get that addressed. I have all the documentation and new identification. Now that everyone knows we're married, I should update everything and use it. And let everyone know my official last name is yours."

He smiles against my neck, and it lightens me even more. "Lance Knight. It sounds even better now than it did before. I'll never get tired of hearing it."

"With Rosie's last name being Knight, it's only fair both of her dad's are, too."

Damon laughs as he pulls away, still keeping me in his arms. "And here I thought the paperwork you filed already reflected that."

I smile even wider. "It does, but it'll be nice having everyone call me Lance Knight, now that they know that's my name."

Damon leans in and kisses me softly, still smiling. "I've never been more happy than I am with you. I'm sorry I made you wait so long, baby. It was a completely stupid thing on my part because I knew this was right long ago. I just fought with myself about it. I apologize for that. It was unfair."

I shake my head and lean my forehead against his. "I've never blamed you. I never will. I'm happy we're out in the open with us and everything, but part of me loving you as much as I do is that I'd never force you into doing something you need time to process. You processed. Now, everyone knows. It's okay."

Damon smiles and kisses me again. I love his lips on me. A little soft. A little rough. The perfect combination. "I noticed a bruise on your arm," he says softly when he pulls away.

My eyes fall to my right arm with a groan. "I may or may not have tripped over myself this morning and run into the wall. In my defense, I was tired and not paying attention."

Damon chuckles. "I don't know why, but that makes me feel better. It's very you."

"See? Totally normal. I bet I wake up tomorrow with a scratchy throat. Thankfully, I have a big strong man to take care of me." I put on my best Southern Belle accent and bat my eyes.

Damon laughs. "I love you. Rosie should be home soon. All of her stuff showed up. I have it downstairs." He stands and pulls me with him and leads me downstairs.

"I'm excited to see how her day went."

"Me too. I hated school, but I'm fucking excited to hear all about hers."

Just as we get her stuff set up on the table downstairs, the front door opens. Rosie and Dallas walk in giggling with Alec right behind them. The two girls take their shoes off as Alec closes the door. They drop their backpacks and hang up their coats, then grab the backpacks off the floor.

As soon as Rosie sees all the boxes, her eyes light up. "Oh my God! Everything is here!"

"We'll have to keep track, but I think this is everything," Damon says. "As you're going through it, we'll make sure it's checked off the order forms on each order."

Both girls squeal as they make a run for the couch in the living room. Damon settles on our loveseat with his tablet. I laugh because there's no way he'll be able to keep up. Good thing I'll be able to.

Alec smiles. "She had a good day. They were chattering the whole way here. Something about a crush on a hot guy."

I raise an eyebrow. "Already?"

"He was really nice to her. She sat next to him in most of her classes. I guess there was assigned seating. Alphabetical. So she and Dallas didn't get to sit next to each other in all but one class."

"Don't tell Damon that. Fuck, he'll show up at the kids house all threatening and shit telling him to stay away from his daughter."

Alec laughs. "I don't blame him. I'm the same with Dallas. She might be my sister, but I'm not afraid to use my reputation to my advantage if it means keeping assholes away from her. Anyway. Speaking of assholes, I need to talk to Gavin. With Josh out, I need his help. Or at least his say on giving me some men. I think we found our rogue."

"Yeah? I heard something about him being around here."

"You'd be right. He's a slippery fucker. I'll give him that. But we think we tracked him. I want to grab him now, but he's got a lot of guys with him, according to my surveillance. We could take him, but I'd rather overpower the fucker and avoid the fight completely."

"I'd prefer that, too. Take him down, less of a threat to Rosie."

Alec nods. "Listen, if you don't mind, can Dallas stay with you guys a couple of days? She has clothes at Josh's and some at Jessa's, too. I'm gonna be gone for a few days, though. I don't want her routine interrupted at all. She hates being in our compound without me, Tag, Ink, or Chaos. They'll all be with me for this. I need the best. And I trust all my guys in the field, but I don't trust all of them with my sister."

"And Hawk? I know Dallas is okay with him."

"Hawk is helping out a friend of ours. Besides, his asshole father is up to his old tricks again. No fucking clue what he's planning, but we've been keeping an eye on him. Don't trust that motherfucker as far as I can throw him. Which isn't far, considering how much he weighs. He's you and me combined."

I glance at him then down at myself. "Oof."

"Yeah. And I'm not fat-shaming, here. Just being truthful."

I laugh. "You don't need to justify yourself. I've seen him. Reminds me a little of the dude in *Austin Powers*."

Alec grins. "Fat Bastard. Hawk literally calls him that."

I smile. "Have fun with Gavin. Don't let him have too much fun. You know how he is."

"I'll keep him on his best behavior." He winks. "Dallas, you good? I'll be gone a few days."

"I'm good!" Dallas calls, barely looking up at him.

"I'd be hurt I'm not getting a hug goodbye, but all that teenage angst and shit...," Alec says with a teasing smirk.

Dallas giggles as she jumps up. She runs to us and hugs Alec. "Have fun, big brother. Promise to check in."

"Always." Alec kisses her head and lets her go. She scurries back to Rosie. He gives me another wink. "Enjoy all the girly shit."

I laugh. "Get out of here." I playfully shove him out the door and close it behind him, locking it. As soon as I sit down, both girls dive into the boxes that they've opened but were waiting on me to dig into.

I sit next to Damon and grab my laptop. It only takes seconds after they start pulling things out of boxes and neatly arranging them on the table for Damon to be lost. Luckily for him, I have all of the orders pulled up and easily toggle through the screens. I'd already created a spreadsheet with each item underneath the corresponding store so I can easily check off each item.

Damon settles into me and watches the show. We both have huge grins on our faces as the girls 'ooh' and 'ahh' over the items. When they're finished getting everything out of the boxes, Damon starts breaking the boxes down and stacking them with all of the other packing used for the items. I finish checking things off the list until I confirm each item has arrived.

When we're done and things are picked up, we both watch Rosie and Dallas putting the stuff in piles. Each pile has its own category. School supplies. Clothing. Undergarments. Personal items. Night clothing. Bedding.

When they're satisfied, they start hauling the stuff upstairs, but they're doing it in such a manner that Damon and I just watch. Neither of us want to interfere with their method without direction from them.

We've both learned a thing or two from our little sister, Lyric. It's important to let Rosie feel like she's both independent enough to express herself, safe enough to be who she truly is, whoever that might end up being, and supported enough to be herself. Quirks that might not make sense to us are things she might feel strange about doing but does naturally. Things like organizing her books multiple times a day might be things she does to settle her mind.

The advice was very welcome because Rosie does do things that Damon and I have questioned. She's rearranged our entire kitchen so that it makes sense to her. We allowed it because we want her to feel at home, but mostly because when she was done she seemed content and settled.

She's rearranged her entire room a few times. We thought it was because she was bored and anxious to start school, but we discovered it's because she wanted her room set up so it was like her own sanctuary. We think she's gotten it the way she wants it to be because she seems very content being in there.

After the two finish putting things away, Damon and I have ordered dinner and put in a movie. Neither have homework tonight, so we all settle together to watch the movie while we eat.

It feels right.

Completely normal.

Like this is how it was always meant to be.

For a little while, I completely forget the danger we all face as long as the Ruthless Warriors are still out there and the Viper's Venom rogue is still roaming and lurking. I allow myself to sink into Damon and watch our daughter bond with her new friend. I forget that the Ruthless Warriors and the VV rogue aren't all the risks we face.

There's one more.

A secret I'm hiding from everyone.

One only my husband knows.

The thing that's so threatening that the thought of having to fight through it again makes my stomach clench in fear and trepidation.

Something that gets harder and harder for me to survive each time it rears its ugly head...

Chapter Ten

☙ Damon ☙

(One Week Later)

"Dad?" Rosie calls softly through the bathroom door.

"We'll be right out," Lance answers weakly, his head leaning on his arm as he hugs the toilet.

I run my fingers through his hair and rub his back. The bathroom has seen Lance in it more often than either of us would like this week. We've decided he really does have the flu, but it's only because we had Doctor Freeman run tests. It's the only thing stopping me from rushing him to Mayo Clinic in Rochester, Minnesota. They're well-known around the world for being one of the best hospitals. They treat a variety of things. I know Lance would be in good hands there.

I can hear Rosie sniffle before her soft footsteps retreat. "We have to tell her, baby," I rumble both soothingly and dominantly. I know he needs me to be both his loving and dominant husband right now.

"Doc says it's just the flu," he says, but I know he knows I'm right.

"She deserves to know. She's our daughter. And you know she's worried about you. So am I." I swallow down that worry, though, because that isn't what he needs to hear from me. He needs strong. He knows he can always count on me to be that for him when he's falling apart.

After a few moments, he nods. "Help me up," he says quietly. "I need to brush my teeth and clean up."

I do as he asks, slowly helping him to his feet. I stay close to him as he brushes his teeth and cleans himself up. Stepping away only long enough to grab him clean sweats and a hoodie from the closet in the bathroom where I always keep an extra set of clothing, I help him get dressed.

He barely made it this time before he lost the contents of his stomach. Tea is apparently too much. We've discovered he can drink plain water and chicken broth. But not just any chicken broth. It has to come from Ryan's kitchen. Ryan isn't just a ruthless mafia boss. He's also one fuck of a cook. Whatever he does to the chicken broth he makes settles Lance's stomach better than anything we've come across.

"Ready?" I rumble deeply with a soft smile. I keep a hand on his hip to steady him.

He closes his eyes with a low groan, but after a few moments, he nods. He opens his eyes and nods again. "Yeah. I'm good."

I kiss him softly and help him to the living room. I smile when I see Rosie in the kitchen. Lance's favorite stainless steel tumbler is sitting on the counter with a straw. Rosie has her head down as the microwave cooks something. I settle Lance onto the couch and put a blanket over him, tucking it around him.

I start the fireplace, thankful that our electricity has been restored and the pipes in the entire compound have been fixed. I'm also grateful that it's starting to warm up and that we haven't gotten any more snow. Lance has spent the past few days either freezing cold or burning up. He's shivering right now.

I watch Rosie put her phone away when the microwave beeps. She carefully pulls out a steaming mug. She stirs it before transferring it to another mug. When she turns, I can't help but smile. It's Lance's new favorite. She had it made for him. It says World's Best Hacker Dad. Lance won't drink anything that's hot out of anything else.

Rosie hands him the mug with a soft smile before curling up next to him. "How about a movie?" she asks quietly.

Lance takes a sip of the broth before clearing his throat. I put my arm around both of them and hug them close. "That sounds good. But first, I think we need to talk," Lance begins.

Rosie nods, visibly apprehensive. "Okay," she says quietly. I squeeze her shoulder in comfort and kiss Lance's temple.

He takes a deep breath. "Um…, this… isn't easy for me." He focuses on his mug. I squeeze his thigh in support. He takes another breath. "When I was six, I got sick. My parents didn't like the diagnosis and abandoned me in the hospital, but it ended up okay because I was adopted by two very loving people who took care of me, guided, and loved me for all the rest of their lives."

Rosie looks down at her hands. "Okay…," she whispers.

"The diagnosis was… Leukemia," Lance pushes on. "I fought through it. My adopted parents, as soon as my social worker contacted them, never left my side. We bonded in the hospital. By the time I got to go home, they'd already filed the paperwork for adoption. It wasn't long after that I was officially theirs. It took a while for me to get clear, but I did go into remission. When I was in my teens, though, I relapsed. It was a lot harder to fight off the second time. I felt a lot weaker. It took longer, but I did go into remission a second time. I've been free of it for nineteen years."

Rosie sniffles and hugs herself cuddling closer to Lance. "But…?"

"A few years ago, I thought I was relapsing," Lance continues. "Thankfully, I wasn't and didn't, but it's a fear." Lance leans forward slowly and puts his mug down. He sits back just as slowly and looks down at Rosie. "It's something I should have told you about. I know it has to be difficult having that thrown at you after the adoption has already been finalized. I don't want you to feel like you're stuck with me. With us. If you -"

As I knew she would, Rosie turns and hugs Lance. Her grip is firm, yet gentle. I know she doesn't want to jostle him. "You're my dad. You both are. You're my family. As crazy as maybe that is since it was so fast, but I don't care. I'm a Knight. We're all Knights." She shakes her head with vigor. "I don't want another family. I have my family. If you get sick, I'll help you fight through it."

I lean in and whisper in his ear as I rub Rosie's back. "Told you."

Lance turns and hugs her just as tightly, though his strength isn't what it usually is. "I'm so happy to hear you say that," he almost whispers. "So happy. Thankful."

I hug them both as they hug each other for a few more moments. "Doctor Freeman did look at him and is confident he has the flu," I say. "But it's still something to be vigilant about."

"Not that you have to worry every time I sneeze," Lance says with a grin as he winks teasingly at me. I smile, but it's accurate. I do worry about him, probably a lot more over the past few years since he opened up to me and had that scare.

Rosie leans forward and grabs his mug. She hands it back to him. "When I was in Brystone Springs, Kody got sick once. Xavier bought him Pedialyte. Maybe we should do that for you. He said it helps with dehydration and balances electrolytes."

Lance smiles. "We'll make sure to get some. That and some Gatorade."

Rosie shakes her head. "X says that stuff is awful for you if you have the flu. Sugar makes you feel more dehydrated."

I grin. "Sounds like you learned a lot from him."

She smiles and nods. "One time when Dylan had a cramp in her calf, X made her drink pickle juice. She hated him for it until about five minutes later when she started feeling better."

Lance smiles. "I've heard pickle juice helps with a lot of different things. Including acid reflux."

"It's so weird. I never would have thought about any of it, but he's really knowledgeable." Rosie smiles.

Lance shifts and sips his broth as Rosie flicks through our many premium subscriptions. After she picks a movie and everyone settles, Lance drops a hand to my thigh. The gesture is completely innocent, but my attraction to him is beyond comprehensible. As usual, he makes me hard as steel in seconds. I've never been so thankful for the blanket we're all snuggled under to help cover my growing problem.

A few minutes later, Lance sighs. "Okay, I've had something playing in my mind. I'm just going to blurt it out. I've been wanting to do something for a while for the kids at Lurie's Children's Hospital. Specifically, the cancer patients. I'd like to do some kind of a fundraiser to raise funds that we'll donate specifically to cancer research treatments, but I want to do a family donation to the hospital as a whole."

It takes me a few seconds to catch up to everything that just fell from his lips. His words were like rapid fire. I grin and look at him. "You want to do some kind of a gala?"

He smiles. "I do. But not just any gala. I don't want it to be the stiff and boring kind. I want it to be fun and kid inclusive. I want a silent auction, but I'd like it to be something kids can bid on. Like maybe each kid who comes gets a hundred dollars in play money at the door and can bid on the kid prizes. And the adults have their own section of prizes to bid on. Vacations. Big prizes. Little prizes. So everyone of all ages and income levels feels included."

I raise an eyebrow. "I see where you're going with that, but what's to say the little prizes meant for those families with the lower income level actually get any of the prizes, big or small?"

"Um... I honestly haven't figured it all out yet. But I was hoping..." His eyes fall to Rosie. He grins when she looks up at him curiously. "Maybe you'd help me out. Fun prizes. Big and small. Games. Food. Anything at all to make this inclusive to everyone and fun."

Rosie's eyes widen. "Oh my God, I have so many ideas!" She jumps up and runs up the stairs.

I laugh. "I think you've gotten her pretty excited." I kiss his neck as he finishes his broth. I take his cup and put it on the table. "How do you feel?"

"Mostly tired. But this is helping."

I smile and hug him closer to my side. "I'll admit you are looking better today than the past couple days. And that bruise on your arm is fading. I do feel a lot more confident this will pass."

Lance smiles. "I told you. I really don't feel like I did then when I had the scare or when I actually had cancer. I mean, I'm tired. But that's the only real symptom that I have. The rest is all flu. Which, by the way, I'm baffled neither of you have gotten it."

I chuckle. "So am I, honestly. Maybe I'm just immune," I tease.

Lance kisses me. "Thank you. For taking care of me."

"In sickness and in health." I kiss his forehead. "But again. I don't really give a shit about that. I'd be here whether I took those vows or not."

"I'm a lucky man."

"No, baby. I'm the lucky one."

He smiles, a slight blush darkens his still too pale cheeks. He kisses my jaw as Rosie comes running back down the stairs. She sits next to him again, but faces him this time as she sets her laptop on her lap. She's changed into her pajamas.

"Okay. So many ideas, dad. So many." She doesn't look up at either of us but we both grin as we shift more towards her. Lance leans into me, and I wrap both arms around him, snuggling his back against my chest.

"What do you got for us?" I ask.

"Well, would you be opposed to two events? Because I have such good ideas, but I don't think they'll work if there are people there who have a lot of money." She looks up at us hopefully.

"I don't mind two events," Lance says.

"Yes!" she cheers. Her fingers fly across the keys of her laptop. "So, I'm thinking for the first event, we could do what you were saying about the family donation to the whole hospital. We could do an event for all the kids there, not just those in the cancer wing." She looks up. "Wait. Would that work? They'd have immunity issues, so they probably wouldn't want them around all of the other kids, would they?"

"Depends, honestly," Lance says. "Some kids are terminal with other types of diseases, so I doubt they'd allow a lot of mixing, but for the others, they'd be okay with something social."

She pouts. "Well, that's okay. We could always do something in each section if we had to."

"I like that idea," I say. "They do Christmas stuff for all the kids separately."

"What if we had like a fancy dinner for everyone? All of the families. Treat it like a gala, except no dress code. No money to get in. When each family enters, they get a super fancy invitation that has a number on it. That number would be for a raffle. We'd have enough prizes for everyone to win."

"I like that," Lance says. He links his fingers with mine. I rub my thumb over the top of his hand.

"The prizes could be something for the adults to do to just relax for a little while and rejuvenate." She nibbles her lip. "Oh! Dinner at somewhere fancy. We could do a tux and dress rental or something for them." She starts typing but stops and looks up at us. "Wait. This costs money. A lot of it, probably."

"Money isn't a barrier, honey," I rumble with a smile. "You write down everything you want. Whatever you think is best."

Her eyes light up. "Okay, I was thinking about the kids." She folds her hands in her lap and smiles brightly. "An auction."

I raise an eyebrow. "An auction?"

"What kind of an auction?" Lance asks.

"I'm so glad you asked!" Rosie giggles. "Picture this. Fun things for kids. Things like story time with a cop. Lunch with a firefighter." She animates her voice like she's talking to a child. It makes me grin. "Something like that brings the kids and our emergency services together. We could do a day with superheroes and princesses. A pizza party. Each of the prizes would be something that everyone could enjoy, but the winner gets something a little extra. Maybe some time with the police officer or firefighter. Maybe the princesses could do a makeover. The superheroes could do… something. Whatever superheroes do, I guess. We could see if the high school drama team would put on a play for the kids."

"How would we auction off the prizes?" I ask genuinely intrigued by our girl's ideas.

"Well, what about play money? We could give them play money, maybe with the Lucinio Family crest or something on it? And then say something about the Lucinio family on it. The parents would get to keep the pretty invitation. The kids could keep the money. It would be commemorative. Anyway, each kid at each table would get an envelope with this play money in it. We'd have a certain amount of prizes. They'd get one hundred dollars for each prize we have. So, if we have twelve prizes to bid on, they'd get twelve hundred dollars. To keep it fair, though, if they win, they can't bid on anything else. But they can use the money to 'buy' other things. Like coloring books, maybe? Or maybe some music? Or comfort items? I don't know what yet, but I'm sure I can figure it out."

"I love all of this so far," Lance says. He squeezes my hand. I continue to rub my thumb over the back of his as I hug him. "What about those that can't attend?"

"Umm…" She tilts her head as she thinks. "Oh! I've got it. We could do a comfort package for them. We could give them things like a specialized fleece blanket or something. Something hypoallergenic. It could have the Lucinio Family Crest on it. We can do teddy bears with a t-shirt that has the crest."

"I kind of like that idea for everyone," I say, positive Josh would be onboard with doing something like that. He'd never tell a soul, but he does a lot of work with kids. Especially the troubled ones.

Rosie nods. "Everyone could get it at the party, but it could also be something that those who didn't attend get, too. Coloring books and things. Books that are age appropriate. Games. And for the adults, we could put in a self-care package. A massage, maybe. A spa package that allows for relaxation. The ones that attend the party would all get something. No one would be left out. It would just be what, exactly, they win. And those that don't attend could get something, too."

"And what about dinner?" Lance asks. "You said something gala-like."

Rosie bounces a little. "We could do a menu when we announce it all. So we'll have an idea of who will be coming. We can keep track of new admissions right up until the night of the event. The caterer might not like that, but I'm sure we can find someone who understands and would be willing to work with us. And we could have extra prizes on hand. Just in case. We could have extra commemorative play money and invitations. And then for the gala itself, not the one we hold at the hospital, we could charge by the plate and do a silent auction. For that, all of the money would go to cancer research instead of the whole hospital."

I grin. "Man. I'm a fan of all that. It'll take time to get it all together, but this could be something we do every year. Raleigh is good at keeping track of everything and getting donations. We could put her in charge of some of this. I bet she'd love working with you on this."

Rosie blushes. "Do you think? I hope so. I bet she can help find the best prizes for everyone."

I smile as Lance and Rosie launch into a little more planning. I keep my arms around him and leave soft kisses against his neck and watch him ease our daughters fears and mine. It's starting to seem more and more like he's coming out of it. Like my fears were unfounded.

Despite how sick Lance is, I'm proud to see him and Rosie planning these events and bringing Lance's vision to life. I don't think I could be more proud to see them both throwing themselves into helping others.

These fundraisers are going to be *epic*.

Chapter Eleven

☙ Lance ☙

(One Week Later)

I grimace, holding my stomach as I lean against the bathroom wall in Josh's house. I have a massive headache, my chest feels like it's being squeezed, and my stomach is cramping so badly, I question if death is imminent.

This is the worst flu I've ever experienced. I've thrown up so much that I'm doing nothing but dry-heaving at this point. I started throwing up chicken broth, so I stopped drinking it and have been living off nothing but water for the past two days.

Despite all of that, though, I am feeling better. My temperature has gone down. I'm less chilled. I'm not as tired, though I still do end up taking a nap in the middle of the day. It's usually only for an hour or so.

"Fuck," I rumble, clutching my stomach tighter as it cramps once more.

The one thing that doesn't make sense is that I've been around others. Rosie and Damon haven't gotten sick. Josh hasn't either. Gavin came down with a cold. I've been working with Robby on some tracking shit and he only felt under the weather a little bit for half a day. I've stayed away from the little kids completely just to be on the safe side, but I've been near Ryan. His son, Christopher, hasn't gotten sick at all. Neither has he or his wife.

I'd be completely stupid to not see Damon and Rosie becoming increasingly more worried about me. Both of them have mentioned to me that they feel like I should go in. Damon has even had Doctor Freeman look at me again. He took more labs just a little bit ago and took them to the hospital to test himself.

Right afterwards, Robby called needing my help. I haven't done a lot to track down our enemies. I haven't had the energy. Robby has been pulled in different directions because he's working on things for Ryan, who is technically his boss, and Josh, who is mine. Just because we're one big, happy family, through blood and bonds, doesn't mean Robby should have to pull my weight.

I need to get back into it. Whether I feel like shit or not.

After a few more agonizing moments, I've managed to breathe through the pain. The cramping and stabbing in my stomach has gotten more frequent, but it hasn't been too bad. I've managed to hide it from both Damon and Rosie. I don't need them worrying more than they already do.

Rosie has school. She's doing incredible and has adjusted very well. I'm very proud of her. Damon has been spending a lot of time chasing down leads with Gavin and Josh. He's even helped out Alec a few times. Everyone has been doing their job except me. I won't let that keep happening.

We have eyes on Gregory Franklin's house. We know he has cameras set up all over the place that can see several feet around his house. If we approach it, he'll know and be able to detonate the couple of explosives we see around the property.

He's very brazen. He has a regular chain link fence around the property. If we were to somehow manage to get through the couple of areas where the explosives are and hop the fence without him seeing, the entire property inside the fence is littered with landmines. As if that isn't enough, the fence itself is electrified.

He has a mailbox on a pole just outside the gate, though. So, maybe there's just a teeny bit of compassion in there. More likely, though, it's because he doesn't want the issues that would come along with electrocuting a federal employee. Maybe he's more scared of the feds after his ass than he is us.

That thought process wouldn't be his first mistake.

I take a careful breath before making my way back to Josh's dining room. Each step is deliberately slow because I don't want to end up right back into the bathroom. I lean against the wall outside the office door catching my breath before I walk in. When I finally get to my seat and pull my laptop back in front of me, it's not lost on me that a lot of people are watching me.

I don't say anything about it, though, because what I see on my screen steals all other thoughts. "Holy... fucking... shit..." I quickly search through the information I'd been waiting to download.

"What?" Robby asks, leaning over.

"I don't think Gregory Franklin is the leader of Ruthless Warriors. I don't know who is yet, but I don't think it's him."

"Why?" Josh asks.

Damon stands behind me and leans over my chair. He puts one hand on the table next to me and kisses my neck. The gesture is as sweet as it is protective. I doubt he knows what he does, but he seems to do it when I need him to. I'd never flat out say I need him close to calm me down. It's not who I am. Damon picks up on it every time. But sometimes, he takes it that extra step, like right now, and makes me feel very much his.

"How the hell did you find that? What is that?" Robby asks, staring at my screen in openmouthed shock.

I grin and lean back in my chair as Josh stands behind us. "This, ladies and gentleman, proves that he's getting funds from someone."

Josh shifts as I look up at him, still grinning. He furrows his brows as he folds his arms across his chest. "Are you telling me that Viper's Venom is funneling money into this random as fuck account that isn't linked in any manner at all to Gregory Franklin?"

"On the contrary, it is linked to him." I toggle to another tab and lean back once more. Everyone falls silent,

Damon clears his throat. "Okay, you're gonna have to explain this one, baby."

"It's an account in Gregory's name. Only, not quite his name." I lean forward. "Robby and I got the idea to run his name through an anagram to see if we could come up with any other names. One name stuck out to us like a sore thumb."

"Ginger Roger," Robby says. "The thing is, I ran that to see what accounts came up. I came up with a lot of possibilities. I had no idea how to go further than that because the accounts I found had no links to anything. I don't know how Lance found this."

I smile. "Lucille Ball is one of Alec's favorite vintage actresses. The other?" I watch everyone's baffled expressions and smile even wider. "Ginger Rogers." I expand the name on the account so everyone can see.

"Ginger Lucille Roger." Josh closes his eyes and shakes his head. "So, you got curious." He grins as he opens them and looks down at me.

"I did. I ran some shit. Dug a little bit. Did a lot of cross-referencing. This account is used frequently. Large cash withdrawals. Good thing they have a lot of large deposits to cover all those withdrawals." I punch a few more keys and pull up a list of deposits into the account. "All from the same account number."

"Wait a second," Damon says. He looks at Josh. "You said Viper's Venom is doing this. How do you know?"

"The account. That company name." He nods to the screen. "It's an obscure one. One that Alec has actually been looking into for a completely different reason. Nothing at all to do with this. He thinks money laundering is happening. He bought this company when his dad was still alive just to piss the fucker off. He hasn't done a lot with it since he took his father down. He was thinking of selling it outright."

Damon laughs. "Alec bought a motorcycle dealership?"

"Yep. His dad was so pissed off. He told him to buy a garage where they could chop up cars and other vehicles. Motorcycles included. The dealership sent him into a rage that Alec told me he sat and laughed at. He didn't have to worry about his dad taking it out on anyone he cared about. Dallas stayed with him, and his mom was gone at that time." Josh nods towards the screen. "No one knows this dealership even belongs to him or is associated with Viper's Venom."

I smile and subtly swallow. I put a hand to my stomach and fight off a stab of pain. "Um…" I clear my throat. "So, this is an account Josh gave us. I plugged it in with the rest and cross-referenced. It was a hunch when I saw the name, but it was actually when I saw this that clinched it for me." I toggle to yet another screen in one of what seems like hundreds of them up on my laptop.

"Fuck me," Robby says, blinking.

"Yep." I nod with a pained smile that I try hard to hide with another swallow. On the screen is a picture of Gregory Franklin. "He has IDs with the name Ginger Lucille Roger. Why he left the 's' at the end off is beyond me. I'd like to think it's because the name Ginger Rogers would be suspicious as hell, but then a guy walking in with the name Ginger Lucille Roger is just as fucking suspicious. But maybe that's just me."

"I wonder if he was born a female," Robby says. He hunches over his laptop. "I'm digging into that right fucking now. Maybe Franklin isn't his and Edward's last name."

"I'm not sure about that," I say. "We dug into that pretty deeply. Let me look into these documents. See if they're forgeries. My instincts are saying he paid someone off. Let's see how long Ms. Roger has been around. Most assholes who give themselves fake aliases aren't smart enough to give themselves a whole life and backstory, too. Most of these aliases just pop up. There's no record of them anywhere. Every human has a record of some sort somewhere."

"I'm fucking impressed," Josh says.

I smile. "You doubted me?"

Josh barks out a laugh. "Hell no. You do things I can't even comprehend."

I grin and glance at Robby. "Time to find a record of Ginger Lucille Roger."

"So, Ginger Rogers and Lucille Ball. Alec's favorites. Are you saying he's calling out Alec?" Damon asks.

I nod. "Yep. That name just clicked something in my mind. I remembered us talking about it because I was watching an episode of I Love Lucy. We got to talking about the old school movies. Clint Eastwood's old stuff. John Wayne. Fred Astair. Then we started talking about the women. I mentioned my favorite was a toss up between Mae West and Marilyn Monroe. He told me he loved Lucille Ball and Ginger Rogers."

"But how the fuck would anyone else know that? Josh is his best friend. He doesn't know that," Damon says.

I grin because I love him playing devil's advocate. It makes me think more clearly. "I'm glad you asked. It would have to be someone close to him who knows. So, we have two options. The first is someone who was around while he was growing up. Gregory Franklin fits that. The other would be someone in his crew is betraying him. Also plausible." I find my other research that I've been doing while I've been up to working, which isn't often. "Gregory worked with Alec's father. He used to be a Viper's Venom pledge. Until he wasn't. Unfortunately, that's all the further I've gotten. I don't know his biker name or anything else. It looks like Alec, though, was around four or so when Gregory left."

"So, how the fuck would he know this shit about his favorite actresses?" Josh asks.

"Another very good question. And one I don't have the answers to, boss. Just hunches." I look up at him. "I'll get the answers. Right now, I think it's probably because little Alec danced around the room to the music from the movies and sat and watched *I Love Lucy* reruns with his mom. We'll figure it out." I sigh because it's then that my bladder decides to strike. How the fuck I'm able to take a piss at all is beyond me. Not like I've been getting all that much water down. I'm surprised my body isn't just using all of it. "After I take a leak."

I stand a little too quickly and regret it instantaneously. The ground underneath me tips. Suddenly, I feel like I'm on a Tilt-O-Whirl. Or an up and down rollercoaster. My stomach lurches and quickly makes its way to my mouth.

"Lance? What the fuck?" Damon's voice seems way too far away considering how close he is. I can feel his hand on my arm. "B…a…b…y…?"

I blink and stare at his mouth. Why does it sound so far away and like it's been slowed to super slow motion? Like we're underwater or some shit.

Damon says something else, but I suddenly can't hear him.

The edges of my vision start to darken. Before I know what's happening, I feel myself falling.

Only the falling sensation doesn't stop.

My vision goes completely dark, but I don't remember closing my eyes. All I can hear is the air passing by me as I endlessly fall and fall and fall.

I try to grip anything, but there's nothing to hold onto. I can't even feel Damon's hand on my arm anymore, but I know it's there. He wouldn't let go of me. He'd never let go.

So, why can't I feel him anymore?

Why can't I feel anything?

Chapter Twelve

❦ Damon ❦

"Lance? You okay, baby?" I ask, alarm filling every fiber of my being. He shakes his head, but slowly. His eyes are completely unfocused. "Oh fuck. Lance! Talk to me, baby." Just as I start to pull him against me, he sinks to the floor. I drop to my knees with him, holding him tightly.

"I'll call Doctor Freeman," Robby says.

"I'll call Ryan," Josh says. "Alex is at work. We need a chopper."

There's a flurry of motion around me, but all I can do is rock with my husband and bury my face in his neck. He's soaked in sweat. "Jesus Christ, baby. Jesus, tell me what's happening."

But Lance is completely silent. Save for the rise and fall of his chest as he viciously shivers and tenses in my arms, I'd have no fucking clue he's even alive. I hug him even tighter, doing everything in my power to wake him. I nuzzle him. Nip his neck. Kiss him.

Nothing works.

"Fuck. Lance, wake up, baby. Please wake up for me. I can't lose you like this. I can't lose you at all. Come on, baby." I rub up and down his back. His groan gives me hope that he's coming to, but it's quickly dashed when he slumps even more.

"What happened?" Doctor Chantau, the Crane Family doctor, asks as he slides next to me and instantly starts checking Lance over.

"He just passed out," I choke through the thickness in my throat.

"How long?" Doctor Chantau asks.

"I don't…" I swallow and hug him tighter.

I can't think.

I can't breathe.

"Seven minutes, doc," Josh says from behind me.

"What…?" I ask, feeling like I'm being suffocated in a thick mass of clouds. It can't have been seven minutes, can it? Have we been sitting like this that long?

I can hear a whirring in my head. It drowns out everything else. All but me and Lance. I close my eyes and press my lips against his neck, willing him awake with my love. Begging him to feel it; to let it bring him back.

"We gotta go, Damon. Help me get him up." Josh's voice is like the calm to my war. The command I need to move. I nod and let him help me.

When we have Lance standing, I lift him in my arms. It's not an easy task. Lance is solid muscle, but I've spent years weightlifting. If I couldn't lift him at all, I'd figure out a way to make it happen. I don't want him in anyone else's arms. He's mine to protect, and I'll stop at nothing to make sure he's safe.

In *my* arms.

Josh and Doctor Chantau lead me out to Ryan's chopper. He's landed it in the middle of the fucking street, but he could have landed it in the fucking front yard on top of a snowbank if it meant getting Lance help. I've never been more grateful for Ryan's multiple skills.

Josh and Doctor Chantau help me get Lance into the chopper. Robby is in the co-pilot seat. Doctor Chantau sits across from me. I hug Lance as tightly as possible and look at Josh. I usually don't need direction, but he knows damn well I do right now.

"I'm going to get Rosie," he says loud enough to be heard over the blades. "Ryan is getting you to the hospital. Doctor Freeman will meet you there. Doctor Chantau will accompany you."

I nod and rock Lance back and forth. I say nothing, but I know I don't need to. Josh closes the door. Doctor Chantau makes sure it's secured. Josh steps away from the chopper. I look out the window briefly and see Arianna with Christopher and Jackson. Everyone else is at work or school. I feel a little bad, but also extremely grateful because it means I don't have to see everyone's concerned faces. The two crying kids and Crane Mafia's Queen is enough.

As Ryan lifts off, Josh wraps his arms around Arianna when she turns to him. She's sobbing just as hard as the kids. I wonder what she'll do when she finds out Lance's childhood diagnosis. What she'll do if the Leukemia is back.

I take deep breath after deep breath as I bury my face in Lance. His masculine, intoxicating scent is strong enough to give me the strength I need but subtle enough to calm me. He smells like the freshest sandalwood.

Doctor Chantau keeps a reassuring smile plastered to his kind face as he keeps checking over Lance. He has some kind of a machine hooked up to him that's monitoring his blood pressure. I can't help but notice it's really fucking high. Lance is breathing heavy. His pulse rate isn't normal. I don't know what normal is, but I know one-hundred-twenty-two isn't it.

I do all I can to breathe steady for him, but it's not easy when I'm so fucking close to panicking. I take more deep breaths just to keep my own heart in check for him. If by some small miracle he can feel me, I want him to feel safe. I want him to feel protected and loved. I want him to know it's okay for him to fall. That I'll catch him.

I'll always catch him.

"You can't leave me," I whisper in his ear. "Don't go. I need you. I love you, baby. I love you."

Lance continues shivering violently, but he does take a deep breath. As I cradle him against my body, his hand splays across my abs. He grips my shirt and cuddles as close as he can. Whether he's consciously doing it, I don't know. All I care about is that he seems to hear me. He's not calming down in the slightest, but at least he feels me.

I hope.

"Come back, baby. I can't lose you. I won't. Fight for me. For us. Our family," I rumble against his neck. Talking to him; holding him is all I can do. I need my love to be enough because it's all I have.

I glance out the window with my lips against Lance's head as Ryan begins our descent. I raise an eyebrow when I see that he's landing right on the roof of the building where the medical choppers would be landing. I would say something, but Lance is all I care about. Insensitive? Maybe, but I don't care. All that matters right now is him and getting him the treatment he needs.

Next to the door is Doctor Freeman. He has a nurse with him, and they are both watching Ryan land. As soon as he touches down, they both dart to the chopper with a hospital bed on wheels. Doctor Chantau opens the door. Ryan shuts the chopper down.

"We moved too quick for me to get an IV in him," Doctor Chantau says. "I couldn't anyway. He's shaking too badly. High fever. High pulse. High blood pressure."

Doctor Freeman nods as I help get Lance out. Robby and Ryan both start to follow. Doctor Freeman stops them. "There's a medical chopper coming in with an accident victim who coded twice on the way in. They're three minutes out. We need to get Lance loaded up. You need to fly out of here. Help get the rest of the family here," he commands.

Ryan nods. "You got it." Without another word, Ryan puts his headset back on. Robby follows. Doctor Chantau and I jump out of the chopper and race after Doctor Freeman and the nurse.

Just as Ryan is lifting off once more, we're entering the building. Another doctor and two nurses rush off the elevator we're stepping into.

"The chopper taking off is mine!" Doctor Freeman calls to them. "Yours is on the way in. I saw them in the distance!"

"Thanks!" the other doctor says back as they shuffle around us and run to the door.

In blurs of motion, Lance is loaded into the elevator. I squeeze in behind everyone fighting myself from getting in their way and wrapping my arms back around him. That's not what he needs right now. He needs them.

Helpless, I watch Doctor Freeman and Doctor Chantau hold Lance's arm down while the nurse quickly gets an IV in him. It's obvious she's a trauma nurse because she's fast and efficient. Despite how tense he is, she gets the needle in his vein on the first try.

I lean against the elevator wall and focus on steadying myself. I'm on the edge. So fucking close to bursting into tears. I've watched people die right in front of me. People I cared about. I've gone to their homes and given the news to their families.

But it's different when the person fighting for life is my own family. When Gavin got shot, it was hard on us all. He's our brother.

Lance.

Lance is so much more. He's part of me. The other half of my heart. The completion to my soul. The calm to my storm.

My whole fucking life.

The elevator doors open. The doctors and nurse rush Lance out of it. I hurriedly follow after them. There are more doctors and nurses in this area of the hospital than I've ever seen in my life. They must have a massive trauma coming in. I thank whoever is listening that we have our own doctors because I'm positive Lance would be triaged at this point. He may not be as important as the people about to be brought in.

Fuck that. Fuck all of them. Lance is the most important person in the world to me. One of the most important people in my life.

Doctor Freeman stops me from following them through a set of doors. "I know you're going to be pissed at me, son, but you can't go back there."

My heart stops beating. "Doc… Please," I beg, my voice barely above a whisper.

"No." He shakes his head, his voice reassuring. "Trust me. We need to stabilize him, then he'll be going to a VIP room upstairs." He nods over my shoulder. "This nurse will take you there."

I take a shaky breath and nod. I know he's right, and my body is starting to weaken. The adrenaline pumping through my veins is quickly subsiding. I feel like I'm going to crash, but no way I'll allow myself to do that. Not until I know my husband is okay.

Once again I step onto the elevator. The nurse scans a card as the doors close. Moments later, we're moving up to another floor. The further I get away from Lance, the further away my heart feels. It's sitting right next to him.

"I'm Amy," she says softly. "And I know it's not what you want to hear, you probably don't want to hear much at all, but the doctors have him. He'll be okay." She gives me a soft smile full of reassurance.

I can't return it. "You're right. The only thing I want to hear is Lance's voice telling me it's all okay."

She nods. "I understand. It's never easy when a loved one is being treated and you can't be with them." She keeps her eyes on the elevator doors in front of us.

I look down at her. "You say that like you know exactly how that feels."

She looks up at me. Her smile is watery, but I can see she's trying to be strong. "My mom is here. I know she has the best care, but…"

I nod, giving her my own soft smile. "But you want to be with her."

She nods. "I was running tests with Doctor Freeman when a multi-car accident call came in. My mom was in it. My attending wouldn't allow me to see her. She was one of the first people taken in."

"That's fucked up. It's your mom. Why would he not allow you to at least check in with her? See how she is?" I'm grateful for the distraction she doesn't know she's giving me.

She smiles a little more. "That's exactly what Doctor Freeman said. He said that since I'm running labs with him, he's my attending. He makes the calls. He really put my actual attending in his place. Dressed him down in front of everyone. Then he got the call of your husband coming in. He told me that he'd get my mom to the VIP wing. Then, when you got here, I could escort you and see her. And have the rest of the night off."

I can't help the chuckle. "Sounds like him. It's not the first time he's done something like this. He went up in front of the board a few times. Lucky for him, he has Lucinio money to back him. He's also lucky the board has a conscience and usually sides with him anyway. Otherwise, I'm sure he'd have been sanctioned a few times and lost his license to practice by now."

She smiles as the doors open. She leads me out of the elevator onto a pristine floor. Security sits to the side of a set of doors. "I'm sure your family wouldn't have let that happen."

"You'd be right," I say with a grin.

She smiles a little more as we reach the desk. "Hey. This is Mr. Knight. His husband isn't up here yet, but his attending doctor told me to take Mr. Knight to the waiting room."

The guard, who looks far too young to actually be one, looks down at his clipboard. He smiles. "Sure. Mr. Knight will be in room thirty-o-seven when they bring him up."

"Thanks. I'm here for my mom, too. Doctor Freeman put her in room thirty-twelve."

He looks down at his clipboard again. "Uh… Oh. Right. He called you in when he called in Mr. Knight. They just brought her up a few minutes ago. I think they're settling her now. Doctor Freeman told me to tell you she's okay. No internal injuries. She has a broken foot and a concussion. He wants to observe her overnight."

Amy breathes a sigh of relief. She smiles up at me as the security guard hands us badges. She leads me to the door and scans hers. Per her direction, I scan hers right behind her and follow her. She shows me to the VIP waiting room and hurries to the room they have her mother. She wipes her eyes as she rushes down the hall.

I walk into the VIP room. I'm grateful no one else is in here as I collapse into a chair rubbing my head and looking around. There's a lot of room for many to sit. That's good news, considering it's about to be invaded with people.

There's a vending machine in the corner with chips and other snacks. There's a coffee vending machine that looks inviting. Insert a credit card and out pops whatever fucking drink I'd desire.

Next to it is a vending machine with a variety of cold sandwiches. There are breakfast sandwiches, burgers, and chicken sandwiches that can be heated in the microwave sitting on the counter. In a small fridge with a clear door, there are hardboiled eggs, milk, both chocolate and regular, and juices. Yogurts.

I blink. "Fuck. It's like a hotel breakfast bar. Only you have to pay for everything." There's even a waffle maker with another fridge next to it with what I assume is waffle mix. There's fruit and other things people could put on waffles.

I break down and stand. I take out my wallet with a sigh and feed my credit card to the coffee vending machine. A vanilla latte sounds fucking amazing right now. I watch as the machine spits out a cup. A piece of plastic comes up and closes the cup inside as the latte starts dispensing. Moments later, the plastic piece drops down, and my latte is finished.

"Maybe I need one of these at home." I chuckle and take the cup. I find a lid and put it on just as the door opens. I look over my shoulder and see Rosie with wide red eyes. Josh is right behind her. I set the cup on the counter and turn.

Rosie wastes no time running to me and leaping in my arms. "Please tell me he's okay. Please!" she sobs into my shoulder.

All I can do is tighten my grip and hug her. "I don't know, cub. I wish I did." I sway with her as I stand next to the counter.

She cries into my shoulder for a long, long while. More and more people trickle into the room until our entire family is here with us. When I finally sit down with her, my latte is long forgotten. I pull her into my side on one of the couches in the room.

It's been at least an hour since I got up here, and there's still no word. I know Doctor Freeman or Doctor Chantau will be up here as soon as they possibly can, but it doesn't help the impatience. It doesn't stop my heart from trying to escape my chest.

Patience isn't my strong suit, but all I can do is wait...

Chapter Thirteen

☙ Lance ☙

(One Week Later)

I push the tray on the hospital table away. "Can't eat anymore," I grumble.

Damon chuckles next to me. "You did pretty damn well, considering it's your first real meal in fuck knows how long."

"Maybe you could try some more yogurt?" Rosie asks hopefully.

The truth is, I'm fucking sick of being here in this hospital. I've had the best care, but I want to go home. I'm tired, which really shouldn't be a thing. I've been sleeping a lot because there's nothing else to do, but I still feel exhausted.

It's frustrating as hell and pisses me off.

I take the yogurt Rosie hands me with a soft smile and do as she silently begs me to because I can't resist her. This past week, she's made the most adorable nurse. After, of course, her mind was put at ease when she was convinced that I'm not dying.

I can't really blame her or anyone for thinking that. I don't remember anything that happened. One minute I was showing Josh,

Damon, and Robby what I'd found that I'd hoped would go a long way in helping us put an end to this Ruthless Warriors bullshit. Next thing I know, I'm waking up in this hospital bed. I lost hours of my life and couldn't figure out why Rosie was curled into me crying and Damon was rubbing her back and my hand.

After Damon told me what happened, I came to two very abrupt conclusions. The first was that I'm incredibly lucky to have Rosie and Damon. My own little family. The second was that I needed to tell the rest of the family what Rosie and Damon already knew. It wasn't fair for me to keep it from them.

So, I did. I told them about what happened with my real parents. I told them about the Leukemia; how I had it twice. I opened up to them about thinking I had it again a few years ago. By the time I'd gotten the words out, there wasn't a single dry eye in the room.

Hours after that and extensive tests later, Doctor Freeman, Doctor Chantau, and a cancer specialist had all given me a clean bill of health. The conclusion was that I just had the flu. A severe case of it. By the time the flu left my system, I was weak and more sick. Dehydrated.

It was the dehydration that led to everything. I couldn't hold down anything more than water. I drank excessive amounts and felt better only briefly. I'd tried Pedialyte to help balance my out of whack electrolytes, but my body was already fucked up. The excessive water made my stomach upset. The lack of fluid gave me cramps from being dehydrated. I had a headache that wouldn't quit. I even got weak and out of breath walking up the stairs to bed.

Eventually, my body just went into shock. It was the only thing it could think of to get itself what it needed to, I guess. It got tired of me ignoring it.

I've been in the hospital now for an entire week out of an abundance of caution. I was hooked up to an IV for a few days being fed fluids, potassium, magnesium, and who the fuck knows what else. I've been taking vitamins every single day to balance all of my dangerously low levels. When they got me where I needed to be, they slowly started weaning me off of everything. Today is the first day I haven't had an IV stuck in me.

It's also the first day I'm eating solid food. I've been on a liquid diet because they wanted to make sure I didn't take too much in at one time. While it's still stuff that is easy on the stomach, it's more than piss water broth and green jello. I'll take yogurt and applesauce any day of the fucking week.

When I finish the yogurt, Rosie is smiling brightly. I chuckle a little because I'd give anything to keep that smile on her face. I haven't seen it much over the week. She has hated every second about leaving and having to go to school. But she comes straight here afterwards. She does her homework and sleeps in the lounge with the rest of the family

I look out the window. Damon cleans up the tray. Rosie tidies everything else. "More snow? This has to be the snowiest season on record in this city," I grumble. I was born and raised in Los Angeles. We had a cabin in the mountains we went to for two weeks at Christmas. That was enough snow for us for the entire year. Chicago is something else entirely.

"You know, I said that to Breetana," Damon says with a grin as he sits next to me. "Her response was something along the lines of be glad it's not Minnesota, and that you weren't around there for the famous Blizzard of '91 that buried parts of Minnesota in over thirty inches of snow. Or the one just a little over three years later that hit them with almost four feet."

"They can keep that shit up there."

"Oh! We actually just learned about that in our history class," Rosie says as she sits on the other side of me. "I don't even know how it came up, but the teacher put aside the lesson and looked up everything about those two storms. I guess the one in '91 happened on Halloween and didn't stop for three days. They've a lot of storms. One of them happened in 1835, and it was so strong over the lake that nineteen ships sank. Two-hundred-fifty-four sailors were killed."

"In comparison," Damon begins, "the worst Chicago has ever seen was in 1967 with twenty-three inches. Well, until this one."

"We're moving to Hawaii. Fuck the snow," I grumble with a small grin.

"I mean, I wouldn't mind Hawaii." She gives a teasing smirk, and I know I'm in for Rosie's cutting and whimsical sarcasm. "I could wear bikinis all day, hula skirts at night, and ogle all the hot guys."

I laugh. "Absolutely not. You aren't allowed to date until you're fifty."

Damon grins. "And I have a few ways to ensure that." He winks at her.

Rosie giggles. "You aren't allowed to scare off my dates."

Damon laughs. "On the contrary, you agreed to that when you signed up for this adoption thing. Daddy's a big bad mafia man. Daughter's men must pass his checks. All of them."

Rosie laughs again just as the door to my room opens. We all watch as Doctor Freeman comes in. Josh follows behind him with Gavin and Alex. "Where's Raleigh and Harleigh?" Rosie asks, peering behind them.

"Sleeping, honey," Gavin says. "I don't think either of them have slept at all in a week. I won't lie and say I may have given them something to knock them out. They can be pissed off at me later."

Rosie's eyes widen at him. "You mean, you drugged them?" she squeaks.

Josh grins. "For their own good. Raleigh is about to take off with Alex on a very important business trip. Harleigh has a huge exam coming up. If she fails, she fails the class."

"They both need sleep, and we got tired of them fighting us on it," Alex rumbles. "At least this way, they'll actually be getting the sleep they need. They can be pissed at all of us if they want, but they both knew it was going to happen. They were warned." He shrugs. Rosie just watches them all gaping in shock. I can't help but laugh because it's adorable.

Damon smiles. "So, what brings you all here?"

Gavin smirks. "We're busting Lance out."

I look up so hopefully that I probably have a nice set of puppy dog eyes going on. "Tell me you're being serious."

"Oh God, not the eyes. Turn them off," Josh says jokingly as he covers his own. Rosie, Gavin, Alex, and Damon all crack up as Josh grins.

My smile widens. "Not a chance. They're the perfect weapon. Not even Kings can resist them," I say with a wink at Rosie.

Doctor Freeman nods and chuckles. "Gavin is being serious. I see no reason to keep you. Your labs have returned to normal. You're still a little tired, but we have you hydrated. We have your system stabilized. I think a few more days rest would be good. Get you slowly eating solid food again. I'd like to keep an eye on you, but we can do that at home. I'll swing by each day."

"Whatever you need to do, Doc. Just get me the fuck out of here."

(One Week Later)

"Has anyone ever told you you're an asshole?" I look up at Josh with a deadpan look. I'm sitting behind the desk in the office in mine and Damon's house.

The dickhead grins as he leans back in the chair in front of me and sticks his feet up on the desk. "I get that a lot. I don't know why. I'm a delight."

My lips twitch because I want to laugh, but I have a point to make. "What you're asking me is completely impractical and impossible. You're asking me to spy on someone who has proven over and over that she can be trusted. Fuck. She's marrying your brother."

Josh sobers and lets out a breath. "Come on. You know this doesn't have shit to do with Raleigh. This has everything to do with the Ruthless Warriors and their goddamn leader."

I sigh and lean back in my chair flipping my chewed up pen between my fingers. It's a bad habit, but I tend to destroy the lids of pens by absently gnawing on them. "Josh, not even I can get past Alex's system. It's not possible. There's a reason governments around the world contract him to protect their computer systems. He has a team who has created an impenetrable system. Hacking into it would not only lead him directly to me, but it would likely completely destroy my system because his would drop a virus on me that would delete and totally crash everything. Everything, Josh."

I don't need to tell him that would include everything I keep for him. Backup files. Accounting. Literally his entire life and that of this whole family. And not even just ours. I have stuff I keep as backup for the Crane Mafia, too. Just as Robby does for us. If I were to hack into Alex's system and lose everything, it's not that I couldn't get it all back. I could with no issue. It would just take days. Days we don't really have for me to be fucking around with that.

"What about Robby? He hacked into the State Department. The United States Government uses Alex's system."

I shake my head. "Not then they didn't. Now? Yeah, they do. And if you ask Robby to do what he did then today? He'll tell you to fuck off, Josh."

He sighs and leans his head back as he thinks. "Fine. But I need some kind of surveillance on her computer without her or Alex being aware of it. I have to know what's going on in the background. I don't think she's doing anything wrong. But I do think something is happening that they aren't aware of. And before you say it, I can't tell them. Because if I do, Alex's immediate reaction will be strengthening his system to keep people out of it."

"You owe me for this." I narrow my eyes at him when he turns to me with an arched eyebrow. I dial Alex's number and put it on speaker. "So owe me." I shake my head as the phone starts ringing. Josh sits up and watches me.

"Lucinio Tech. Alex Lucinio's office. How can I help?" Raleigh's sweet yet professional voice fills the room.

"Raleigh, it's Lance."

She sucks in breath. "Lance! How are you feeling? Okay?"

"I'm a lot better, sweetheart. Listen, I need Alex. Is he in?"

"He is. Just a minute. I'll transfer you." She puts me on hold.

I glare at Josh again. "Owe me."

"Whatever you want as long as you get me what I need."

"You're about to regret those words." I wait a few seconds longer before Alex picks up.

"Hey, Lance. What's up? Feeling alright?"

"Yeah. I'm good. I ate a whole burger today and didn't puke or shit my guts out."

Alex dramatically gags, but I can hear him laughing. "Fucker. What's up?"

I hate what I'm about to do, but I steal my nerves because I trust Josh. "I was doing a little work today and saw some random as fuck anomaly. Would you be opposed at all to me using your system to do a bit of digging? I mean let me remote access in? You have a little more software that I can use to boost my own. I also wanted to update my own security. I thought I could download your latest stuff now instead of ordering the software like I usually do."

"I keep telling you that you don't need to do that. I have no idea why you insist on it." Alex chuckles. "Besides. The software you'd order isn't the shit you should have on yours anyway. You need the government grade program. You know I'd have to send a tech to do it unless you do it yourself."

"Maybe with this entire Ruthless Warrior bullshit, I decided to listen to you. I could do Robby's while I'm at it. He hasn't upgraded yet. I could just remotely give it to him so it updates automatically on his end."

"Yeah. Whatever you need to do. Anything to help out. Listen, I have a meeting. Raleigh just popped in and said he showed up."

"Want to transfer me down to tech first so when I remote access in, they don't blow up my fucking system?"

Alex laughs. "I'll take care of it. Hang tight." Alex puts me on another hold.

Josh is grinning from ear to ear. "I've never doubted you, but damn, I'm fucking proud of you right now."

"Man, you fucking owe me. Something huge. Like a fucking vacation." I take out my phone and text Robby that I'll send him the system update for our security remotely so when it starts to download, he doesn't freak out.

"Mr. Knight," a male voice rumbles over the phone. "I'm Sam. I'm the head of the Tech Department. Mr. Lucinio told me to give you full system access. May I ask why?"

I glance at Josh with furrowed brows. He mimics me and leans forward silently. "You may not," I say. "I've explained that to Mr. Lucinio. He's the only one who needs to know. Your job is to follow your boss' orders."

Sam pauses. Josh and I watch the phone suspiciously. Instincts are tingling. Something about this guy isn't right.

Finally, after a few moments, Sam sighs. "I'm sure you can understand my hesitation."

I raise an eyebrow. "Considering I'm family to Mr. Lucinio, no. I don't understand your hesitation. I suggest you do what your boss told you to. Unless you'd like to be in the unemployment line by the end of the day because I assure you I have that power."

He sighs again. "I'm going on record as being completely opposed to this, Mr. Knight. I have texted you at the phone number Mr. Lucinio provided. Please use that login information to access remotely. Once you're in, I'll see you and grant you the permissions you need to use the system freely. I will then text you a code. Should you run into any area that restricts your access, please enter that code. It will allow you through."

"Got it." I look at my cellphone and follow the directions in the text. Josh squirms uncomfortably, but I know he doesn't want to say anything to alert the asshole on the other line that he's in the room.

"There you are. I have texted you your access code and granted you system access. Is there anything else I can do for you, Mr. Knight?"

"Nope. Thank you." I hang up and instantly get to work.

"A code in case you run into something restricted? Isn't that what your access is all about?"

"Yes. I think that code will allow him to track what I'm accessing." My eyes fly across the green code on my screen. Suddenly, though, I find the red I'm looking for. "There you are," I rumble.

Josh watches me, confused. "What?"

I quickly access the page. "Employee files. It's restricted. I'm going to enter the code he gave me to see what he does, but first…" I pull up a second screen so I can quickly find the information I need after I enter this code.

"Why are we looking at employee records?"

"Because it's restricted and far from what you actually want me looking into. It allows me to see if he's watching me. And if he is, then I'll have a reason to watch him."

Josh leans back. "Huh. How? If he's watching you, how are you going to watch him?"

"By cloaking." I grin after entering the code. I switch to my other screen and watch what he does. I'm sure he has no idea that it's possible to watch him behind the curtains of where he's watching me. As I thought he would, he enters code to stop me from looking at certain files. I just chuckle. "Good boy. Give me what I need." I take out my pen and write down the files he's restricting me from, his included.

A few moments later, I go back to reading code on my screen, looking for more red. Accounts Lucinio Tech holds. Security footage. Programs they're working on. All of it gets written in my notebook because when I cloak myself, I'm looking into all of this.

To him, it will look like I logged out. He'll take the restriction off the files. By that time, I'll have already planted the trackers I need to, one of them being on his very own computer.

"I wonder why the fuck he blocked access to the security cameras for his office and Raleigh's desk...," I mumble.

As I work, I barely notice that water and food has appeared in front of me seemingly out of nowhere. I eat and drink absently. My only real conscious thoughts are unraveling the mystery I suddenly found myself in.

As the sun sinks deeper and deeper below the horizon, I find myself further and further behind the dark walls of Lucinio Tech.

And the shit I find makes my blood boil.

Chapter Fourteen

❦ Damon ❦

I yawn. It's three in the morning and Lance has just finished the digging he was doing. And then proceeded to drop one fuck of a bomb on us all. I rub my eyes.

"Are you sure about this?" Alex asks for the fifteenth time.

"Dude," Lance growls low.

Alex sighs and holds out his hands to ward off an imminent blow-up. Lance doesn't like being questioned. He's more tolerant if it's family because he knows we don't question. We just can't wrap our heads around the information he shares sometimes. Like Alex in this very moment.

Alex locks his hands behind his head as he paces. "Fuck, how the fuck? How the fuck are they still somehow using her?" He's asking himself, but it's a question we're all wondering.

"It's not that they're using her, A," Lance says. "They're trying to cast doubt in her from you and us. It's obvious she has nothing to do with it, but all of this is happening from her computer."

"But how? I don't fucking understand how. Raleigh isn't a part of this."

"She is, Alex," Josh says. "This all fucking started with her. She was promised as a baby to Edward Franklin, remember? We thwarted those plans. Franklin got fucking pissed. Now, he's dead, and his brother is exacting his revenge."

"Why not go after Harleigh?" Gavin asks. "I mean, I get the fucker is trying to tear us all apart by driving a wedge between us. He's counting on Alex choosing his girl over us. But why not Harleigh? This shit with Gregory Franklin started with her. He bought her for his douchedick son, Charles. Remember? So, why hasn't he gone after her?"

"He has, Gav," I say. "In case you've forgotten, we've had to tighten her security because her lead bodyguard got suspicious of people following her. Not only that, Lance looked into her. She has a ghost account."

Gavin's eyes snap to Lance's. "The fuck?"

"I haven't gotten that far yet. Thanks for the segue, baby." Lance smiles and flips to more screens. "Harleigh has a ghost account. Deposits from the same account depositing money into that Ginger Lucille Roger account are being deposited into this account. The account wasn't hard to find. It's a ghost account, but they wanted to make sure it could be found. There are deposits into it, large withdrawals. And then more deposits. What's interesting is the deposits happen once a day for the whole month. The large withdrawal is the entire amount of the month's deposits. The next month is full of more deposits each day. All of the deposits total one million dollars. The withdrawal is one million. I think they've taken the million and just keep breaking it up to deposit it and withdraw it. I think it's the same million being deposited and withdrawn over and over."

Alex growls as he drops next to me. "How fucked up does this actually get?"

"You remember the other day when Nicole was distracted and she fucked the cake measurements up? The cake basically blew up in the oven and caused a huge mess?"

"I remember," Alex says. "I'd laugh because it's fucking funny, but I'm too pissed off."

Lance gives a half smile. "It's like that level of fucked up. I pulled the footage your guy blocked me from. Did you know he doesn't leave until ten o' clock every single night?"

"Yeah, but that's not unusual for my tech guys. They're staffed twenty-four-seven. They have to be." Alex shrugs and points to Lance. "Hackers don't sleep. They do their best work at night."

I chuckle. "So fucking true. Anyway, Lance pulled the footage. The footage from his office shows how late he stays. The camera angle wasn't that great to see what he does on his computer, which I don't think for a second is unintentional. I think he moved it so it doesn't show as it should. But regardless, he stays until exactly ten each night. Every night at nine o'clock, something interesting happens to her desktop."

Alex raises an eyebrow as I nod towards Lance. He looks at Lance. "What?"

Lance turns his laptop. "This."

Alex, Josh, Gavin, Dane, and Cole all gather around his laptop. I've already seen this. I know what's happening. It's nine o' clock. It's pitch black in Raleigh's area and the entire top floor of Lucinio Tech. There's no light at all because there are no windows in that area.

As if a poltergeist was there, Raleigh's computer turns on. The cameras are set up so they see over her shoulder. There's no angle on the entire top floor that isn't covered, save for the bathrooms and Alex's office. The only light in the entire area is from her screen. No one is sitting in her chair, but the cameras clearly pick up our family's bank's website being pulled up.

As if someone is doing it from her chair, another bank account is pulled up using different credentials but from the same bank. The next thing we see is the withdrawal from the account we connected to Alec and VV and the deposit into the ghost account. Like clockwork, it happens at the same exact time each and every night.

When it's done, Raleigh's computer gets shut down once more, and it's like nothing at all ever happened. Sam stays in the office for another fifty-five minutes putzing around and doing actual work. Raleigh's computer goes right back to being idle.

"How the hell does security not see this shit?" Alex growls. "Do I have another leak?"

Lance shakes his head. "I don't think so. Let me show you what your security team actually sees during this time." He pulls up side by side footage of the security feed for the exact same time. The feed security sees is nothing but blackness. The computer never comes on. Lance points to a tiny speck on the screen. It quickly disappears.

"What was that? Dust?" Gavin asks.

"That was a glitch. It signals feed that's been looped," Dane says. "If you aren't looking for it, you'd never see it." He nods to the screen as Lance backtracks, then pauses it right when the glitch appears. "See how it just randomly showed up?"

"Still looks like dust," Josh says. "Or a fucking ghost. It shows up right before the computer turns on in the other feed."

Dane nods again. "A few years ago while Taylor and I were working a case involving a gang that targeted his wife, we had set up surveillance on her bakery. We sat there for hours watching her. We had an undercover man in there. We thought we had all of our bases covered. But we were wrong. We noticed she'd been in the back decorating a cake for a pretty extensive period of time. That her motions were repetitive. There's no way she'd take that long on one cake. Then we noticed just a very tiny speck in a corner. Next thing we saw is Nicole doing exactly the same thing she'd just done. But it was so subtle that we hadn't noticed what was happening."

"So, this ghostly phenomenon is a glitch." Cole chuckles. "Fuck."

Dane leans forward and points to the speck. "If you're paying attention, you'd see this doesn't have any kind of pattern. Dust flies around. It doesn't just appear like that in a random as fuck part of the room, then disappear less than a second later."

Lance grins. "Exactly. This video is looped every single night. And after he shuts things down again, he makes sure the room is completely dark. That the screen isn't glowing or anything signaling that it had been on. He makes sure all of the lights are off on the tower underneath her desk. Then he puts back the live feed. No one is going to pay attention to a random white dot that shows up at obscure times in a different part of the screen." Lance pauses the video again and points near the corner where I know there's another white dot because he showed me before we called anyone here.

Alex breathes a huge sigh of relief. "It's not that I didn't trust Raleigh, but none of this made any fucking sense. I get it now. All of it."

Gavin nods his agreement. "I'm going to kill that fucker when I get my hands on him."

I laugh. "Before you kill him, we need to question him first. Lance is gathering a little more information."

Lance looks at Alex hesitantly. "I dropped what I'll call a tracker on Raleigh's system. Now before you freak out on me, hear me out. We have the video evidence that it's happening. But we don't have the remote access information. The tracker will give me a record of literally everything that happens on her computer, but not just at night. It will show me everything that happens in the background during the day. It will show me what she accesses, but it will also show me if he copies what she's doing or looks at what she's doing."

Alex just watches him, confused as fuck. "Layman's terms would be great."

I laugh. "Basically, if Sam is watching Raleigh's movements on her computer, Lance will know. If she accesses someone's employee record, he'll know. If she accesses a huge account, he'll know. Or at least we think he knows because we think he's paying very close attention to what she does since she's connected to you."

"Why wouldn't he just look at me?" Alex asks.

Josh leans against the desk. "Well, we think he is. After some of the shit Lance found today, especially the remote access to her computer, we don't think he's stopped with her. We think he's looking at you, too."

Alex rubs his eyes. "I still don't get what this has to do with anything."

Lance leans back in his chair and meets my eyes. I give him a slight nod and reassuring smile because his theory is good. He's just hesitant to share it. Lance takes a breath. "I think Gregory Franklin believes that we're using your company to track him. I don't have hard evidence. At least not yet. The instincts and hunches are there, though. I think he thinks that you're more than just a security software firm. It's well-known you work with the government. Many from around the world, not just here. I believe he thinks your company is able to find him and his hiding places. Spy on him. I'll be able to tell once I do more digging. Especially into him. The trackers I have on you both show me a lot of stuff, but it also allows me free reign in and out of the back end of Lucinio Tech without your system destroying mine if I were to try and hack it."

Everyone is silent for a few moments as they mull over the words. After a few moments of it rolling around in their minds, I smile. "It's a good theory."

"A damn good theory," Josh says. I watch as my husband's cheeks pinken at the praise. He lives for it. Praise is what he thrives on.

Even though he'd never in his life admit it.

It makes me want to reward him for all his hard work. In fact, I want to show him all of our gratitude so badly, I find myself standing. "Okay, everyone. It's late. Lance has been working on this for almost ten hours. We're all fucking exhausted. Time for bed. Everyone go home. We can talk more about this tomorrow night after he gets more information after he's rested."

Everyone tiredly agrees. I show everyone out as Lance shuts down his equipment. By the time I have everything locked up, Lance is finished shutting down and has two bottles of water for us. I take one of them and his hand with the other.

"You're right. It's been an exhausting day," he says raspily. We're both tired, but he deserves some attention before we both pass out.

After quickly checking in on Rosie, I quietly close her door. We have six bedrooms in this house. Rosie decided she likes the other master suite on the opposite end of the house from mine and Lance's. While the two of us were playing the pretend we aren't attracted to each other game, we had the house built with two suites for the both of us. By the time it was completed, we were not only married, but I'd already worked past the shock of being gay. We both have been sleeping in the same room ever since we moved in. The room Rosie is using has never been used by anyone else.

I rub my thumb over the top of his hand as I pull him into our bedroom. I close the door and push him against it. My lips are on his before he has a chance to realize what's happening. He quickly adjusts and starts kissing me back. Our hands are all over each other. With Lance being sick, this is the first time we've really done much more than kiss.

And fuck do I miss him. His tongue diving into my mouth hungrily is all I need for my own blood to heat for him. We grasp at each other, fighting for control over ourselves and one another, but neither of us are going to win. We're too starved for each other. Like rabid animals digging into their first meal in months.

Seconds later, we're tearing off each other's clothes near our bed. Our lips still move against one another's, getting rougher and more needy. The moans and gasps emanating from deep within him spur me on. It's not just my dick that's become rigid. It's my whole damn body. I'm wound so tight that all he'd have to do is touch me, and I'd be coming down his throat.

It's not about me, though. Not this time.

It's all about him.

I slow things down. My body protests hard, but I ignore it. I kiss down his jaw, nipping at his stubble until I get to his neck. "Time for me to worship you."

"Da-" He cuts himself off with a surprised moan when I suddenly drop to my knees and take his dick in my mouth. "Oh fuck…"

I look up and smile when his head drops back. His eyes close. His fingers spear my hair. His hard cock is a stark contrast to the smoothness of the skin encasing him. I take him as deeply as I can before pulling back slowly, gently scraping my teeth along the underside of his dick. I flick my tongue over him. When I reach his tip, I suck hard.

It's the guttural moan that has me gripping my own cock hard. I jerk myself at the same pace I'm sucking him, slow and hard. I smile when he moans again and looks down at me. His fingers grip my hair a little tighter. His other cups my cheek. His stomach clenches as his dick thickens and gets even harder for me.

I grip his balls and tug just a little as I roll them in my palm. He starts thrusting into my mouth. I let him and stroke myself to the pace he sets. I flick my tongue erratically around him, scraping my teeth lightly when he moves himself out of my mouth, and suck hard around his tip.

"Mmm…," I rumble around him when he thrusts to the back of my throat. I swallow.

"Holy fuck." He starts thrusting faster, panting.

"There we go." I growl low and deep around him. I know it sends vibrations through his dick and makes him feel really good because his balls immediately draw up.

"Baby, holy fuck, I'm gonna come!" He thrusts faster and faster. I twist my wrist around myself as I let him fuck my mouth to his heart's content.

Seconds later, he stiffens with a moan and thrusts himself one more time into my mouth. His tip meets the back of my throat. I swallow with a wicked growl. Just as I want him to, he comes hard for me. He shoots his come into my mouth, and I take all he gives, swallowing greedily as I suck him dry.

I lick him clean with a grin as I slowly pull my mouth off him. "Has anyone ever told you that your taste is fucking addictive? You're like a drug."

I kiss his dick. I stopped stroking mine as soon as he started coming, but I'm regretting the action now because it's fucking painful. As I stand. I give myself a couple of squeezes to ease myself, but that never works. Especially when Lance's eyes drop and focus entirely on my cock.

"You know that's going in my mouth," Lance says as he sits. "Now." He grips my hips and pulls me closer to him.

I groan. "Baby, that wasn't the intention. You found so much shit today and worked so hard that I wanted to reward you in some small way."

Lance smirks and looks up at me. "Damon, I haven't had your dick in my mouth, in my ass, or against my dick while we stroke each other off in weeks. I need your come down my throat right now."

My dick jerks at his words. I'm no stranger to a little dirty talk, but when it comes out of Lance's mouth, it always turns my rock solid cock into pure granite. So, I waste no time feeding him my dick and fucking his mouth fast.

I groan again as I watch him take me. His eyes never leave mine, but his mouth is like a damn hoover. He licks and sucks at the perfect pace and pressure. His teeth graze me as I thrust until I jerk hard into him. A jolt shoots down my spine, and I come hard for him. As he gave me moments ago, three weeks worth of come escape me. He swallows every drop with a smirk and licks me clean when I'm emptied.

"Oh fuck. Fuck, baby."

"Mmm…" He licks his lips when he pulls away. "Yep. I should've just been eating you this whole time. Best medicine."

I laugh and lean down. I kiss him deeply, tangling my tongue with his and sharing both of our combined tastes. He might be right. I don't think there's anything better tasting than the two of us together.

I pull back slowly and crawl into bed with him. I set the alarm so we wake up to get Rosie off to school. Like he always does, Lance snuggles back into me and melts in my arms. I kiss his shoulder and back then snuggle him close.

"I love you," Lance murmurs.

"I love you, too," I rumble back.

A shiver runs down his spine. Hugging him as tightly as I can and burying my face in his neck is the last conscious action I take before sleep overtakes us both.

Chapter Fifteen

☏ Lance ☏

(Four Months Later)

"I don't give a shit if you have to tear Rome upside down!" Josh screams into his phone. I just blink at him as I watch him pace his office as I set up my laptop. "Find Gregory Franklin! Because if I have to fly out there again, you all are going to end up at the bottom of the fucking sea! Got me?" I say nothing when he hangs up and throws his phone onto the couch completely across the room from where he's standing.

Damon picks that moment to walk in. Gavin is right behind him. Both have blood on their hands and a little on their clothes. Damon has some speckled on his neck and cheek. Josh is too busy pacing and growling underneath his breath about incompetent people to notice.

"You, uh, have fun down there?" I ask. As I hoped he would, Josh snaps his eyes towards the door instead of focusing on the war going on in his mind.

Gavin grins. "He was tough to crack."

"Literally. Crack," Damon says. He shakes his head with a half smile. "In half by the time Gavin finished with him."

"First of all, gross," I say as I laugh. "Second, go clean up. I'm not getting into this with you two tracking blood all over the place."

"What information did he give?" Josh asks. His blue eyes are sharp and stormy. "Fucking give me something because I'm about to hop a plane to Rome and kill a few people because I'm tired of chasing Gregory fucking Franklin."

"Well, lucky for you, we got some information," Gavin says. "Right as I started carving out his ribcage."

Josh blinks a few times. "What the fuck is wrong with you?"

Gavin laughs. "I'm sorry. Wasn't it you who told me to let out my dark side on that fucker?"

"Well, yeah, but I didn't say enjoy it!" Josh runs his fingers through his hair. "I've employed a sociopath."

"I'm not a fucking sociopath, you fucker. Franklin landed an hour ago. I have a team at his house waiting on his ass." Gavin turns on his heel. "I'm using your shower! Harleigh will be over with some clothes for me!" His voice fades the further down the hall he gets from us.

Damon laughs as he grabs Josh's arm when he starts darting out of his office. "Don't. You're about to be needed for something else."

"Franklin is my number one priority right now. I really want to be the one to haul his ass in," Josh says.

"Trust me. You want to hear what Lance says." He nods to a chair.

Josh eyes us both but slowly takes a seat. "What could possibly be better than me choking the life out of that smug motherfucker?"

"By the time you get there, they'll have him. Trust me," Damon says as he sits next to me. He drops his arm over the back of the two seater couch I'm sitting in. Thankfully, he's not as covered in blood as Gavin is.

I decide to dive right in. "Remember Sam?"

Josh nods. "Yes. Lucinio Tech's lead tech guy. Father of two. Wife is some big time executive for a worldwide entertainment firm."

I nod. "Correct. After he was caught trying to set up Raleigh, he was fired. But something about the entire thing struck me as very odd. How does a guy who never had a speeding ticket, never been in trouble, never been handed a pink slip at any of his jobs suddenly just up and do something with such serious consequences? It doesn't make sense at all, right?"

"Admittedly, no. But I don't blame Alex for firing him." Josh shrugs.

"I don't either, but I kept investigating. I wanted to know what the hell happened to make this seemingly law-abiding man who has been described as a good father and husband do something this serious. And I figured it out. It took a while because of all the other tracking and shit with Franklin. I'm glad I stuck with this, though, because he's the link."

Josh raises an eyebrow. "We proved he had nothing to do with it. He was being blackmailed."

I nod as Damon starts rubbing the back of my stiff neck. I don't know how he does it, but he knows exactly when I start feeling cramps in my neck and shoulders. "He had a very convincing story and some good evidence to back it up. But it still didn't sit right with me. He was too… willing. Despite being blackmailed, he put up very little fight. After we changed his name and the name of his family members and relocated them, I kept track."

"As any good member of the mafia would," Josh teases. "Where are you going with this, Lance?"

"You're no fun." I smirk. "Fine. It's his wife."

Josh is quiet for a long while. Damon keeps rubbing my neck and shoulders grinning like the Cheshire cat. Finally, Josh clears his throat. "Okay. Color me intrigued."

"Don't mind if I do. Mafia King, meet Edward and Gregory Franklin's younger sister." I turn my laptop towards him. His eyes narrow. "The fuck is happening right now? Why didn't we know about her?"

"Because, like Raleigh, there's no record of her being born. I found a forged birth certificate in her employment file, but her license and everything else is completely faked. The only thing that connects her to the Franklin's is something so buried, that I needed Robby's help. She was adopted from…" I trail off. "You know what? Just guess." I watch him. Damon rests his foot on his knee.

Josh thinks for a moment. I can see the exact second that realization hits him. "Rome. We relocated her to Rome, and that's where Gregory spends a lot of his time."

"Ding! Ding! Ding! Ding!" I press another button. "The celebrity's favorite manager was born Allesandra Bellini. She was illegally adopted as a newborn by Brenda and Phillip Franklin. Her name was changed to Sandra Belle Franklin. When she married, her last name became Franklin-Vincenti."

"So, tell me how the fuck you figured that out," Josh says.

"I was looking at missing persons. Same as we did with Raleigh. Except this time, I got a hit on Interpol. Sandra bears a very strong resemblance to a baby who was reported missing. They did an aged image, what she may look like, and Sandra hit on that. So, I asked Robby to help from there because I can't hack Interpol. I tried. I'm good, but that kid has some skills I'm still learning. He got through. We found the report and everything for Allesandra's disappearance."

"When we relocated them, Sandra mentioned family friends she hasn't seen since she was a child. She wondered if they were still around," Damon says leaning forward. "I didn't think anything of it at all. Gavin and I got the names, looked them up, gave her an address for them, and that was the end of it. But then they found this report and family information." Damon nods to my screen. "Including her parents."

Josh leans back. "Let me guess. The same people Sandra wanted to see."

I grin. "Yep. And that's not all. Her name. She wanted their family name to be Bellini. She wanted hers to be Allesandra."

Josh rubs his hands over his face. "So, she knew she was adopted. How does Sam come into this shit?"

"I'm so glad you asked. Vito Bellini, as he's now called, was born to Italian immigrants, Valentino and Nicolette Rossi."

Josh nearly chokes. He coughs hard. Josh looks at me in horror. "The Italian mob. The fucking leaders of the Italian fucking mob. Is that what you're saying to me? He's son of the leader of the fucking Italian mob?"

I nod. "La Cosa Nostra. His coronation? Two nights. He's meant to revive them from the ruins they've been left in by you and Ryan. And then go after you both."

"Mother fuck!" Josh stands and quickly grabs his phone from the couch where he threw it. "Gavin! Damon! Both of you with me!" he bellows into the hall. He turns his eyes back to me. "I'll have Dane or Cole

133

pick up Rosie. We need to move. I'll call Ryan. We need to get some guys together now and go after them." He turns back out of the room like a whirlwind. Damon looks at me, then chases after him.

I stand up and scurry after them. "Josh, for Christ's sake. Would you think this through for five minutes? You can't go tearing out to Italy!"

"The fuck I can't!" He runs towards the front room of his house. I glance at Damon as we both follow.

"Josh! Fuck, would you stop and listen to me?" I catch up to him and grab his arm.

"I'm not letting the goddamn Italian mob come after this family!" Josh says as he pulls open the front door. Standing on the other side is Alec with a sobbing Dallas and hysterical Rosie. Dallas leaps at him, knocking him back a foot before he regains his footing. "What the hell?"

Rosie runs to me and Damon, slamming into us full force. We both wrap our arms around her and look at Alec completely confused. He's wiping blood from his mouth as he slams the door closed behind him.

"The fuck?" I look at Alec.

"We found your fucking Gregory fucking Franklin. He's outside in one of your guard's SUVs along with seven of his cohorts," Alec growls.

"That explains one thing," Josh says. "Now explain why Dallas is clinging to me like an octopus and Rosie is scream-sobbing."

He tightens his grip on Dallas just as we do on Rosie. He's not wrong. She's screaming and sobbing so hard that she's choking on her sobs and coughing before she goes right back to screaming and sobbing all over again.

I tangle my fingers in her hair and hug her harder. Damon shifts so she's sandwiched between us. So she's surrounded by us and feels protected. I lean my cheek against the top of her head and close my eyes as we both sway with her.

"We got you, sweetie," I whisper soothingly. "You're okay. You're safe."

"What the fuck?" Gavin comes into the room putting on his shirt.

Harleigh is next to him staring at us all with wide eyes. "What's happening?"

"Harleigh," Alec says. "Can you do me a favor and take the girls upstairs, please?" He looks over his shoulder and opens the door just a little bit. "Ink, with me. The rest of you, wait until I get the girls secured."

He turns back to us as Ink slips inside and closes the door. "I need you to go with Harleigh. Take the girls. They don't need to be here for this."

Damon glances at me as Josh whispers in Dallas' ear. "Sweet girl, we need you to go with Ink," Damon says softly to Rosie. She shakes her head and clings to him. "Rosie, honey, something is happening here, and we need to figure it out quick. You need to be a good girl and help us out. Ink is a good person. He'll protect you from whatever you're afraid of. I promise. You trust us, right?"

She nods but doesn't loosen her grip in the slightest. "They... tr-tried... t-to k-k-k-kidnap us!" She whispers, but it's still a very obvious shriek that sends chills right through me. Not because of how haunting it sounds, but because someone made an attempt on our daughter.

I kiss her head. "Go with Ink," I whisper in her ear. "You can cling to him all you want to. He'll protect you. And Harleigh will be right there. Dallas will be with you. We'll be right out here. Nothing will happen to you, honey. I promise."

It takes both girls several minutes to calm down enough to leave us. Harleigh hugs them both and leads them upstairs to the bedroom Dallas uses when she's at Josh's. Not a single one of us makes a sound until we hear her door close. As soon as it does, though, all eyes turn to Alec.

"What the hell is happening?" I ask, my chest tight. "Kidnap them?"

"As you know, Rosie and Dallas are very good friends and hang out at school," Alec begins, gritting his teeth. He's pissed. "They share a locker. Most of their classes are together. They are always together. Fuck, they both even have a few guys from the baseball team protecting them. Which I didn't know until today when I went to pick them up. As soon as I pulled through the fucking gates to the school, I knew something was wrong. Next thing I know, the school's security is running towards the back of the school, and the guards we had at the front are getting into position with their weapons drawn prepared to shoot anyone who attempted to leave. So, I ran after the guards."

I run my fingers through my hair. "Don't like where this is going."

Alec's cold stair turns venomous. "I got around the back and heard screaming. Blood-curdling screaming. There's a black SUV that crashed through the wall behind the school totaled out, and another one near the door. Two guys are trying to shove Dallas into the back. Another two have

Rosie right behind her. There's a guy in the driver's seat screaming to hurry up. And there's three guys in baseball uniforms trying to fight off two other guys. One of the kids has one of the fucker's guns, but instead of shooting, he throws it and kicks the fucker so hard in the balls that his scream could shatter glass. I jumped into the mix with the guards. Ended up shooting the driver when he attempted to drive off. You're lucky I aimed low because the driver was Franklin."

Josh growls low. "All of them. Bring them all to the interrogation compound. I'll be there with Gavin and Damon in a few minutes."

Alec nods and says nothing as he walks out the door. Josh stands still for several moments with his eyes closed. We all know better than to ask him if he's okay or needs anything. This is Josh's way of reigning in his satanic side.

Damon squeezes my hand and leans in. He kisses my neck. "Stay here with the girls. Dallas is fine with Ink, I'm sure, but Rosie needs one of us."

"And you know what's about to happen is something I prefer to stay away from," I whisper with a smile.

I can handle mafia shit, but I'm the hacker for a reason. Staying behind the computer screen is my preference. I'm good at it. I'm not good with the gorey scene about to play out. I can handle it, but I don't really like being a part of that side of the mafia.

Josh takes out his phone and walks to his office. He motions for us to follow him. "Ry, we have an Italian mob issue."

We all follow Josh as he fills Ryan in on everything he just learned and all that just happened. After coordinating with him to set up teams, the coronation happening in two nights will be crashed. Sam/Vito and his wife will not be making it out alive. Their two lovely children will be rehomed. Thankfully, they're too young to really remember what's about to happen to their parents and grandparents.

It's a good thing for us that we're larger than the Italian mob, and they know it. We can easily overpower them and take them out. Many will die tomorrow night. It will be a show of power on our part, and it's not the first time we've done it. They tend to stay away from us, but sometimes, they think they can rise up and show their muscles. Anyone who shows up at this coronation is directly betraying us and the agreement we have with them to leave them alone as long as they fall in line and don't fuck with us.

It's going to be a bloodbath. We have things here that need to be taken care of. More important shit than the Italian Mafia trying to flash their big dick energy around. I hope he makes the decision to not go and send in teams instead.

We all stay in Josh's office while he formulates a plan to take down those who will be at the coronation. It needs to be a coordinated attack. They have to be taken by complete surprise, and the kids need to be out of harm's way. Which means we'll need to get them placed in good homes with good people.

When he and Ryan finish discussing their plans, he hangs up. "Okay. That's finished. Lance, I need you and Robby on adoption papers and setting things up. There's going to be a lot of displaced kids. Meet him at his house. He's already starting. He was with Ryan when I called."

I glance a little frantically at Damon. "Josh, uh…" I start as I look back at him.

"Problem?" Josh glares.

I'd shrink back at how harsh and deadly he looks right now, but I'm used to it. So, I stand tall instead. "Yeah. I have a terrified child to think about. You can have him come here, but I'm not leaving my daughter."

"Fine. Have him come here." Josh shrugs before turning to Damon and Gavin. "As for us, we need to finish this shit quick with Franklin. I'm not leaving a takedown of this magnitude in anyone else's hands but ours. I need you both. We'll fly out with Ryan and Luke tonight."

Damon nearly chokes. "Josh, what about Rosie? She was almost fucking kidnapped! You want me to just fly off and leave her after something like that?"

Josh sighs and softens, but only a little. "Do you think I want to leave Dallas alone after that? She was kidnapped once, remember?" His voice betrays him when it cracks. I'm completely taken aback. It might be the first time any of us has seen him look like that.

Torn.

Almost completely shattered at his own decision.

He shakes his head. "There's no getting around this one. We have to take out the threat. I need my best by my side." He glances at me, Damon, and Gavin before striding out of the office. Gavin looks at us before following him.

Damon takes a breath and leans down. He kisses me. I feel all of the love and reassurance he pours into it. "Can you pack me an overnight bag?" he asks with more conviction than I'm positive he actually feels. "I'll come back before we go. Maybe grab something for me to change into."

"Yeah. Of course." I give him a reassuring smile, but I know damn well it's unconvincing. I've never been able to hold anything back from him. As soon as he leaves the room, I close my eyes. I don't feel like being strong, but I have a kid to think about now.

Almost every single battle Damon has gone in, I've either been with him or close by. Watching him. Having his back. This is the first time in a very, very long time he'll be miles away from me, depending on someone else to keep him safe.

And that thought alone tightens my chest and makes me sick to my stomach…

Chapter Sixteen

☙ Damon ☙

"We're really doing this the hard way, aren't we?" I say from where I'm perched on the metal table in the middle of the room. Of the eight people we have chained up in this room, only three are breathing. The others had been carved up torturously slowly.

Gregory Franklin himself stares at me with a vicious glare. I'd laugh but I'm fucking tired as hell and pissed off that we're even still in this room. Gavin is leaning against the wall behind me. Josh is kneeling in front of Gregory.

We haven't gotten a single one of these motherfuckers to talk, and that's really saying a lot. Gavin gouged out the eyes of one of them because he said something about Harleigh being hot; how he'd throw her against the wall and fuck her brains out. With a knife. Gavin made him watch as he took a knife and stabbed through his ballsack, pinning him to the floor, just before he gouged out his eyes. The howling coming out of him was deafening. We thought he'd slowly bleed out and shut up after a while, but he refused to die. Making him guzzle a bottle of turpentine seemed to do the trick.

A few of the others are missing limbs. Not a single one of them, though, has answered questions. It means there is a lot more at work than just a few assholes in a motorcycle crew. I have a bad feeling this MC isn't just any MC. Someone is pulling the strings.

I look at my watch with a sigh. "Josh, time to end this shit. We have a plane to catch."

Josh sighs dramatically. "I know." His fierce gaze lands on the guy we have on the backside of the room. He points his bloodied knife at him. "We're going to play a game. Hangman. Heard of it?"

The guys eyes narrow. "Fuck you. Everyone's heard of Hangman."

Josh's eyes light up as he stands. "Good. Then you know how it goes. My version is a little bit different. See, my guys only answer in the event that yours don't. So, you better hope they do because my guys will intentionally guess wrong letters in the word we put up." He kneels in front of the guy and flips his knife in his hand.

Gavin sits next to me on the table grinning from ear to ear. "I love this game. If they guess wrong, you lose a limb."

I get off the table and kneel in front of the other guy next to Gregory. He hasn't said a damn word this entire time. He hasn't even made eye contact. We've all decided he's our weak link and have left him completely alone.

"Time for the fun to begin," I say as demonically as possible as I grin sardonically. "You know they say Josh is satanic. Gavin is demonic. I'm the fucking crazy one." I flip my own knife in my hand and then slash it along the leg of his jeans deep enough so the knife cuts the top couple of layers of skin.

"Ah!" the guy screams. His eyes light up in pure terror when they jerk to mine.

"Oh shit." I look down mock apologetically. "Fuck. I always do that." I glance at Josh with a half-smile. "Sorry, boss. Knife got away from me. Too excited."

"Dammit, Damon," Gavin says.

"Don't do that again over there," Josh says. Both of them have teasing undertones in their voice that makes me grin.

"Promise." I put my left hand up in a Scout's Honor motion. I wink once more at my terrified, panting victim. "Forgive me?" I pout my lips and bat my eyes as he pants and trembles. I cut through his other pant leg as gently as possible. "There. See? Just to show no hard feelings." I tap his face with a wink, then cut the rest of the legs of his jeans off him. "Okay, here we go. My word." I quickly slash five lines in the thigh that has no marks.

"Ah! Please!" he screams and fights his restraints to grab his thigh. That won't be happening. His hands are secured behind his back.

I raise an eyebrow. "I'll spare you. Please is six letters. My word is only five letters, and we haven't started yet, so I'll let that one go. Five letters, boss. And go!" I shake my head at him. "We're not going to get through this if you can't handle a few scratches. Come on, tough biker guy. Grin and bear it." I look at Josh as my guy grimaces and groans.

"Alright, first letter!" Gavin says with a grin. "If you don't at least take a guess, I'll start cutting you." He glares directly at Gregory.

Gregory glares right back before looking at his wide-eyed associate. "Fine. You want a letter? F. For fuck you."

"Oof… F. Nope. Not in my word. Josh?"

Josh grins and stands. "This is about to get messy. Be quick. Don't want him to die before we get through the word." Josh stands and finds a chainsaw. "I fucking hate messes." He starts the chainsaw up and lowers it slowly over the asshole's leg.

"Ah! Fuck! Don't! Don't! R! S! T! L! N! E! T! I choose T!"

"Well, too late for your leg, but there are two Ts." I carve in two Ts, one in the first spot; the second in the fourth space.

"Ah!" my guy screams. He closes his eyes and grunts as he clenches his teeth and trembles with the effort to not scream out in pain.

The other guy isn't so lucky.

"Ah! Fuck! Stop! Ah!" he screams as Josh starts cutting through his leg. Gregory turns his face. The blood from his cohort's leg splatters hitting Josh, the asshole he's cutting up, and the wall.

Gregory doesn't look back at him and clamps his mouth shut as his guy screams. My guy has his eyes squeezed shut. He refuses to make a sound other than the deep breathing that's turned more into Lamaze.

"Such a trooper," I say loudly over the chainsaw. I tap my knife against his cheek. "You don't get to guess. You're part of the game. Guess again, motherfucker," I say to Gregory with a twisted grin.

Gavin rolls his eyes when Gregory stays silent. My guy looks around at all of us frantically. "No one's gonna guess?" Gavin asks. "Okay. Well, we have a plane to catch. C."

I laugh. "No C."

Josh cuts off his guy's other leg with a shrug. The guy screams in agony as Gavin nonchalantly looks at his watch. Once again, blood flies everywhere, reaching me this time. Gregory visibly cringes, but my guy keeps his eyes tight and forces himself to stay silent.

"We don't have time for this," Gavin says as he looks at me. "My guesses. O, M, and S."

"Nope. Negative. Incorrect." I nod to Josh.

The guy has gone into shock. His mouth is frozen open in horror. I'd say he's dead, but as soon as the chainsaw's teeth touch his arm near his shoulder, his eyes get wider. He tries to get away, but Josh is quicker. The chainsaw easily cuts through his bone, turning the room into even more of a bloody disaster.

"Shit...," my guy whispers. Gregory is starting to look green. He swallows hard as more blood hits him.

Josh goes after the guy's other arm. It's a damn good thing none of us are squeamish of blood or anything. If we were, there'd be a lot of puke to go with the pools and spatters of the sticky, red substance. The guy still doesn't scream, but he's fading fast because of the blood loss.

"Just kill him, King!" Gavin says.

Josh grins. "Gladly." He uses the chainsaw to cut through the guy's neck. None of us cared to figure out names. We simply don't give a shit.

The guy's head falls off his body and rolls towards Gregory. The eyes are open. The mouth is frozen in terror. Gavin watches the guy's body twitch and fall limp. Josh stops the chainsaw and drops it next to the limbless and headless corpse.

"I was gonna continue this game of bloody Hangman, but Gavin is right. We have other shit to do, and I'm fucking sick of the bullshit." My eyes darken as I glare venomously at my terrified Ruthless Warrior. I put my knife under his throat. "Tell me everything I want to know, and your death will be quick. Fuck around, and I'll make it as painful as I have time for. Maybe we'll have you drink bleach instead of turpentine. That sounds fun, doesn't it?"

"I'll talk!" he yells. "I'll talk! I'll tell whatever I can!"

"The fuck you will!" Gregory yells. "No one is allowed to say a fucking word! I'll kill you myself, asshole! I'm the leader! You obey me!"

"You're not the leader!" my guy spits. It's enough to make me pull my knife back from his throat. I'm completely floored by that information, but fuck if he'll know that.

"Talk," Josh growls as he kneels next to me. Gavin stays put, looking bored out of his mind. It's a ruse that should never be fallen for.

"Don't say a damn word, or I'll cut out your tongue!" Gregory screams.

Quick as a flash, Gavin is kneeling next to Gregory. "Say another word." He presses his gun against Gregory's throat. "I fucking dare you," Gavin snarls. I grin. Gregory shuts his mouth.

"Now, talk," Josh commands.

"He's not the real leader. We all knew it," the guy begins. "He's always talking on the phone to someone. Taking orders. He doesn't think anyone has seen him, but we all have at least once. We go along with it because we figure the real leader has a reason."

"Who's the real leader?" I ask.

"I don't know. All I know is his biker name. It's Tits."

I glance at Josh. "That's a fuck of an embarrasing name."

"No shit," Josh rumbles. He looks back at our guy as Gavin holds the gun tight against Gregory's throat. "What else?"

"He got it because he likes big tits on his women. That's what Abyss said." He nods towards Gregory. Gregory growls, but our guy just keeps talking. "Abyss wasn't even the second. He was the third in command, but he played the leader because those were his orders. I heard him on speaker one day at the clubhouse."

"Well, now we're getting somewhere," Josh says with a grin.

"Tell me why you fuckers went after two little girls today." I'm done playing games. I want to get this shit done with so I can go home to my family.

"We only went after one. Rosie. The other girl got in the way and fought us, so we grabbed both, but then their boyfriend's started fighting us, too. We didn't have time to do anything because we were descended on immediately by school security and your men. Rosie was our assignment. She was bought by the leader."

"So, this Tits guy. He bought a sixteen-year-old girl? Almost seventeen?" I ask, bile rising in my throat at the thought of my daughter being sold like a piece of property. Before I can stop myself, my knife is against his throat once more.

"Wait! Wait! That's not all."

Josh puts a hand on my wrist and shakes his head. I drop the knife with a low, protective growl. "Tits is the leader and bought a young girl. Why? Because his plan of getting Raleigh and Harleigh fell through?"

Our guy shakes his head. "No! Just her. Just Rosie. Harleigh was supposed to become Abyss' son's girl. Charles. Blobfish wanted her. His biker name was Blobfish because he was so fucking ugly. Raleigh was meant for Abyss' brother, Quackers, but when you all killed him, Abyss decided to take her for himself. He hasn't been able to get to her because the security on her is too high. We were going to grab Rosie first and then go after Harleigh and Raleigh when your guard was down."

"A sexy little harem, huh?" Gavin looks at Josh. "I love how Abyss here thinks he has a chance in hell of making that happen."

"Better chance of walking on the fucking sun," Josh rumbles. "What else do you know?"

"That's all. It's all I know. I swear. Tits wanted Rosie. Abyss wanted Raleigh and Harleigh."

"Tits is the actual leader, according to him. He wants the girls. So, we need Lance on him," I say. "Doesn't matter if we kill them or not. He's the one pulling strings."

Josh turns his attention to Gregory. "Where is he?"

Gregory laughs. "Closer than you think, but you'll never find him."

Gavin glares at our talker. "Where is he?"

"I don't know. I've never been privy to that information, and I haven't heard any recent phone conversations."

"I don't think we're getting any more information from these two," I say.

"Me either," Josh says. We all stand. Josh looks at Gavin. "End it. We need to get the fuck out of here."

Gavin nods and shoots both of them in the head. The three of us leave the room. We walk past the guards outside the door.

Josh directs them to get our cleaners in there before turning to us. "We'll shower and change at my house since everyone is there before we head out. We're going in the back. I don't want the girls seeing us like this."

We all look down at ourselves. We look like we just left a slaughterhouse. I suppose it's not that far off. Gavin picks something off my arm and holds it up as we walk to Josh's. Chuckling, he places it back on my shoulder.

I laugh. "Wouldn't want a tendril of bloody-whatever-the-fuck all over the compound."

Gavin glances back with a grin. "Not like we aren't getting blood all over the damn place anyway."

We all fall silent, but walk faster to Josh's house. I've thought many times I have to be some kind of a psychopath to not be bothered by shit like this. Today is no different, but as usual, I tell myself over and over again that I'm ridding the world of bad people.

The world be even more fucked up if it weren't for people like us and our own brand of vigilante justice.

"I'm actually really glad to see such few people here," I rumble low in the earpiece as I lay prone next to one of our guys. Josh is near the front of the building. Gavin is at the side where there's another door. I'm at the back entrance. We're all hidden.

"The others were smart not to show up," Josh whispers.

"Even smarter to start calling us and letting us know," Ryan whispers. He's on the other side of the house opposite of Gavin. Between us all, everything is covered.

"Do we have absolute confirmation that the parents are here?" Gavin asks just as low as all of us. "Because I'm gonna be pissed if they ended up staying home or some shit. I don't know how these fuckers do their coronations."

"They're here," Ryan says. "We had eyes on them as soon as I got off the phone with Josh."

I chuckle and silently take out my phone. I take a picture of the back entrance of the house. Just inside the doors are the parents. I've had my eyes on them ever since I've been laying here. They've only moved one time, and it was to walk outside to share a cigar. It would've been so fucking easy to take them both out.

I put my phone away after sending the picture I took of them to Gavin, Josh, and Ryan. "There's your confirmation, you paranoid asshole," I tease.

"I'm the paranoid asshole?" Gavin teases right back. "Was that you who asked Ryan on the plane a hundred and twelve fucking times if we were sure the parents didn't decide to stay back in New York? Or am I imagining things?"

"I mean, you are getting old. What are you now? Forty?" I grin.

"Fuck you. I'm the same age as you, prick," Gavin growls.

I grin at the quiet chuckles over the earpiece, but the seriousness quickly returns. "They're starting. The leader just met his dick son at the podium." I grin even wider. "And he's looking right at me. How nice of him." He can't see me, but I do enjoy how he's trying to be cautious and see if anyone is lurking outside. There's only about a hundred of us.

"As we talked about, they'll flee out the back when we hit the sides and front," Ryan says. "They won't expect another team there, considering the force we're going in with. They all think they're safe with all that bulletproof glass."

"They're in the middle of fucking nowhere. I bet they have no clue we even know about this place," Josh says.

"Thanks in large part to the ones who decided to ally with the correct side," Gavin says.

I chuckle. "Coronation has officially started. Looks like everyone is pretty settled inside."

"Two guards on the inside of each door," our surveillance guy says. That's usually Lance. I miss his voice and am far from ashamed at admitting that. "Twenty-three people inside the ballroom of the house. There are two more guards outside the entrance of the ballroom on the west side. Two inside the entrance. South side entrance has two guards out and in. And I have two more on the inside of the ballroom by the entrance to the backyard. All are carrying ARs except the two at the backyard entrance. They both have 270s with a scope. The audio I have inside is faint, but everyone is silent as they listen to daddy give his speech."

"Quiet my ass," Josh says. "Time to make a little noise. Sniper Two. Ready to go?"

"Ready," I say with a grin.

"Sniper One, ready?" Ryan asks.

"Ready," Robby growls.

I watch as our teams descend on the house. The back of it remains completely silent, but the sides and front are about to have a very rude and loud awakening. I grin when I see grenades thrown. Doors blow off the hinges simultaneously. Though I can only see the door that Gavin and his team just went through, I know all of the other doors met the same fate.

The team calls out their kills. Each team of two guards by the doors are down. The noise has caused distraction in the ballroom and everyone is looking around. The guards by the doors are looking outside.

"You won't see a thing, asshole," I rumble.

Everyone inside the ballroom continues to look around. A few jump when they hear the shots coming from outside the ballroom. All of them start taking out their guns. The guards by the doors drop to a knee and ready their guns.

"The two guards at the outside ballroom entrance are trained on each door," Robby says. "Watch yourselves because our bullets won't penetrate the glass."

"Got it," Ryan rumbles. "Doors open now!"

I grin as the ballroom doors are kicked open. Our guys immediately start shooting as they come in low. People drop and run or crawl towards the back door.

Robby laughs when two grenades land near the guards by the door. They both scatter. "Run, little piggies! But you won't get far!"

The grenades explode. The glass shatters but doesn't break. Blood splatters all over the place. "Well, that's fucking disgusting. Is that brain matter?" I ask.

At that moment, the door flies open, and the current leader and his son come barreling out. "I got the leader," I rumble, calling out my target. I take my shot. He drops at the same time as his son.

"No survivors inside," Josh says. "Tell me you got the leader and his son. They slipped out after the third grenade explosion."

"We got them," Robby says. "Where's the kids?"

"Still have them in the nursery next to the ballroom," surveillance says. "The nanny is cradling them in a corner. Watch her. She's holding a handgun on the door."

"Got her," Josh says.

"Clean up crew is good to come in. It's a fucking mess," Ryan rumbles.

Moments later, Josh comes out with the kids screaming in his arms. "Where's my adoptive parents?" he asks over the earpieces. "We need to get these two away from here. Nanny is down. She was definitely not friendly."

I can't help but chuckle as I stand from my hiding place. I dust myself off and lead the guard with me down the slight slope of the hill we were perched on to Josh. "They're at the airport," I say when we reach him.

He glares. "Tell me we have car seats."

I shake my head. "Nope. But someone can hold them in the backseat."

Josh watches me for a long moment before huffing and turning away. I laugh. Kids flock to him. He makes them feel safe and protected. It's the reason the two he's holding have calmed down considerably.

I follow with a huge smile but wisely keep my mouth shut as I climb into the driver's seat. He's not a fan of no car seats. Josh slides in the back. Gavin grins as he climbs into the passenger seat. He shoots me a wink, but he knows better than to say anything either.

So, as we drive in silence to the airport, I allow my mind to wander to my own family.

I've been away too long. I can't wait to get home.

Chapter Seventeen

☙ Lance ☙

It's not often I'm nervously waiting at home for Damon, but I find myself sitting in Josh's house trying to keep myself busy. Damon texted a little while ago and said they were on the way home, so I've been pulling up all of my research to go over with Josh when he gets back. Rosie is in the pool with Dallas, Raleigh, and Harleigh. Alex is grilling. Dane is reading a book. Skyla, Alex's CFO who has become a good friend of the family, is doing some kind of work on her tablet. Cole is lounging in the sun. Something about working on his tan.

I've holed myself up in Josh's office because I can't seem to think. I hate not being out there with them. Watching Damon's and my family's back is what I do. It's how I feel like I pull my weight out there. And how I know everyone is safe. I'm good at what I do. I watch everything. If someone sneezes, I know about it. It's not that I don't trust anyone else. It's that I know they aren't as good as I am.

"They're almost here. The girl's are getting out of the pool now."

"Thanks, Alec," I say. I don't look up, though.

"Listen, I know being here and not with them has to be hard, but you know they're okay, right?"

I sigh and look up at him. He's leaning against the doorframe with his arms crossed over his chest. "I know. But I'm not good at sitting around waiting for them to get here. I've been forced on the sidelines too much lately with that fucking flu that took me down. I hate not being out there. I need to distract myself until they get here because if I don't, the guilt is going to eat me alive."

"What the fuck? Dude, come on. You have nothing to feel guilty for." He drops his hands to his side and strides towards me. "I got some information for you, though. To help you distract yourself." He grins as he drops some papers on the desk.

I pick them up and flip through them. "What is this?" I shake my head, slightly baffled.

"Abyss. When you said that, it just triggered something I couldn't let go. I looked it up in our records. We had an Abyss years ago. It was before the shit with Jessa. We were both young. I barely have memories of him."

I smile as I look at what he gave me. Alec's father was going to kill Jessa, Alec's sister, because he had no use for her. Her mother secretly found a family who would take her. They had enough money to mask her so his father would never find her.

And he never did. Up until just a couple of years ago, Alec thought she was dead. Jessa, however, always knew she was adopted. She never really stopped looking for her family, but it was hard because she didn't have much information to go off of. All she had was a few things from her childhood and a picture of her and Alec as kids.

It was that picture that triggered Alec. He has the same one. It's all he had of her.

I guess Matthew Lucinio did one good thing throughout his life. He brought family together. Inadvertently, but if it hadn't been for his treachery, we probably never would have known half the shit we do. Like how Alec and Jessa are related. How Josh is the older twin, though we all thought he was the younger one because that's what Matthew wanted us all to believe. And how Nick Crane and Dane Michaels are Alex's and Josh's half-brothers.

Truthfully, if it hadn't been for him, Rebekkah never would have been reunited with her family. She never would have rekindled her romance with Kent, her long lost love, and never would have known that her son with him, Dane, was alive. She never would have seen Ryan, Jason, and Nick, her nephews, again.

I suppose it's because of all of that, that it doesn't really surprise me Abyss, or Gregory Franklin as we know him, is somehow connected to Alec and this whole entire fucking mess we have going on.

I rub my head and lean back in Josh's chair. "Are you telling me he was a Viper's Venom at one point?"

Alec nods. "Yep. It was right after Jessa's disappearance that he also disappeared. But you also mentioned that shit about the name on that account being Ginger Lucille. I started thinking about that, too. The older I got, the less likely it was for anyone to catch me dancing to old musicals, especially after I lost Jessa, but before that? One of my first memories was standing on my mom's feet and her dancing around the bedroom and quoting Ginger Rogers' lines or singing along with her. That's shit that I've never told another soul except you. Anyone who knows that would only know it if they were around when I was a kid." He nods to the papers in my hand. "He was."

"It says here that his brother was also a member."

"Yep. But he left years after. I remember him now. The name didn't ring a bell before because I never knew him as Edward. I knew him as Quackers. He had duck feet and liked to feed the ducks crackers at the pond behind the compound. He left because he had a business venture. I was a teenager around then."

"Business adventure," I rumble as I think. "Wait. You were a teen. How old are you now?"

"Thirty-seven. I'm a year older than Josh almost exactly. Our birthdays are four days apart. Well, four days and a year."

I spin the pen in my hand around with my fingers. "Raleigh is about twenty..."

"I was seventeen, if that helps."

I grin. "Immensely. It would mean that Edward left the MC and joined Matthew when he adopted Raleigh. And I use that term loosely. It would mean we have that timeline down. We know when Harleigh was sold off to the Ruthless Warriors to become Charles' wife. And we know that Gregory planned to take both Hareligh and Raleigh as his own after his brother and son were taken out. And from our interview, we know some fucker named Tits is the real leader of the Ruthless Warriors. Rosie was sold to him."

"And you got a lot of other shit on this Tits guy."

"Just need a location. Robby is working on that. But I know he's in Chicago because his debit card transactions are coming from area ATMs and businesses. I guess they aren't aware I know of the Ginger Lucille account."

"I'm just glad you're still monitoring it. I got my guys on that hotel downtown. Haven't seen him yet."

"It could be a ploy. A just in case thing to throw us if he thinks there's a chance we're watching. He did take out a large sum of cash. He could be anywhere, really. That's what annoys me so damn much. And there's still one thing that makes no fucking sense to me."

"Well, talk it out. That's what you do with Josh, right? Or Damon or Gavin?" Alec sits in a chair in front of me and props his feet on the desk.

"The fire. If the leader wanted Rosie, why the fuck would they set the house on fire?"

"They didn't know she was there. Didn't the grandparents tell them she was gone?"

"Yeah, but they didn't even check the house. The first fucking thing I would have done is checked the house for her. The grandparents loved her. How would I know they weren't hiding her? I mean, when we got there, they were already rolling out. They couldn't have checked outside for her. She could have been in the fields. Or the basement. Or even the storm cellar. They had one of those about a hundred feet from the front door. But they didn't check. Why?"

"Honestly, I think it's because they didn't think to. I don't think the intention was to kill her. You said that the mother said something that you could hear on the phone about going to her friend's house or something. It won't take much to find her because she doesn't have many friends."

"Yeah, it's just hard to wrap my head around that kind of stupidity. Anyway, at least we have a name. Sort of. Hopefully, Robby will have better luck than me when he gets in. I know he's been working on it some. He made some headway on the plane."

"I hate to say this, but we're doing all we can right now. Do I want to go into every motel and hotel in the city? Fuck yes. But the more and more I think about it, I don't think he's even staying in one. I think they have a hideout."

I blink. "Why the ever living fuck didn't I think of that? Gregory's house."

"No one's been in and out. We have some of my guys rotating out with teams from both Crane and Lucinio Mafias. The house is dark."

I sigh and rub my head. "They have to be somewhere. It's not possible for them to just vanish into thin air. There's always a trail. Always."

"I agree. And we have the best of them on the trail." He grins and looks towards the office door. "Sounds like they just got in. Maybe put this shit away and come greet your husband."

I smile. "You don't have to tell me twice." I close my laptop and follow Alec as he heads out to the living room.

"Something smells good," Gavin says. "Barbecue?"

"Alex is grilling as we speak," I say.

Gavin's eyebrows shoot up. "Fuck me. You let Alex near a grill? The last time that happened, we all ended up with hockey pucks instead of steaks." He hurries out of the house. "Alex! Take them off! They're done! I don't even have to look at them!"

Josh cracks up and follows him, Alec close behind. Damon's eyes land on me, and I shiver. I don't move, though. I'm rooted to my spot because I'm overcome with emotions I can't place. They're all racing through me.

Damon makes the first move and crosses the room to me. He wraps his arms around me and kisses my neck. "I missed you. Fuck, I missed you, baby."

I throw my arms around him and let the words tumble out. "I hated not being there. I was worried as hell that the surveillance guys would miss someone or something that would get someone killed. Or you. I love you so much, Damon. I was debating using satellites to keep tabs on everything. I -"

"Baby," Damon rumbles. His dominant voice soothes me instantly. If it's possible for a human to melt, I'm pretty sure I just did. "I'm okay." He kisses my neck and hugs me tighter. "We're all okay. We went in with three teams of thirty-two people, baby. Four of us were outside. Me and Robby, and our spotters. We went in with such force, I don't think anyone managed to get a shot off. They threw grenades in there. The kids were in a nursery next to the ballroom. Not a lot of people showed up for the coronation. A lot of people called us and Ryan about it. The location was kept secret until the morning of the coronation. Only twenty-seven people showed up. The guards they had were pitiful for that kind of an event. No one survived except the kids."

I let out a breath. My fingers grip his shirt, and I breathe in his masculine scent, letting it calm me. "I'm just so happy you're home." I need him. I have to feel him just to convince myself that he's really here, but I know it's not the time. I'll have to wait.

Of course, Damon knows what I need. "We have time," he says with a grin. He takes my hand and tugs me to the bathroom at the opposite end of the house from where everyone is.

"Damon, I can wait," I say a little hesitantly.

"I know." He tugs me into the bathroom and closes the door. "But I also know you. You don't need to be the one doing the fucking very often. You do right now."

"Rosie has been dying to see you," I say quietly. "I don't want to take you away from her. She needs you, too."

"Baby, stop. Josh will cover for us. She'll be okay. There's plenty of me to go around." He keeps his gorgeous dark eyes on me as he unbuckles the belt on his jeans. "Now, are you going to fuck me? Or do I need to beg?"

"Damon, Jesus Christ." I reach down and adjust my hard as steel cock.

He grins. "I know what you like." He drops his jeans and boxer briefs to his knees as he turns around. He braces his hands against the wall in front of him and teasingly wiggles his ass as he looks over his shoulder.

I groan, then growl as I watch him. Seconds later, my jeans and underwear are around my knees, and I'm slamming my dick deep inside his ass. An ass I love being nestled inside of when I need the control.

Like I do right now.

"Holy fuck, Lance…," Damon moans. To his credit, he stays relatively quiet.

It only turns me on more. His consideration for others has always been a huge part of my attraction to him.

I give him long and hard thrusts as I wrap my arms around him. I close my eyes and rest my cheek against his shoulder blades. Sometimes when I need this, I take him hard and fast. Others, it's this I need. I need him to feel every inch of me, just as I have to allow myself to feel him.

His tightness with each thrust I give him eases me more and more. I kiss the back of his neck as I slip my hands under his shirt and run my fingers over his washboard abs. He turns his head, and I kiss him deeply, letting our tongues thrash against one another. I let my hands wander lower.

Lower.

Lower.

Damon's body is well-groomed. His chest and stomach are as hairless as his back. His base above his thick and long cock is always shaved. There's no hair around his dick because he hates how it makes him feel less than perfect. Even his balls are hairless.

Damon moans into my mouth and pushes back against me when I start stroking his cock with one hand and rolling his balls around in the palm of my other. "Baby, fuck yes."

I smile against his lips. "You always feel so good." I plunge my tongue into his mouth. I start stroking him faster as I thrust harder and deeper.

I rotate my wrist as I stroke him and shift my hips side to side as I roll them against his ass. I roll his balls and squeeze a little as I tug them. I nip his tongue and suck on it as he starts to pull away from the kiss.

But then his mouth is back on mine once more. And as I fuck his ass with everything I am, he kisses me, pouring all of the love he knows I need to feel into it. I stroke his cock as fast as I'm thrusting until we're both thick. Precome drips from his tip. I refuse to waste it, so I make sure to catch it and coat his dick with it. I'm going to fill his ass, but his come is getting swallowed. It's too good to let spray against the wall.

"Ah…, Damon. I'm gonna come so hard for you," I rumble against his lips. I kiss along his jaw as that all too familiar jolt shoots down my spine. My dick stiffens as I thrust one last time. "So fucking hard, baby." I let my head fall back as I bury myself inside his tight ass and come hard. "Ah! Fuck, Damon!"

I hold back from screaming his name. My hips jerk against his ass as I come inside him.

Filling him.

Claiming him.

I pant against his neck while my dick jerks and spasms. His ass clenches and tightens as he moans. I keep stroking him as I come, but I know he's close. I stop stroking and squeeze his dick just enough to keep him from blowing his load too soon. Not until my mouth is around his cock.

As soon as I finish, I pull out of him slowly. I love seeing my come drip from his ass, but I don't take the time to watch it as much as I usually would. I'm too hungry for his delicious taste. I drop to my knees as he turns. I shift my grip and start stroking again as I take him in my mouth.

"Oh fuck, Lance. Fuck, baby. My dick looks so good in your mouth."

He gets harder for me as his fingers tangle in my hair. I take him to the back of my throat and swallow as my tongue darts around his dick. I smile around him and look up at him. I stroke the part of his length that I can't fit in my mouth. I bob my head and suck hard on his tip. Each time he touches the back of my throat, I swallow and moan low.

With my other hand, I go back to rolling, tugging, massaging, and playing with his balls. It doesn't take long for them to draw up tight. His dick gets even thicker. His fingers tighten in my hair. He lets his head fall back and groans.

"Damn, baby. You know how to work my dick." He stops my bobbing motions and thrusts into my mouth. As soon as his tip touches the back of my throat, he's coming. "Oh... fuck... yes..."

As he comes, his dick throbs in my mouth. I keep massaging his balls and stroking his dick, but I slow my pace. I swallow around him as he comes, drinking everything that slides down my throat. I moan because he tastes so fucking good.

When he finishes, he slowly pulls out and helps me up. With our pants still down, he pulls me in for a deep kiss. Our dicks press against one another and immediately react to each other. They grow painfully hard once more. I'd love for him to bend me over this counter, but instead, I pull away from the kiss with a groan.

He grins and reaches for the paper towels. We both clean up and quickly get dressed. After checking ourselves in the mirror to make sure we don't have the freshly fucked look, or at least the toned down version of it, we leave the bathroom and head back to our family.

I take Damon's hand and squeeze it, silently thanking him for what he just allowed me to do. For knowing me well enough to know what I needed. Damon smiles and kisses my hand as he leads me outside.

Feeling a lot more like me, calm and collected, I let myself breathe in the fresh air, thankful that I have a family as accepting and loving as this one.

Chapter Eighteen

🌶 Damon 🌶

I lead Lance outside into the backyard. The sun is warm and beating down on us, making the day feel calm and peaceful. After the shit we've gone through over the last couple of days, I'll be the first to admit I need this. I need to feel grounded once more. Being a vigilante might fill me with some kind of satisfaction at making the world a better place, but I still need the normalcy to make me feel like myself again.

"Alex! Get off the grill! Fuck, you're banned. Completely fucking banned," Gavin says as he waves a spatula at Alex.

I laugh. "Are you two still fighting over the grill?"

"There's nothing to fight over. Alex is a terrible griller," Gavin growls.

"I've been grilling most of my damn life!" Alex retorts. "You all are still alive!"

"Alive?" Gavin stares at him a moment before taking something off the grill. "Would you eat this?"

Lance nearly chokes. "Is that a hotdog?"

"Was. It was a hotdog. Until Alex murdered it in cold blood and laughed in its face." Gavin starts throwing the burnt stuff away and flips the other unburnt stuff over. "If we ate that, we'd be as dead as the hotdog."

Alex cracks up as he walks away. "Fuck you, grillmaster! Have at it! I'll be over here cuddling my girl while yours gets cold."

Gavin laughs. Harleigh slithers up to him with her beach towel wrapped around her. She giggles as he drops an arm over her and kisses the top of her head.

Rosie squeals as she runs to me. "Dad!" She hits me full force and wraps her arms around me, effectively soaking my t-shirt.

I laugh and hug her back. "Guess I'll be sans t-shirt today. Did you enjoy the pool? Where's Dallas?" I kiss the top of her head as she pulls away.

"I think she went inside to change. She was shivering a little." Rosie smiles and finds a pool lounger in the sun next to Cole.

"Where's Josh? I wanted to tell him the shit I found while he was gone."

I raise an eyebrow when I don't see him. "He's probably inside changing. I might head home and change myself. It's warmer out here than I thought. It's definitely a nice June day."

"I brought you shorts, actually. They're in the office. I can change, too. We can have a pool day to go with the grill day." Lance turns and tugs me back into the house.

I laugh. "If you wanted to get me alone, you just had to say so." I swat his ass teasingly.

He grins over his shoulder and winks. "Already had my way with you."

"Yeah, like that's enough."

"Okay, true. I'll never get my fill of you."

I watch his ass as he drags me into Josh's office and will my dick to behave for once. The effect Lance has on me is simply like no one else. I used to be completely embarrassed by it. Years ago, I'd hide for a period of time and silently berate myself and my dick for allowing a reaction to him to happen in the first place.

Now, all I want is him.

All of the time and in any way he'll let me have it.

We quickly get dressed so we can join our family again outside. When we're finished, we start heading down the hall, but pause before we reach the living room. I pull Lance back a little bit because I don't want to interrupt whatever is going on.

"I know. I do. I'm sorry for that, Dallas, but you know the rules and why."

"They're stupid rules, Josh," Dallas whispers. I can hear the tears in her voice. "You know they are. You've said it yourself."

"It doesn't mean I'm letting up on them. I can't. You're too good for... Fuck, just don't. Please don't push it. Just... go outside. Please. I don't beg for anyone, baby. You know that better than anyone, but I am for you."

I glance at Lance. It's obvious he's just as uncomfortable as me, but this isn't a conversation that should be interrupted. I take Lance's hand and quietly tug his hand so he follows me back to the office.

"Josh, this just isn't right. You're ignoring me and my feelings. Both of -"

"Dallas, enough!" Josh hisses. The dominance in his voice makes us both jump and freeze in place, but it's the underlying hurt and sadness that really strikes me. "Go outside and enjoy what's going on out there. The rules are non-negotiable no matter how fucking much they hurt. It's for the best. Now, go."

Hearing her sniffle pains me. Lance drops his head. Neither one of us make a single move, though. I don't want Josh to hear us shuffling or Dallas to be embarrassed that we heard all of that. At least the tail end of what seemed like an upsetting conversation.

"That didn't sound good," Lance mouths.

I shake my head. "Nope," I mouth back. But I don't have a clue what that could have been about.

"You two can come out now," Josh rumbles.

I glance at my shocked husband. Still holding his hand, I take a deep breath and lead him out to face Josh. "We weren't eavesdropping," I start. "We were coming out of the -"

Josh holds up a hand. "Stop. I don't care. How much did you hear?"

Lance keeps his eyes lowered. He's good about standing up to anyone, even Josh, if he knows he's in the right. If he feels like he's been caught doing something he shouldn't have been, he hides. "Uh... The end, mostly," he says quietly.

"Lance, I'm not mad," Josh says almost sadly. We both look at him, confused. He sighs. "It's… a long story. But you don't need to worry. Everything is fine. What you heard…" He trails off and looks down. I've never in my life seen Josh off his game or unsure of himself. Even years ago when his father was fucking with his head, he still had an aire of confidence about him. "Just keep it between us, okay? I don't want her to be embarrassed or hurt if everyone finds out."

"Does this have something to do with her crush on you?" I ask him, keeping my voice low. I rub my thumb over the back of Lance's hand to calm him even more. He really doesn't like when he feels like he messed up.

Josh says nothing for a long moment, but he does nod slightly. I don't think he knows I caught it. "I'll be out in a minute. I just need to grab something." He looks up at us with a grin that doesn't reach his haunted eyes. "I'll grab more things to drink out there. It's warm."

But instead of heading for the kitchen, Josh takes out his phone and walks down the hall towards his office with his head. We can hear his voice low when he greets the person who answers the phone as he closes his office door. I don't even need to guess who he's calling. There's only one person he talks to when he's like this.

Lance nods. "Lyric always helps get him out of his head. Looks like he's berating himself for something again."

I nod and lead Lance to the kitchen. One thing about Josh that none of us have been able to break through is the barrier he keeps up around himself. The one he retreats behind just when we think he's making forward progress. What Matthew did to him is completely unspeakable. The brainwashing and serum were only the start of the damage he caused. Josh has severe post-traumatic stress from all of the mental and physical anguish he endured. It's a struggle he faces down each day.

He knows he has help in us, but sometimes, he needs his ex to talk him down. Lyric knows him in a way so many others aren't capable of understanding. She was with him right after everything that happened to him. While their love faded, their friendship grew even stronger. I kind of think Dallas has that same talent. I'm sure it's why they get along so well.

Lance and I grab a few more drinks and bring them outside. Gavin is just taking things off the grill. Dallas and Rosie are huddled together over Rosie's tablet. Lance and I drop the drinks in the cooler, keeping one for ourselves. Dallas looks up when she sees Lance striding towards her and Rosie with drinks in his hands for them. Her smile fades slightly as she looks past me. It doesn't take much to see she's looking for Josh, but she hides it well. It makes me wonder what's really going on between those two, but I know our brother. Josh will tell us when he's ready.

"Josh okay?" Gavin asks me as I help him set everything up buffet style on the table on the patio. "I saw Dallas come out wiping her eyes."

"He's fighting some of his demons. I'm pretty sure he just called Lyric."

Gavin nods. "I thought today might be a good day to talk more about the project Lance wants to do. I know Raleigh has been helping Rosie with donations and things, but you wanted to have this before the school year starts. We only have a couple of months to really get the details down. Might be a good distraction for whatever is going on if we can get Josh to participate."

"Nothing is going on. I'm tired. Just like everyone else. Get me to participate in what?" Josh's deep baritone voice behind us makes us both turn slightly.

"You made Dallas cry, you moody asshole," Gavin says with a teasing grin.

"I'll make it up to her. What were you two talking about?"

"The charity events Lance wants to do," I tell him. I turn towards everyone. "Food is up!"

We step aside as the girls hurry towards the food laughing and giggling. All the guys follow. We wait until the girls grab their plates before any of us make a move for ours. It's what we do. It's what we've always done.

After we're all settled in a circle with our pool chairs, I decide it's time to do exactly what Gavin suggested. "So, about the event for the hospital. We probably have to finalize details because it's coming up quick. I know Lance scheduled it already with the hospital, but we need to start getting the donations together. We probably should start looking into the Gala, too."

"Oh, about the Gala," Raleigh says. "I know a lot of places we can get some great donations, but if you want to go really big, a lot of places won't donate the huge packages that you're looking for. I mean, they will, but there will be conditions. Like there's a resort in Kissimmee, Florida, near Disney that has some really great packages that I was looking into, but the condition is a timeshare tour. They want people to buy them, and they're super pushy."

"What's your solution to that?" Alex asks after he swallows a bite of his potato salad.

"I was thinking about just buying it outright and saying that it's a donation from Lucinio Tech. In fact, I was thinking about doing that with a lot of them and saying they are donations from companies that the Lucinio family owns. A lot of the small businesses and restaurants the family owns have donated things. Which gives them super great publicity. I also talked to Ryan about doing the same for the Crane family businesses. And to Jason and Chase about doing huge prize packages from their companies. They're totally on board."

"Actually, I don't know if this is something you'd want to do or not," Skyla begins. She bites her lip. She's still unsure if she can just speak out or not. Dane nudges her with a reassuring smile as he eats. She smiles back at him. "Um... the companies can write them off on their taxes, as I'm sure you know. I was thinking for the prizes from the companies themselves, they could just come from company money. What if each family, instead of using their own money for the prizes, those ones at least, just got together and donated a large sum of money to the hospital itself? Like that would come from the family and not the company. Would that mean more? I guess I don't really know what you'd like to do, but I thought that was a good idea."

"Actually, I do like that," Josh says. "It would be more heartfelt if the family did a big donation on our own. Something not related to companies, but to us. But going through and getting these large packages and big ticket items from the companies is a good idea."

"What if we asked Jason to do a house remodel for the one for the gala?" Lance asks.

"Oh, I like that," I agree.

"What if we asked him to do that for the smaller event for the kids and their parents?" Rosie asks. "Oh my God, I bet you a lot of those families would truly appreciate something like that. I bet some of them would be in need of a remodel."

"Actually, I bet Jas would just offer that to everyone," Dallas says with a soft smile. "He's super generous."

I grin. "I think you're right, actually. That could be his company donation if he's up for that."

Alec leans back in his chair. "What about medical bills? I bet a lot of these families could use help with them. What if we paid off the medical debt of these kids? We could all get together and pay off the bills of those kids for a whole year, and it wouldn't touch our bank accounts. Well, maybe mine, but not big enough to really hurt me if everyone came together on it, too."

"We could do that," I say.

"What about a goodie bag?" Lance asks. "When I was at the hospital in L.A., I remember we got a goodie bag one day. Can't remember who it was from, but we were told a family wanted to give it to all the kids. We all got things to keep us occupied. Coloring books and crayons. Colored pencils. We all got this really cool kit that you could make this design with yarn and hang up in the room. Mine was a dreamcatcher. It was like a paint by number, but it was like sewing. We also got paint by numbers and a teddy bear. There were a few other things in there, too. Books to read. It was a mood booster."

"I know this company that does custom bears," Harleigh says. "I just used them to get one for a friend at the University for her birthday. If we get to them now with a number of bears we need, they can have the order ready by the end of the summer. They're super high quality, too."

Rosie nods as she types the ideas into her tablet. "I really want to do blankets, too. I think non-allergenic blankets that maybe have something cool related to the family would be awesome. Maybe we could do one with the Lucinio family on the front and Crane family on the back. It would show family unity and just be a cool gift." She looks up at us.

I smile. "I like that idea. I think we mentioned that before. I know the Crane's have a family crest. Josh had one created a few years ago. It's a Phoenix." I look at Josh. "What do you think? You're head of the family, so it's your decision."

Josh grins and nods. "I love the idea. I'm all for it. I think we could do our crest on the front of the bear and the Crane's on the back. It would match the blanket and theme of our unity."

Rosie squeals and claps before typing it into her tablet. "Yes! I'm so excited! Raleigh helped me get a lot of the donations for everything so far for the event with the kids."

"We've been keeping it all at our house," Alex says. "But with having almost all of it already, maybe we should have some kind of a party where everyone comes by and helps get the baskets and stuff together. A wrapping party."

"We'll have to get pretty baskets," Harleigh says.

"Oh! And that metallic, thin paper. We could even do that really pretty colored tulle," Dallas says with a much brighter smile than what she has had since she left the living room after talking to Josh. "We could do that for my birthday!"

"You want to do a wrapping party for your Sweet Sixteen instead of having some big thing with all your friends?" Alec asks in almost pure disbelief.

I have to laugh. "Alec, come on. Even I know she hates being the center of attention and much prefers to do things with people she's close to. We could make it a family party. If she wants to invite a couple friends or something she can. We can send them home before we do the wrapping party."

"We could do a pool party," Josh rumbles. His eyes fall on Dallas. "Or maybe a midday movie party. You love my theater. We could do a taco and nacho bar."

Dallas eyes sparkle, and she smiles as she nods. "I'd love that."

I smile because whatever was happening between them seems to have ended. "What about food and everything?" I ask.

Lance sets his plate down and twines his fingers with mine. We sit back together and chip in ideas as the girls grow more and more excited in their planning. The more excited they get, the happier and more at peace Lance becomes.

I squeeze his hand. I know how important this is to him. Seeing everyone come together on a project he's passionate about fills me with a sense of serious gratitude. But looking at Lance, it's pretty obvious by his beaming smile that he feels honored and even more grateful.

Everyone is showing him how much he means to them.

He's seeing what I've known all along.

How loved and cared for he really is.

Chapter Nineteen

☙ Lance ☙

"Jesus, honey. How much tulle do you actually need?" I ask Rosie when she continues piling more of it in Damon's arms.

"A lot. Do you know how many kids there are?" She tilts her head and picks another darker blue color.

"Navy blue?" Damon asks when she puts it in his arms. "Rosie, that's like four shades of blue."

She nods, much to my amusement. "I know." She finds a hot pink and adds that to the pile. "Now, I need green. And maybe black. Definitely some white."

I look at Damon with a grin. "Remember when she was talking about limits?"

"Now is the fucking time," he grumbles. "Your allowance is ten dollars a week. That seems fair, right?"

She giggles. "Yep! But this isn't for me. It's for the kids."

"The sad thing is I can't even argue with that." Damon shakes his head and shifts the stuff in his arms.

I quickly catch one of the rolls of tulle that almost tumbles to the ground. "She's gonna have this piled high." I grin when she adds two more rolls to the thirty she already has.

"I want to make sure that everything is perfect and pretty. They might not be paying for this, but I want them to feel like royalty. They deserve that."

I smile at our girl. "I knew there was a reason I liked you."

She places her hand on her heart as she looks up and bats her lashes adorably. "Just like?" she asks, pouring on the Southern to her Southern accent. "And here I thought you loved me." She shakes her head with a teasing smile. "I mean, the adoption and everything."

Damon laughs. "You're such a brat. Why did we adopt you again?"

"Because you love me." She smiles brightly and rolls her eyes. "Obviously."

We both laugh as she smiles and heads for the metallic paper. Damon takes all of the tulle to the friendly older woman behind the counter. Ever since Raleigh came here for her decorations for a huge event she planned for Lucinio Tech, we've all come here for any decorations we need for any event.

Anabelle, the older woman who owns this place, told us we're keeping her in business and helping her pay her husband's medical bills. Of course, we just paid them off for her. Chase found out how much she was in debt and cleared her debt. Then, helped her invest so when she was ready to retire, they'd have something extra to help them out.

I take out my phone and chuckle when I look at the text. I smile at Rosie. "The blankets are being worked on, but Lyric said she printed out the magnets you thought were so cool for the gift basket. She also sent some other things both for the fundraiser and for the kids that she made."

"Oh my God! Was she working all night?" Rosie asks with wide eyes. "I just asked her yesterday!"

Damon laughs. "Knowing her? Probably. And it probably drove her husbands insane."

"She's amazing. I don't think anyone can keep up with her." Rosie shakes her head and turns back to the metallic papers. "Seriously, I want to just buy all of this. We would use it with the amount of stuff we have."

"Get what you need, honey," I tell her.

She simply nods and starts piling it all in my arms. I can't help but smile as my heart fills with love for her. Her dedication to this is touching. It's something very important to me, but seeing others care about it just as much and wanting it to be as special as I do really is a beautiful thing.

As Damon follows Rosie to the baskets and giftbags section, I bring the paper up to Anabelle. She smiles a brilliant smile as she helps me set everything on the counter. I glance towards the door for the thousandth time. Something about seeing our guards there sets me at ease. I don't like not knowing where this Tits fucker is hiding. We all know better than anyone that he could just show up whenever the hell he wants.

"This event is going to be fabulous," Anabelle says. "I'm sorry I'll be missing it."

"Who says you have to miss it? We could use all the help we can get." I grin as her smile gets even brighter. "I'd love to. The hospital means the world to me. They saved my husband's life. We might not have kids or anything, but it would be nice to have a night out."

"Then consider yourself invited." I take out my phone and text myself to add her to the invite list for the Gala as well.

"Dad? Do they have metallic balloons? I need silver, purple, blue, gold, pink, and red. And I decided against the black. Can you take the black tulle out? Dad said it might make them think of death. That made me cringe."

"Black is out." I grin at Anabelle. "She bought you out of every single metallic tissue paper stuff."

"Except black." Anabelle smiles. "I got this. I'll take it out. We have lots of balloons. You tell me what you need and how many. I'll make sure to have it when you need to pick them up."

"Thank you, Anabelle." I wink at her and walk back to Damon and Rosie. I burst out laughing when all I can see is the top of Damon's head, his eyes, and the lower half of his body. "Need some help?"

Damon blinks. "I won't be able to see pretty soon."

I laugh again. "Go get those to the counter. A hundred bucks if you don't drop any."

Damon slowly turns and walks towards the counter. "A hundred dollars off her allowance, and you're on."

Rosie's mouth drops as she starts handing me giftbags. "Then I'll owe you money!"

"Should've thought of that before you thought a thousand bags were necessary!" Damon calls back. He grins over his shoulder as he carefully sets the bags on the counter.

Rosie giggles and turns back to the giftbags. "Do they have more of the pink and navy blue?"

I stare in disbelief at the shelf. "Honey, do you really think we need to clear her out of everything?"

She blows her bangs out of her face and looks up at me. "Dad...," she starts. I bite back the smile because when she gets that tone of voice, she's about to do her best to set me straight in her own way. "There are six-hundred and forty-two kids in that hospital right now. We have to compensate if more kids are added. Everyone has to have something. So I have to get extra things. If we end up not using them, then we can donate them to the hospital for new kids that might end up being admitted."

I nod and let the smile break free. "Okay. You've done your research."

"And that doesn't even count the parents. I need one for each of them, too. And I'm shipping these to Lyric because she promised she'd do the family crests on each side of the bags."

"Honey, I think we'll need to ask Anabelle to do an order then. I really don't think she has fourteen hundred bags." I look down at the packages in my hand. "Each of these are a fifty count. How many did you give Damon?"

"She had four packs of each color I needed. So, two hundred for each color. Um..." She stops and thinks for a moment. "He has a thousand. I just need the pink and navy blue."

I glance at the counter. "Huh. Maybe she does. Hey, Anabelle?" I call. "Do you have any more of these bags in the stockroom? Pink and navy blue. I need two packs of each, and she cleared your shelf again."

"Don't worry about that, handsome," Anabelle says as she bustles off.

Damon looks down at Rosie a little on the stern side as he comes back. "I think we need to offer to help her restock these shelves."

Rosie blushes and nods as she shuffles her feet. "Yes, sir."

A few moments later, Anabelle comes out of the stockroom with the bags I asked for and adds them to the pile I just put on her counter. "Did you need anything else, sweetheart?" she asks Rosie.

"No, ma'am. Well, the balloons. But I would like to offer our help in restocking your shelves. I really did clean them out."

"Don't be silly, honey. I can do it."

"Really, Anabelle. I insist," Damon jumps in. "You have no more of these colors of tulle she picked. And you definitely have no more bags or that tissue paper. It's important to look stocked up in a business like yours. You point us in the right direction, and we'll happily help replenish the stock."

She smiles. "Very well."

After a bit of debate on how many balloons we're going to need and putting in an order for a special shipment of the vases Rosie liked and several other things, I finally pay for the product. All five-thousand of it. I may not be a billionaire, but I am paid well. If I weren't, though, I'd be crying at that total. Especially since we still have a few caterers to visit in a few days.

A few of the guards start hauling everything out to the SUVs as we follow Anabelle to the back room. As she directs us, we start restocking for her. It doesn't take us long, but I noticed that Anabelle is getting slower and slower on her feet.

"Anabelle, I thought you had some help? You're not working seven days a week, are you?" I ask her as I finish stocking the bags.

"I have a young man who comes in on the weekends. He's in school over at Kingston University. He's very nice. A business student. He helps me out a little bit with the books."

I stand and nod. "Well, if you need anything, you can reach out anytime. And you know the family will buy the business when you're ready to step away."

"Actually…, I have been thinking more and more about that," Anabelle says. She sits on her chair behind the counter. "I'm almost seventy now. I love this business. We built it from the ground up, but I can't work forever. My feet get pretty sore by the end of the day, and I'm starting to get some arthritis in my hands. It might be a good idea to talk to Chase about our retirement fund. It would be nice to be able to step away. But I'd never be able to completely leave. I love this little shop too much."

"Well, talk to Chase and name your price," Damon says. "We'll make it work. And you can work here as long as you want to."

"I'd love to work here part time," Rosie says, looking around the store. "I love this place. I love how it's a small town feeling in such a great part of the city. And it's close to home. The flower boutique next door is so perfect."

I glance at Damon with a raised eyebrow. He grins. "Are you thinking what I am?" I ask.

"Buy it and give it to Rosie when she's finished with college?"

I grin and nod. Rosie's eyes widen with hope. "She wants to be a business major. And not like she wouldn't have help. Josh, Alex, Chase, Jason, Ryan, and even Gavin all have experience." I look down at Rosie. "What do you think?"

She makes no other noise but a squeak somewhere in her throat before she launches at us both. She hugs us hard as she jumps up and down, still speaking in squeaks and other noises that make us both laugh.

Anabelle gives us all another smile. "I'd like that. I'd like that a lot."

Damon and I hug an excited Rosie. "Thank you! Thank you! Thank you! So much!" She kisses us both on the cheek and runs behind the counter to hug Anabelle. "Thank you so much! I'll make sure it stays just as perfect as it is forever!"

"I'm sure you will, dear. I can tell you have that small town feeling about you."

I smile as Damon glances out the window. I follow his gaze when I notice his entire demeanor change. "What?" I ask, peering past him.

"The guards look very on edge," he says loud enough for only me to hear. "Rosie? We need to go, sweetheart."

"Okay. Bye, Anabelle! Thank you so much again!" Rosie hugs Anabelle again and hurries towards us with a huge smile.

"Cover! Cover!" one of our guards yells.

I watch in horror as guards scatter.

Instincts kick in.

I grab Rosie around the waist just as a guard kicks something away from her and the door to the shop. Everyone ducks and covers. Damon throws his body into mine so he's covering me and Rosie.

Something explodes.

"Ah!" Rosie screams.

"Up! Behind the counter!" Damon commands.

But there's no chance.

Gunfire shots ricochet all around us. Anabelle's knick-knacks explode over our heads. I can hear Anabelle screaming. I want to get to her, but we can't move.

"Stay down, Anabelle!" Damon yells.

"Ah!" Rosie screams as she cries.

"Shh… I got you, baby girl," I whisper. I hug her tighter.

I feel Damon shift. I know he's going for his gun. I glance around as Damon pushes us towards the backroom. "Run!" he yells. "Anabelle, on me!"

Damon shoves us towards the backroom. I stay wrapped around Rosie as much as I can be as I grab my own gun. I push her towards the back door. Damon is right behind me with Anabelle in front of him.

"Get down behind the shelves," I hiss in Rosie's ear. "Don't move until -"

I'm cut off by a loud explosion that sends the back door hurtling off its hinges. It blows me back several feet. I hit a set of shelves with my body and fall with it to the ground. I land with a hard thud, hitting my head.

Everything goes dark, but I hear a high-pitched ringing in both of my ears. I can hear myself groan. I feel the pain of hard wood digging into me. But I hear and feel nothing else. I see just midnight black.

I shake my head, trying to clear the cobwebs. "Fuck…," I rumble. I force my eyes to open. The ringing is loud as fuck. The pain is excruciating. "Rosie…"

Slowly, my vision starts to clear. There are a lot of people in black running around this room, but they're doing it in slow motion. I furrow my brows in confusion, trying to get my brain to function.

Damon is on his hands and knees. The people in black suddenly start fleeing.

Why is everything moving so slow? I feel like I'm trying to fight through Jello.

I see some more people running into the room from the store as I sit up. The more I move, the easier it becomes. The ringing is lessening. People are screaming. Yelling. Commands are being barked. I put my hands against my ears and feel blood on the back of my hand.

I watch as Damon looks towards me. Seeing I'm okay, he stands and stumbles towards the door screaming from Rosie, but I haven't come back enough to figure out just what the fuck is going on.

One of our guards kneels next to me. His lips move, but I still can't fully hear him. My eyes are on Damon as he limps his way out the door.

I look around for Rosie. Guards are around Anabelle. A couple are around me. Several follow Damon out the back door. Someone is on the phone, presumably to Josh.

No Rosie.

And then it hits me like a train.

"Rosie!" I yell as I fight my way up. I nearly fall backwards, but the guards hold me steady. I try running for the door. The nausea takes me to my knees. "Rosie!" I scramble back up and ignore the dizziness, nausea, pounding head and everything.

When I finally reach it, two of the guards on my heels making sure I don't fall on my face again, Damon is running down the alley after a black SUV without plates.

"Rosie!" we both yell at the same time.

My heart leaps into my mouth as I hit my knees once more.

"This is happening. This can't be happening."

But Jesus fuck it is. It's happening. She was taken right under our noses, despite the amount of protection we had on her. I can't even be pissed at any of them. I look down at the two dead guards who were guarding the back door. Their SUV was damaged by the explosion. The two of them are hardly recognizable.

No.

They didn't fail. We're supposed to protect her. She's our daughter.

We failed.

I failed.

Chapter Twenty

☙ Damon ☙

"Rosie!" I yell as I run after the black SUV with no plates I saw them throw Rosie into. I want to shoot at it, but I don't want to risk her getting hurt. If I shoot out a window, the bullet could hit her. If I aim for a tire, it could cause a crash, which could hurt her. Either scenario could cause death, and I'm not willing to risk it. "Rosie!"

I keep pounding the pavement as I run after her, but the SUV keeps getting further and further away. If I can't get a vehicle, I'm going to lose them. And if I chase them, Lance is going to be here alone. I saw he was hurt. He was closer to the door than I was when the explosion hit. He didn't look nearly as bad as he could have, but he had blood coming from his nose and head.

I'm torn. So fucking torn on what to do. There are people here who could help Lance, but just leaving the love of my life to chase our daughter breaks my heart. Even though I know damn well it's what he would want me to do.

As soon as I reach the end of the alley, I immediately start looking for a vehicle as I keep one eye on the vehicle that holds my daughter. My eyes fall on the guards outside who look a little dazed. After the explosion, there was instant shooting. It was a complete distraction because the real culprits were coming in through the back. It was fucking smart, and it pisses me off.

"Where is she?" Lance asks weakly when he catches up to me.

"Fuck, baby," I murmur. I want to take him in my arms, but I can't. There's no time. "We need a vehicle. They're heading South." I take his hand and start pulling him towards where we have several SUVs parked.

Suddenly, one skids to a stop in front of us. "Get in!" one of our guards yells. I've never been so grateful to see a vehicle in my life.

I tug Lance to the SUV and open the back door. He climbs in as quickly as he can as I run to the front. We both close the door as Fallon, one of our only female guards, takes off like a fucking Nascar driver. The girl can fight. She's tough as nails. She used to be in the Air Force but got out a few years ago when she found out her husband was abusing their daughter while she was deployed.

I guess the military has some kind of hardship guideline where a service member can be released if they can prove some kind of a hardship. Fallon had no family to take her daughter. The military released her because of that. She almost immediately asked to join us because she found out that her husband had connections to another mafia. We usually recruit. She's one of the ones who came to us asking for help and joined us as soon as she realized what we were about. Fallon is very loyal.

She's also one hell of a driver. Within a few moments and a lot of turns, she has managed to catch up to the SUV. "Someone should get a hold of Josh," she says. She holds back at a good distance so we're not seen.

"Shit," Lance says. "I'm so fucking concerned with catching them, I didn't even think."

"I didn't either, baby." I reach behind me as I turn. "Tell me you're okay." I swallow hard when I see the blood all over him. It's stopped. Judging from the stain on the sleeve of his favorite green shirt, I'd say he used it to stop the flow.

"I'm fine. Just dizzy as fuck. I probably have a concussion, but that's not the important thing right now."

"Lance, you're just as important," I say quietly.

"I have some medical training from my time in the military," Fallon says. "If you can figure out a way to switch seats with me while driving, I can tend to him."

We've hit the freeway. The SUV is five cars in front of us. "Okay. Quickly. Climb into the back. You're small enough. Hurry up."

Fallon nods and unbuckles her seatbelt. She maneuvers herself out of her seat and slides into the back. Thank fuck she's a small woman. With the center console and gear shift in between the passenger's and driver's seat, it will take a lot more for me to get myself to the driver's seat. I'm twice her size and a lot taller.

I don't let that stop me. Having already removed my seatbelt, I shift and put one leg over the center console. As I move myself into the driver's seat, I take the wheel and shift so I'm mostly against the door. I bring my other leg over after I adjust the seat, moving it back.

In the time it took for her to get in the back and me in the driver's seat, we've slowed down to almost forty miles an hour. I quickly speed back up to the speed limit, making sure to maintain a good distance so we can't be seen.

Once I'm settled, I command the vehicle to call Josh. Thank fuck for autoconnecting Bluetooth. It's one of the best features Ford and any other car company decided to implement. I don't even have to take my phone out of my pocket.

"Damon? Fuck, where are you?" Josh answers. "I just got to the scene."

"Get Anabelle some help. She has to be shaken up," I tell him. "It's not everyday a person gets shot at and almost blown up."

"Okay. She's okay, by the way. Hit her head. Why the fuck aren't you here? What's going on? No one can tell me shit right now except I have two dead guards and several who damn near lost their lives because of a grenade thrown at them. No one knows what the hell happened. Just that there was an attack."

"They got Rosie."

"The fuck? How?"

"We were just getting ready to leave when I noticed Fallon tense. She was outside the window in full view of me. She shifted and caught my attention. She was looking around. A couple others were doing the same thing. I don't know what the fuck they saw, but the next thing I know,

Fallon is screaming at everyone to take cover. She kicked something away from her. It exploded. I didn't see what it was, but I'd say grenade."

"You'd be right," Fallon chips in. "I saw some kind of reflection that caught my attention. Like sun glinting off a mirror or metal surface. A couple of us looked up because it seemed like it was coming from a roof. Next thing I know, someone is throwing something at us and diving between a few cars. I started yelling at everyone to take cover. The grenade landed near me. I kicked it away from me and the guards. It blew in the air and shattered the window of the shop. Right after that, we were being shot at."

"Fuck," Josh rumbles.

"We were still inside," I continue. "Glass and bullets were flying everywhere. Knick-knacks and other stuff in her store was being destroyed. We were finally able to get to the backroom. We had two guards out back and a getaway SUV just in case, just as we always do. Right when I got near the door, there was another explosion."

"Jesus. Is that what happened to these guys back here?" Josh asks.

I slow as a vehicle in front of me turns off the exit. As I expect, I'm quickly passed by someone who doesn't like my speed limit. He whips around me and slides into the empty space in front of me. I glance in the rearview mirror at Lance and breathe a sigh of relief when I see he's looking a lot less injured with all the blood cleaned up.

"We were all blown backwards and away from each other. Lance went through a shelf. Rosie ended up the opposite direction of him. Anabelle was behind me and mostly took my weight when I was thrown into her, but we're all okay. I'm chasing the SUV that has our daughter in it. Doing all I fucking can not to run his ass off the road. I would if there was no chance of hurting Rosie."

"I know. Fuck, I know. Robby just texted and said he has you almost three miles out of town."

"Yeah, we just left city limits. I don't know where the hell these assholes are taking her, but I'm not letting them out of my sight."

"Robby is guiding me. I have Gavin, Dane, and Cole. Won't be long until you have some backup," Josh says. "Just keep your eye on them and stay out of sight. We don't want them getting spooked. No telling what they'll do then."

"People are unpredictable when they're backed in a corner," I rumble. I watch as the SUV turns off on an exit. Thankfully a car behind him follows. I look behind me at Fallon. "I need your ball cap. I hate them, but it'll disguise me a little."

"What's happening?" Josh asks.

I put the cap Fallon hands me on my head as I slow down. "We turned off. I don't know what the fuck he's doing right now, but we just hit the 355 heading back into the city."

"Is Robby tracking Rosie?" Lance asks.

"Her phone was thrown a block away from the shop," Josh says.

Lance lets out a frustrated growl. He runs his fingers through his hair. "Oh, shit. Wait. I put a tracker in her purse. She asked me if there were other ways to find her if we couldn't track her phone. She has one in her purse, and one on the bracelet she wears on her wrist." He takes out his phone, mumbling about hoping it still works.

"I'll have Robby grab your laptop and meet us wherever we end up. You'll need it because we'll be going in fast and hard," Josh says. "We're going to need you both watching out for us."

"You got it. Anything to get our daughter back," Lance says.

I grin as I follow the assholes. I fall back a little more when only one car remains in front of us. "It's absurdly deserted for this time of day. There are only a few cars."

"By a few, he means less than what he'd like there to be to remain as concealed as he wants to be," Fallon teases.

I smile as she tries to lighten the mood. "Sure. That."

"I have Rosie," Lance says. "Fall back more. Let them get ahead, but not so far that we completely lose them. Just in case they figure out she's being tracked."

I slow as Lance says. We all fall silent. Josh stays on the line with me. I can hear Robby on speaker from someone else's phone in the background. The traffic gets thicker, and I feel like we're driving forever.

"When I get my hands on whoever did this," I grumble with a low growl.

"He's turning on 290," Lance says.

"What the fuck is he doing? He's heading right back into town," I say confused as I watch for the exit I need. "He's got a lot of traffic behind him," I say when I see him merge into traffic.

"It's okay, baby. I got him. I'm tracking Rosie on my phone," Lance says.

"He looks good," Fallon says. "The wounds are mostly superficial. I think there might be some bruising on his back but nothing is broken that I can tell. X-Ray might be a good idea."

"We'll have Doc on standby," Josh says.

"I'm ready to go, Josh," Robby says. "Ryan is with me. So is Luke. We'll grab Nick on the way or he'll meet us."

"He's criss-crossing, Robby," Lance says. "We were just South of the city. He's swung around and is on 290 now. He might dart back down. I don't have a fucking clue."

"I want to tell you to stay put," Josh says. "But I don't want you guys taking an hour to get where I need you either. Go get Nick. He's in the middle of the city. Almost anyway. Should be able to tell you which direction from there."

"On it," Robby says. "Lance, I have your laptop. When everyone goes in, we'll need to be looking everywhere at once. It would be better to have two of us."

"Couldn't agree more," Lance says.

I weave through traffic until I'm a little closer to the motherfuckers as I chew on my cheek. After a few moments, it hits me. "La Selle. Isn't that just off 90?" I glance in the rearview mirror at Lance.

"Uh…" He furrows his brows. "I don't know, but I don't want to look either because I might lose Rosie."

"Yes," Fallon says a few moments later. "Depends which part, but there is an area that runs near the Expressway overpass."

"What about 57th Street and La Selle?" Josh asks.

"Um… I… Yes!" she says with a grin. "Yes, 57th goes right under the overpass. La Selle is like two blocks from it."

"That's where he's going," I say. "He's making sure he wasn't followed. He doesn't believe he was, so he's going back."

"Can't be a hundred percent on that, but we still have a team out there," Josh says.

"Alert them," I say. I feel this on a deep level. He's going to that hideout. "There's no chance he's not going there. I know it."

"I'll alert the team, Damon, but don't put all of our eggs in that basket. We know that's not where he was. No one has been there. He could have another hideout."

I shake my head, adamant. "He probably does, but that's where he's going. It's the safest fucking place for him. At least that's what he thinks. He was probably casing the place to make sure we weren't there and nothing was out of the ordinary. Just because we didn't see him, doesn't mean he wasn't there somewhere."

"You really think so?" Gavin asks after a few moments. "Josh and I both spent some time out there. We never saw anything. Not even a fucking bird shit. It's dark."

"I used satellites and other technical imaging I won't bore you with to see if there were any tunnels. There's nothing. No other way in or out of that place," Robby says."

"Instincts," I say. "I just have that feeling."

Josh sighs. "Okay. I sent a text. They're on alert. We're not far behind you."

"We're grabbing Nick now," Ryan says. He must be on Robby's phone or something. "We'll head that way."

"You know, if you think about it, Damon is probably onto something," Fallon says. "They have landmines all over the property. An electric fence. Cameras. There's one way into the house, and that's through the front door. To them, everything is protected and locked down. The windows are bulletproof. I'm sure they think they have it made by going there."

"They just hit 90," Lance says. "I'm with Damon. They're heading straight there."

"Meet in the rendezvous spot," Josh says. "Close but can't be spotted. Our lead commander for surveillance will meet us there. Dane has him on the phone now."

I make the turn onto 90 and speed up just a little bit. I don't want to be so far behind, but I also know that now is the time to trust my team. No matter how badly I want to get closer, I know I can't. It could cause a lot of problems. Lance is tracking them, so I don't need to be so close, but there's always the chance they could figure it all out and throw Rosie's bracelet out the window. I need to be close enough that I can still see them, at the very least.

A few minutes later, he takes another exit. I follow and fall back even more. He heads straight for La Selle and turns up.

"Motherfucker. Your time is up," I rumble dangerously.

Fuck with my family, I'll bring all of Hell straight to Earth.

Chapter Twenty One

❦ Lance ❦

I sit in the backseat of Fallon's SUV with Robby as our team makes a plan to mobilize. Damon was absolutely right. They took her to Gregory's hideout. They were very careful when they showed up. They spent a lot of time looking around. There's nothing around this area. Behind them is a dry cleaners, which is where some of our team is located.

The rest are down the block. We've rented four houses since we found the hideout. During the school year we rented a nice apartment for each family. When the lease came up in June, we rented it for the rest of the summer but sent them all to Disney World for an extended vacation. One that lasts the entire summer.

While they've been gone, we've had construction going on at the houses. While our guys were surveying, they were fixing things up. One had a leaky roof. Another had a few things going on inside. We replaced a rickety porch on another and stairs in the other. When they come back, their houses will have been completely updated on the inside. More modern and not a fucking death trap. Our rent offer was enough to pay off their homes and cover their property taxes for an entire year. All in all, I think they decided it was a fair trade.

I glance at Robby's laptop and whistle through my teeth. "You asshole. You hacked the fucking State Department again."

Robby grins. "Not exactly. They gave me credentials in exchange of me helping them out in keeping people like me out."

"I'm fucking jealous."

"I know people. I'll get you an in."

"Do you know how much I could do with fucking United States satellites?"

Robby laughs. "Yeah. I do. These satellites helped me save Jess and Dallas. When I told them what I used them for and they figured out who I work for, things went a lot smoother. I probably should have just asked in the first place. Lots easier than having the Feds show up at my door."

I crack up because that's exactly what happened. It was like a day after he did it that the FBI showed up and arrested him. We had just gotten back from taking Matthew down. Robby was dead asleep when the FBI showed up. Ryan wasn't far behind with an attorney.

"So, they gave you credentials to use the satellites in exchange for your ass helping them keep hackers out."

"Yep. So, I hired Alex. His team developed something fucking impenetrable. He rolled it out to all Government offices and uses me in his damn advertising because he's an asshole. But now I have to beg Ryan to use his resources to get me creds whenever I need information from certain Government sources that I don't have access to, or call Alex when I need to do things on the downlow. Which is far more often than not."

"I wonder if anyone realizes the type of power that Alex holds over their security. If Alex was a bad guy, he'd be in literal control of the entire world."

"Really, it's their own fault for outsourcing it to a company. I mean, I'm sure they vet Alex like no other, but they'd have to know his ties to the mafia."

"Honestly, I think things have changed a lot over the years. Ryan has been working with so many different Government offices for so long. And everyone knows the relationship he has with Josh. I think people are innately too trusting, but when you put your trust in a person with a reputation like Ryan or Josh, those that work with them or are related to them or whatever just sort of come with the package. Ryan did a lot to build Alex's company up when he first started it. And Matthew never knew how any of it worked. So, his extent was just money laundering. He had no clue the level of power he could have had just with Alex's company."

Robby shakes his head. "His mind was always on money as power. Not power as power. The more money, the more power. Doesn't work like that." He claps his hands and rubs them together. "I'm in. Give me a minute to grab a satellite."

I look over as Damon leans against the door and reaches in with our earpieces. "We're ready to go. Just need you to tell us when."

I take the earpieces and hand one to Robby. I put mine in and lean over, kissing my husband. "Be careful. This is going to be one of the most dangerous missions I think we've ever been involved in. Small-time gang of douchebags or not."

He smiles and cups my cheek, bringing me in for another kiss. "I'm always careful, but it will be helpful knowing I have you watching out for me. All of us. I always feel a lot more confident knowing you're our eyes."

I smile as Robby scoffs. "What the fuck am I? Dog shit on the bottom of your shoe?" He grins teasingly as we laugh.

"More like gum. A step up from dog shit." Damon gives him a toothy grin as Robby laughs. "Keep our asses safe, and I'll up you to gum under a table." He winks as he kisses me again and heads back to the team.

"Your husband is a dickhead," Robbie teases.

I laugh then wink. "His dick head is pretty nice."

Robby laughs and shakes his head. "Get to work, pretty boy. We need those cameras down."

"Just waiting on my code to finish. Then it's all mine."

The two of us work in complete silence for several moments. Robby angles his satellite on the house and zooms in while I hack into the security system. Within seconds, I have control of the entire operation. I loop the camera feed, so if anyone is watching, which I'm sure someone is, all they'll see is absolutely nothing more than an empty yard and sidewalk.

We both adjust our earpieces after putting them in and turn them on. "Surveillance One. You have me?" I ask the team.

"Got you," Josh says.

"Surveillance Two. Hear me?" Robby asks.

"Loud and clear," Ryan answers.

"Get ready to move in," I say. I watch as they all pile into SUVs. I know the people at the other houses are doing exactly the same.

"Team One ready to roll," Josh rumbles.

"Team Two ready," Ryan says in his deep, almost always growly voice.

"Team Three ready," Luke says.

"Team Four ready." Gavin chuckles. "Assholes are about to have a very rude awakening."

"Couldn't agree more," Nick says. "Team Five ready."

"Team Six is ready," Damon growls. "Let's go get our daughter."

"Listen up," Robby begins. "Satellite shows two levels. One is a basement. I switched to thermal imaging. You have six guards on the main level. They are all pretty much in the area near the door. There's a huge hotspot. I think that's where they have their monitors for the security system. There are four people under them. One of them is sitting in a corner on the South side of the house. It looks more like a blob on the screen, so I'm sure it's Rosie, and she's wrapped around herself in the corner. The other four are spread out in the room, but no one is near Rosie."

"There are two cameras in the basement," I start. "Robby is correct. Rosie is in the corner with her knees drawn up to her chest. No bindings. Guards described her going in docile with her hands clasped in front of her and her head down. Rosie knows she has a tracker on that bracelet. She knows we're here. I don't doubt she's playing cooperative because she knows we're coming. She also knows we've been watching this place. She'll stay in that corner unless they force her out of it. I'll be watching. I have control of their entire system except those landmines. I'll shut the power to the fence off. We'll need a diversion. We need them to go running to the back of the house. I see a backdoor, but it doesn't look usable. I'm really hoping it is."

"We could set the landmines off," Nick says. "Where are they?"

"All over," Robby says.

"Team Three," Ryan says. "You're at the dry cleaners behind the house. Your team can throw a few grenades back there. The explosion of one should set off several others and send them running to the back. I see no basement windows, so I see no way Rosie could be injured. All of the landmines are near the middle of the property, and all around the house. I'm sure it's in case someone manages to breach the fence."

"Got it. We'll throw on your command and get the hell out quickly to join the teams going in," Luke says.

I look at Robby. "Ready?" I mouth to him.

He nods. "Yep," he mouths back.

I take a deep breath. It's not often that anything is done on my command. I don't usually lead the show, but this is very different. We don't usually have something this large scale in such a small area. And we don't typically rely almost solely on technology and surveillance like this. Yes, surveillance plays a huge role, but not like this.

Maybe it's because this is personal. Not like I've never been on personal missions before, but it's different when the person involved is my very own child. This has to be how it felt for Jason when we were rescuing his wife. Or to Alex when attempts were made on his fiance. Or to any of the other people in this family who have had something happen to a loved one. It's a horrible fucking feeling.

I take one last look at the live feed. "Now or never. Team Three. Go." I swallow as I watch Luke drive up to the back of the house and throw a grenade out. Without stopping, he throws two more into the yard.

"Grenades thrown!" Luke says.

"All teams, move in!" Robby commands. "The little piggies are moving to the back of the house just like we thought they would."

I keep a close eye on all the cameras as I cut the power to the fence. "Fence is off. The guards are nervous. They're looking all over the place."

"Time to give them something to look at," Josh says sardonically.

All of our teams speed up to the house and skid to a stop. In the basement, Rosie is still wrapped around herself. The guards are all nervous and have their guns on the bathroom door. My eyes about bulge out of my head when I see everyone wearing Viper's Venom patches.

"What the fuck?" I whisper. I point to my screen with wide eyes.

"They're all wearing Viper's Venom patches," Robby says. "And one is a female."

"Probably the rogue VV is looking for," Damon growls.

I watch our teams run up to the house. They stay low and have their guns ready. "One of them sees you. He's opening the door with an AR-15."

Josh, who is leading the teams, raises his own AR-15 and shoots the guy before he even has a chance to raise his weapon. Stupidly, two other assholes take his place. They try using the door for cover, but Josh is already on them. He takes out one. Another of our guards takes the other.

In a hail of gunfire, our team enters the house, spraying the entire room with bullets. Within seconds of entering, all six guards are dead.

"Top floor is clear," Robby says. "I texted Alec. He's on the way. I took pictures for him off Lance's screen. Hoping one of them is the fucking rogue."

"The interrogation just became Alec's game," Josh says.

"The fuck if you think I won't be there when that happens," Damon rumbles dangerously, daring Josh to disagree.

"Calm your ass down and focus," Josh commands. "One mission at a time. Where am I going, Surveillance One?"

"Right," I answer, thankful he's able to pull my pissed off husband back from the ledge. "Back of the house. The door to the basement looks like a closet door, but it's not. It will be the second door on the left when you get to the hallway. The woman is Rosie's mother. Just got a better look at her. She looks terrified."

"Good," Damon growls.

I watch the team reach the door. "They have guns on the door. As soon as you open it, they have the advantage."

"Where's Rosie?" Josh whispers.

"Still in the corner on the South side. Opposite end of where you are. Her mother is near her now. You have three guns pointed at you. One of them has a leader patch. Looks almost identical to Alec's. He's the one wearing a red bandana."

I hear a few breaths before I watch the door open. Josh and Gavin both kneel down on either side of the door as bullets start flying and hitting the wall behind them. Ryan is on the other side of Josh. Luke is behind Gavin. No one moves until the shooting stops, and then it's like a standoff. Our team stays still. The Viper's watch the stairs closely.

"Gavin, go prone," Robby says after a few moments. "Silently. It looks like they're about to discuss going up the stairs. Alec said try not to kill them."

Gavin does as Robby says. Josh follows his lead. They both lie silently on the ground waiting for their next move. The guy I've decided is the leader of this operation takes a few steps towards Rosie's mother. He has no idea he's just put himself into Josh's line of fire.

"Josh, I know you probably can't see him, but the leader is in your line of fire. Grab your handgun. Use the wall for your guidance. Aim low." I pull up a trajectory program quickly and lay it over the surveillance. Josh puts his hand against the wall and raises it just slightly, tilting his gun down. "Move your hand up about six inches." I line up the shot. "Stop. Right there. Muzzle down just a hair." I watch carefully. "There. You'll hit him in the knee."

Josh takes the shot.

The bullet travels exactly how I'd hoped and hits the leader in the knee. He drops and writhes in agony.

"Ah! Fuck!" he screams. "Fuck! Holy fuck!" He drops his gun and grabs his knee. "Fuck!"

Rosie's mother covers her mouth, trembling, and drops to her knees with wide eyes. The other two just watch the entire thing happen in complete awe and confusion. Neither seem to really know what to do but stay rooted to the spot they're in. Gawking.

I just smile. "Poor fuckers. Gavin and Josh. If you move forward just a little, you can take out both guards at the bottom of the stairs. Neither are looking at you. You can use either a handgun or AR. Won't matter. They won't see it coming."

Gavin chuckles as they both move forward with their rifles. "Bye bye, little piggies," he whispers.

"Shoot," I say.

They both take their shot. The guards drop dead to the ground, not having a clue what hit them. The leader is still screaming. Rosie slowly raises her head. Until now, she's jumped a few times at the gunshots, but hasn't moved. Her mother has the leader's head in her lap. It looks like she's crying, but I can't hear her over anyone's audio like I could the screaming asshole in her arms.

Rosie very gingerly moves from the corner. I furrow my brows, having no fucking clue what the hell she's doing, until I see the gun on the floor in front of her. She crawls towards it, keeping her eyes focused on her mother and the leader.

"No one move," I command when I see Josh and Gavin standing. Everyone freezes. "Come on, baby girl. You can do it," I encourage her, even though I know she can't hear me.

"What the fuck is happening, Lance?" Damon whispers.

"She's going for the dropped gun. No one sees her," I say. "The leader is still grimacing and holding his blown out kneecap. Her mother has his head in her lap. Come on, baby girl." I grin. I can't possibly be more proud. Especially when her hand falls on the gun.

She quickly moves to her feet and backs up to the corner. "No one move an inch!" she screams. The gun shakes in her hand, but the desired effect is all we needed. Her mother's and the leader's heads snap to her.

"Put that down! What are you doing?" her mother screams at her.

"I said don't move!" Rosie yells. She lowers the gun and shoots the ground. Her arms recoil wildly from the kick she wasn't expecting, but she holds onto the gun.

"Ah! You stupid bitch! You could have shot me!" her mother screams at her.

Rosie points the gun right at her head. "Next time, I won't miss."

"Bad ass girl." I grin with pride. "She's got them at gunpoint."

"Rosie?" Josh calls. "You hear me? Do you know who I am?"

"Josh?" she says after a couple of moments.

"Yes. Josh. We're coming down, honey. Don't shoot me, okay?" He smiles. I can hear the laughter in his voice. It does what he meant it to.

She relaxes and nods. "I won't."

"Keep the gun on them until we get there," he says.

Like the very much in sync team we are, Josh leads Gavin, Ryan, Luke, and Damon down the stairs. Everyone else stays up. Josh makes sure to sweep the room for threats, just in case. Every single person who follows him down does the same thing.

Rosie runs right to Damon. He lifts her in his arms. She wraps completely around him and bursts into tears. My heart breaks as Damon whispers in her ear as he hugs her. Josh carefully grabs her gun as Gavin and Ryan secure the leader and Rosie's mother. They both better start praying to whatever God or demon they believe in because their lives are about to make a complete turnaround.

Fallon drives to the house as Damon is carrying our sobbing daughter out of it. As soon as she stops, I'm out of the SUV and running to my family. Just outside the gate, I meet them and wrap them both in my arms.

"I thought I was going to die," Rosie cries. "They told me they were going to kill me!"

I meet Damon's eyes because there's a lot more to this story than we've told her. We've told the line between being completely honest with her, and withholding information to protect her. I don't think either of us can do that anymore. She deserves to know it all.

The problem is that I'm not sure we know the whole truth…

Chapter Twenty Two

🐚 Damon 🐚

"I'm not going to count to three. Fuck, I won't even count to one," Josh growls. "You will tell me everything I want to know. Or I will cut you into pieces and feed your fucking intestines to your boyfriend over there while you watch yourself bleed out."

I chuckle and stand against the wall with my arms crossed over my chest. It's been just over an hour since we pulled off our damn near completely unplanned mission in the name of saving my daughter. We brought Rosie's mother and the asshole VV member back to our compound and have thrown them in our interrogation compound. Alec met us here. He and Gavin are sitting next to each other on our metal table in the room.

Rosie's mother's eyes widen. She whimpers as she cowers. "O-okay."

"You don't have permission to do that, bitch!" the VV member spits.

"And you don't have the fucking authority over me to tell her she can't," Alec growls dangerously at him. "I'm the president of Viper's

Venom. This entire fucking crew belongs to me. I control it. All the ins and outs. Not you or whoever the fuck you answer to."

"I don't work for you! You have no authority over me!" he screams right back.

"Okay. I'm sick of your mouth." I push off the wall and grab some duct tape. I rip a piece off and stride across the room to him. "Not a fucking word, or I knock your ass out until we're done with your little toy." I slap the tape over his mouth. He bites at it and screams, so I slap another piece over it. "Next piece goes over your nose."

For some reason, the threat shuts him up, even though he glares at me. It makes me wonder if I just found a fear I can exploit. Not being able to breathe and suffocating to death is definitely something a lot of people are terrified of. I'll have to file that away for later.

Alec jumps off the table. "Now. You." He points to Rosie's mother. "Name. Fucking lie to me, and I won't hold Mr. Lucinio back this time when he decides slitting your throat is the better option."

She sniffles. "Jacqueline."

"See?" Josh says with a grin. "I'm not a bad guy when you give me what I ask for. Now." Josh points to the duct taped jackass. "Him. What's his name?"

Her lip trembles. "I…" She looks away.

Josh grips her chin and forces her to look back at him. "Name."

"T-t-tits."

I look at Gavin. His mouth drops. "Well, fuck me," he rumbles. A slow grin spreads across his face as he looks at Tits. "You and I are gonna have so much fun."

I laugh. "You're a fucking sociopath."

"Ain't the first time I heard that," Gavin winks as I sit next to him.

"Tits. Okay," Alec says. He looks at Josh. "He's not one of mine. I've been pouring over members for six months. I'd know."

"I believe you," Josh says looking back at Jacqueline. "I bet she'll confirm that for us." He drags the tip of the knife in his hand up her bare thigh to wear her Daisy Duke jean cutoffs begin. She visibly trembles. "Won't you?"

She nods as Tits screams through the duct tape. I roll my eyes and ignore him. Jacqueline sits up slightly. "He's n-not V-V-Vipers's V-Venom."

"He's Ruthless Warriors and playing pretend," Josh says. It's not a question. He knows the answer. Just wants the confirmation.

She nods again. "He's th-the l-leader."

"And he was using Gregory Franklin as a front." Josh smiles encouragingly. Sometimes, it takes charm and finesse to get information. Josh Lucinio could charm the pants right off a person in Alaska in the middle of a blizzard and convince that person they have fur and will always be warm.

"Y-yes." She swallows hard. Her hands are cuffed behind her back. I made certain they're tight enough to dig painfully into her wrist.

"He's not really Viper's Venom at all." Josh's voice has dropped to some sexy as fuck, flirty level that she seems to be responding to very well. Despite Tits screaming shit at her despite the gag, her eyes are focused completely on Josh.

She shakes her head. "He's th-the leader of R-Ruthless Warriors. Th-they thought using V-Viper's Venom would throw y-you all off. And we could g-get Rosie."

Just her name on this bitch's tongue makes me tense up and coil. I narrow my eyes at her. She must see me looking because she instantly lowers her eyes again and avoids me. Good. This whiny little puta needs to get a fucking life. Preferably one in a different realm. I'd be okay with death, too.

"Tell me everything, Jacqueline," Josh says, a slight dominance to his voice that she responds to like a fucking purring kitten. "From the beginning. How did a beautiful woman like you end up in this mess? Tell me all you know. Let me help." He gives her a smile as Alec stands, shaking his head. I roll my eyes. She's so far from Josh's type, it's comical. But whatever gets her talking.

She nods and takes a breath. "It s-started with my husband. I found out he had a lot of money he'd never told me about. When I brought it up, he told me he'd put it away for Rosie's college. That he didn't think it was necessary for me to know about it because he knew I'd spend it." She shakes her head. "He always said I had a spending problem. I didn't. He had a being frugal problem. He never bought anything for the house or me. But if Rosie wanted, you bet your ass she got it."

"As she should. She's a fucking kid. And not like she'd demand diamond fucking panties and a golden bra," I growl out through gritted teeth, unable to hold back. She shrinks into herself even more, and I give her a devilish grin.

Gavin puts a hand on my knee and squeezes. "Chill, bro. You'll get your time with her."

The very thought of that makes her whimper. I just grin more. She takes a shaky breath. "I r-ran into Tits at a b-bar in town. We danced and talked and started an affair. I opened u-up about my m-marital issues. He h-helped with a plan." Her eyes darken. I can see the fury under the fear. "But he found out about the affair. He planned on divorcing me and taking Rosie. I couldn't touch the money, but I could force her to give it to me when she turned eighteen."

"Man, your grave keeps getting deeper and deeper," Gavin says mock sadly with a grin.

Josh nods. "So, you got pissed at your husband for having hidden money he'd put in an account for your daughter's college education, and you were jealous."

"You don't understand!" she yells, finally losing it just like I knew she would. Her fake tears weren't fooling anyone. The fear is real, but she's a fucking bitter little whore. There's no remorse. "She always had everything! She was daddy's little girl ever since she took her first breath! I was suddenly nothing to him! Rosie got all of his love and attention and affection! I finally found a way out and to get back at her for stealing him away from me!"

"By killing him?" Josh asks with a raised brow and a grin. "I like your style."

Her eyes widen at him. I can see the exact moment she thinks she's found a friend in him, and it makes me grin. "Yes! You understand?"

"Revenge. I get it. It's what I do."

She bobs her head, her attention solely on him now. Even the man throwing a temper in the corner screaming at her to shut-up doesn't keep her from talking. "All I had to do was keep her around until she was eighteen, then force her to give me the money. Tits said someone in his crew would buy her for a pretty penny, and I'd get more money! I could retire in the Swiss Alps. Have no worries at all!"

The more she talks, the sicker she makes me. Bile rises up my throat with each word she speaks. Her fake as fuck Southern Belle accent fades more and more the angrier and less guarded she becomes. I just want to cut out her tongue and shove it in her ear.

Maybe I still will.

"What happened the night you killed that asshole?" Josh says, playing right to her. His hand is even caressing her thigh. She's all but sitting in his fucking lap. "Tits did it. We came back from a walk. Tits was hiding and choked him out. We dug a grave for him together a couple of days before. We buried him in it that night. Tits had to take care of some other things. I don't know what. All he told me was that it was biker stuff. He said he'd be back the next day." She glares. "Rosie saw me coming back with the shovel. She questioned me. She asked where her dad was. I tried to tell her that he left, but she called the police on me. The bitch called them while I was sleeping! I woke up, and they were arresting me!"

"That must have pissed you off even more." Josh shakes his head.

"They combed the property and found him almost right away. Tits bailed me out of jail, but I hated her even more for what she did to me! When we moved, we did it because everyone was judging me. Tits wanted us to start over and be happy while we waited for her to be of age to get the money he left for her. He left her everything! I found out about more money than just that!"

I bite back the chuckle because I know damn well just how much he left her. Her father didn't have a lot, but she's getting a total of twenty-five thousand dollars. Why this fucking cow thinks that's an amount to kill over is beyond my comprehension.

"How much did you sell Rosie for? And to who?"

"Someone named Tick or something. I don't really know. I didn't care. I still don't. Tits said he'd give me a million dollars for her. That we'd run away afterwards and live like a King and Queen."

"You've been a huge help," Josh drawls. "Thank you for telling me all of this. What else do you know? Can you tell me anything else?"

She shakes her head, but then her eyes widen again. "Wait! The rest of Tits' crew. It's not as big as he tries to tell everyone. I always thought it was so strange how he said we'd have more guys showing up but none ever came. The only ones I ever saw were the ones you killed."

Josh gives her a brilliant smile as he stands. "You've been such a good girl, I think I'll let you go." He pulls her up so she's standing. She looks at him adoringly as he steps back and turns her like he's going to remove the cuffs.

It's my turn.

I slide off the table and stalk towards her like she's my prey. She shrinks into Josh, and that fear I'm feeding off of shines in her eyes. I chuckle because she thinks Josh is going to save her. She saw his flirty side and cooperated with him because it's the type of puta she is. She probably thinks she has a chance of ending up in his bed.

"He said he'd let you go," I growl as I stop right in front of her and grip her hips roughly as Josh steps back. She looks at him. That sense of betrayal so obviously fills her, and I can tell when her body slumps. I shove her back from me.

She hits the wall so hard, her head bounces off it. Instead of screaming, she moans and slinks to the ground. "Ugnh..."

I kneel and tug her legs so they're straight out. I straddle her and take my knife out of the holder strapped to my thigh that I keep it in. "Selling a little girl because you're money hungry fucking puta is so low in my book. But selling your own fucking daughter for the money? That's so fucking ridiculous that I might have to set the bar lower."

"I... I'm..."

I lean forward so my lips are just a breath away from hers. "I've been wanting to do this ever since I heard you on the phone telling your fucktoy that Rosie was probably at a friends and that she didn't have many. Right before you burned the house down. The house that Rosie was in the whole time."

Her fear turns to fury once more. "She should have fucking died in that fire."

"But then you wouldn't have gotten that money." I press my knife against the thin fabric of her barely there tank top. "And you wouldn't have gotten to run away and fuck your boy on a bed of it."

I watch her eyes widen. Her mouth forms a perfect 'O.' No sound leaves it. Nothing but a whoosh of breath. I push it in further and further. I can feel it slicing through the soft flesh of her stomach and sliding deeper and deeper until it's buried to the hilt. She makes some kind of a gurgling noise as she chokes on her own blood.

Her body spasms a couple of times as I yank the knife out of her. Dark red blood spills from her mouth as she falls to her side. It won't take her long to bleed out. I stand and take a step back as I admire my handy work.

"You next, asshole," Josh says. I look over as he rips the duct tape off Tits. Gavin and Alec are standing next to him with two containers.

"Fuck you!" Tits yells. "You think everything she told you was the truth? You're fucking stupid!"

Gavin and Alec both tip the containers. A liquid comes out. I watch as it hits Tits' chest. They both step back. Josh is standing a good distance away watching. It's then I notice that Gavin and Alec have put on a rubber apron that covers the front of them all the way down to the floor. They're wearing a heavy set of leather gloves.

Tits screams in agony when the liquid soaks through his clothes. At first, it's more of a surprised kind of yelp. But it turns into a much more higher pitched animalistic howl of agony as the battery acid in the containers soaks his skin.

Josh looks down at him with his arms crossed over his chest. Jacqueline is still gurgling. Her body jerks. "What was she lying about, Tits? Was she the one who killed her husband?" Josh growls.

"No, you stupid cunt!" Tits yells. "Ah! It fucking hurts!"

"Good. It's supposed to. You answer my goddamn questions, or I'll let these two fuckers cover you in acid and watch as it burns you alive."

I'll give him credit. Tits spits at Josh, but he's shaking so badly, the spit gets on him instead. "It hurts! Get it off me!"

Josh nods to Gavin. "Cut the shirt. Show him some good faith or some bullshit like that."

Gavin grins and sets the container down. Jacquine's body jerks once more. Gavin leans down and cuts the shirt, but leaves a superficial wound all the way up Tits' chest. Tits shouts again as he tries to get away from the blade. Gavin doesn't say a word. He just grins demonically as he stands.

"Acid is going to fucking hurt in that," Alec remarks. "I'd hate to be you."

Tits gasps for air, but he glares at Josh. "The bitch thought her little slut daughter was meant for some other person on the crew. She's mine," he growls. "Mine. I planned on killing the whore as soon as Rosie was in my possession. I didn't want to wait until she was eighteen. I went after her as soon as I could."

197

I bark out a bitter laugh. "Yeah? You almost fucking killed her. For someone who wanted her that badly, you did a piss poor job of searching the house." I glare at him. I watch Jacqueline's body start jerking violently. She's still alive and just heard every fucking word.

Good.

I hope to fuck she realizes what a fucked up person she is. And that Karma was going to bite her in the fucking ass. While Rosie would have been in his possession if we hadn't intervened, this bitch would have been dead.

I'm thanking my lucky stars that things went as they did and I got to be the one who twisted that knife inside her.

"We searched that house up and down!" Tits screams. "She wasn't in there!"

"You didn't search it enough!" I yell right back as I join Josh. Jacqueline is no longer moving. The life in her eyes diminished second by second until there was none left. "She was cowered in a closet five fucking feet away from you!"

"You think that bitch didn't get a beating when I figured that out?"

Josh kicks his foot. "What don't I know? Lie to me, and I'll make you drink that shit."

Tits contemplates the words before finally deciding to speak. "You can fucking kill me because I'm not telling you shit. You think it ends with me? Think again, asshole." He shoots her a glare. "Good riddance."

Josh chuckles. "I agree. Good riddance." He nods to Gavin and Alec, then turns to me. "Get home. Be with your daughter. We'll finish here."

I nod as Gavin and Alec pour the rest of the battery acid over Tits. His screams of agony as the battery acid eats at him hits my ears as I turn and head for the door.

None of it matters.

All that matters to me is telling Rosie that this chapter of her life is over. He said it doesn't end with him, but I've seen more people try to leave us with empty threats to scare us as they take their last breath.

We never take them lightly and always take necessary precautions. I know Josh will have our team on finding out if there's anyone above him. We know there are other factions around the Upper Midwest area and are more than happy to keep a close watch over them.

The truth is, though, no one is getting to Rosie. He was the one who bought her. Her mother is the one who sold her. They're both dead and so are the fuckers they worked with here. If Jacqueline's words can be trusted, then we know we took out Tits' whole team.

I believe Jacqueline was telling Josh the truth because she fell for his seduction and the unspoken promise of protection he gave her through that seduction. I believe she told us all she knew and even added something we hadn't even asked about.

I make a beeline for the shower as soon as I walk into the house. I smile when Lance gives me a quick peck on the cheek on my way up the stairs to our bedroom. I hear Rosie's laughter and some giggling and smile even wider.

It's going to be alright.

Our little girl is going to be just fine.

We all are.

Chapter Twenty Three

🍎 Lance 🍎

(Two Months Later)

"Mmm…," I moan around Damon's dick as I swallow all he gives me while he sucks my cock dry.

"There's something about being on my back with your dick in my mouth while you're swallowing my come that makes the day just start right," Damon says as he pops off me. He kisses my tip and taps my ass.

I have to laugh as I climb off him. "I mean, if you'd like to start each day sucking my dick, I won't stop you." I grin.

Damon growls and licks his lips. His eyes fall to my semi-hard cock. "How did I live so long without you?" He smiles as he sits up. "All my life fighting who I am, and here you were the whole fucking time." He grips the back of my neck and kisses me roughly. It's not long before my cock is standing at full mast again.

"Dads! Are you ever getting up? People are showing!" Rosie yells down the hall to us.

I smile against Damon's lips. "She's a cockblocker."

"Fuck yes." Damon laughs and shakes his head. "Be down in a few minutes!" he calls.

"Hurry up! Dallas and Josh brought all of the blankets and bears over, so we can finally get all the gift bags set up and blankets all nice and ribboned with the pretty ribbon Lyric sent!"

I laugh. "She's on a warpath today. It's only eight in the morning."

Damon slides to the edge of the bed with a smile. "After what she went through, I'm just happy to see her taking some control."

I follow him to the shower. He's not wrong. After she was taken by Tits and Jacqueline, she cried for days. She didn't leave the house for anything except Dallas' birthday party, and that was only after she begged me and Damon to go with. We planned to anyway, but hearing us promise we'd be there was something she needed. We were more than happy to give it to her. Even if it meant sitting with her during the movie, which we did.

After the party, she started to come out of it. She never shut down on us. She talked to us about it everyday. She spilled her feelings about what had happened and admitted to how scared she was. She asked us over and over again how it happened. It was like she needed to piece it all together in order to make it all make sense.

In the end, it took watching the surveillance we had from the house. She watched herself in the corner and recalled everything she was thinking and feeling. How she was making a plan; listening to everything being done and said so she could figure out a way to escape if she needed. She knew we'd be there. There was never a doubt in her mind. But she still actively attempted to think of a way out.

She remembered that when they grabbed her, she fought until she saw her mother with a gun pointed at her and a sneer on her face. She was so shocked at the hatred she saw that she cooperated and got in the van. They took her phone and threw it out the window in the alley by the shop we were at.

What she had trouble grasping is how calm she was in the face of it all, and just how much that helped us. She subtly dropped her bracelet on the sidewalk outside the house because she wasn't sure if the GPS tracker would work inside. She was also afraid they'd figure it out and crush her bracelet or something. She wanted to make sure we could find her.

In the end, watching the surveillance of everything that happened from the second she got there until we carried her out and left with her was what she needed to truly understand how brave and strong she was and is. She didn't remember picking up the gun or yelling at them. She had no recollection of facing down her mother. She just remembered listening and hearing Josh's voice telling her that we were there. She remembered Damon carrying her outside and being wrapped in our arms. When she saw the video, it all came rushing back to her.

As the past couple months have passed, Rosie has gone back to her bubbly self, but she's also blossomed into this fiercely strong woman. It's a side of her that we knew was there and are proud as hell to see coming out.

I pull on my shirt after quickly showering with Damon and getting dressed after. "Think she'll be like a drill sergeant down there again?" I ask with a grin. "Like she was at that wrapping party?"

Damon laughs. "I'm not going to lie. That was nice to see after everything. She's so excited that the blankets are done now so she can finish the gift bags." He takes my hand and leads me downstairs. "I'm really hoping Josh brought breakfast. I'm fucking starving."

I laugh. "My come didn't satiate you today? I must not be trying hard enough."

He throws me a sexy as hell grin that has me almost coming in my jeans. "You and your come make me want more. It'll never be enough."

I return his smile with a little heat snaking to my cheeks. I follow him down the stairs. He greets everyone as he sniffs the air. I laugh because Damon is a closet foodie. He loves food almost as much as he loves me and Rosie, my dick, working out, and the mafia… in that order. Give anything Josh puts in front of him, he's in complete food heaven.

He drags me with him to the kitchen. I follow because I planned on grabbing something to drink, but I wouldn't miss anything that's about to happen anyway. I love watching his excitement over Josh's cooking.

"It smells so good, and I'm starving." Damon inhales deeply and closes his eyes. He smiles as he opens in. "Tell me it's those baked egg things you do with the peppers, onions, mushrooms and all of that delicious stuff in it."

Josh grins as he pulls something out of the oven in a large baking pan with dividers. "You mean this?" He puts a cutting board on the counter on top of a hot sheet.

Damon groans. "Fuck yes."

Josh jerks his head towards the fridge. "Get some orange juice and apple juice out. I brought over some chocolate milk for Dallas since everyone in this house is so fucking oddly against it."

I laugh. "We're not against it. Just don't eat chocolate. Or drink it."

Josh shakes his head. "Get everyone what they want to drink. Set up in the dining room. I'll bring the plates out. Raleigh is allergic to onions and doesn't like peppers, and Dallas hates peppers and onions, so I made theirs separate from the others. Lance, take this one. The dividers are in there to separate by portions so Damon doesn't eat it all."

I laugh. "I know you're fucking with him, but I think he probably could eat this entire thing himself."

Josh laughs as he pulls a smaller pan out of the oven. I take the pan, cutting board and everything to the dining room. It's a room we rarely ever use, but Josh has really started to like family dinners. Ryan does his every Sunday. Josh has followed this practice, but not because he's mimicking anyone.

It's because it helps him feel grounded and deeply rooted. It's something he's confided in us all. He's had family dinners, but they were always forced and stiff. Formal. For the most part, no one talked unless Matthew had something to say. If anyone else did, they'd face consequences. He enjoyed his dinners quiet.

Gavin and Damon were a part of many of them. They were unfortunate bystanders to a few of the beatings Alex and Josh took. Some of them were on their hands. They made the mistake of talking when they weren't supposed to. He took it out on Alex and Josh. Damon once told me that it only took twice before they understood the severity of breaking the rules.

Any of them.

I put the pan on the table and go back to the kitchen to help with plates and cups. Once the table is set and everyone is settled, Josh at the head of the table where he belongs, Josh starts our conversation. He likes to know how everyone is doing. This is his chance to catch up. Especially when he's been gone.

"So, how is everyone? Sorry we didn't get to do dinner last week," he starts.

Gavin, sitting on Josh's right side as his second in command, smiles. "Harleigh is on a fast track to her degree." He looks at her adoringly.

She smiles and blushes. "I finished my summer classes. Gavin is impressed by my grades."

Josh smiles. "Straight A's?"

"Mmhmm. But the classes weren't that hard."

Gavin laughs. "It was a biochemistry and some kind of anatomy class. Some of her homework had me feeling like my college education was seriously lacking."

Alex grins. "We went to UCLA. I assure you. It wasn't lacking. But we weren't there to become Veterinarians either."

"Thank God for that. You're the only person I know who can kill a cactus," Josh teases.

Alex's mouth drops as Raleigh cracks up. "Oh my God, the poor cactus!" she says through the laughs.

"I maintain that it wasn't my fault. The cactus just doesn't like Chicago," Alex grumbles.

I smile. "I'd believe that. Except the cactus was perfectly fine when it was living here."

Damon laughs. "It was thriving. Nice and green."

"For the record, the cactus is doing just fine now," Alex says with a glare and teasing smile that takes away all the viciousness.

"Because of Raleigh," Rosie says. "Raleigh is the one who saved its life by showing it some love."

"Yeah, Coldhearted CEO. Because of me." Raleigh leans into Alex, jabbing him in the arm.

"What about you, Alec?" Josh asks. "Were you able to get your bike fixed?"

"Man, I wish, bro. It's fucked. I'm probably just going to have to build a new one or something. Sucks because I love that bike. But I guess I can't keep my first one forever. Probably time to give myself an upgrade anyway."

"We all deserve to be spoiled sometimes. Raleigh, how's the wedding planning?" Josh asks.

Raleigh lights up. "So, so good. We finally agreed on the venue. We're going to do it on the lake on the yacht Alex just bought. I thought he was insane for doing that, but then he took me out on the water, and now I just want to live on it and sail around the world. Big time businessmen can work from anywhere, right?"

Josh grins as he finishes his dinner. "They can. But Alex would never be able to stay away from us that long." He wiggles his eyebrows at Alex. We all laugh when Alex rolls his eyes. "Oh come on. You love me."

"Satan only knows why," Alex rumbles with a deadpan expression.

"Good thing I know why then, since I am the fucking devil himself." Josh leans back in his chair after finishing his breakfast. We all laugh again because he's right. Josh has one hell of a reputation on the streets. I think people seriously call him Satan. Some straight to his face. After a few moments Josh turns to Rosie. "How are you doing, sweetheart? Last we talked, you wanted to kick some ass."

"I still do," Rosie says with a shrug. "I feel like I'll just never have some of the answers I want. Which is fine. I'll live with that. I just still have no idea how my mom could want nothing but money. She wasn't all bad, you know. She used to be an amazing mom. That kind of a change is so horrible. I mean, she basically said she was jealous of me my whole life, but she didn't act like that for a lot of it."

"I think maybe she tried for a while. But her true colors shone," Dallas says. "But truthfully, you're where you belong now. And I'm so happy I got to meet you." She reaches over and squeezes Rosie's hand.

Josh smiles as he picks up his drink. "What about you, honey? How's your week gone?" His eyes meet Dallas'.

She blushes and looks down. "U-um... Well, I..." she looks at Rosie. "W-we... have a date... um... to... the kid's gala tomorrow." She keeps her eyes on Rosie, making sure not to look at Josh.

"Yeah, it's something they've both been looking forward to," Damon says. "Can't say I like it."

I look at Josh with a proud smile. "Took them forever to ask. I -" I cut myself off when I see the look on his face. He's paused with the drink halfway to his lips. His face has gone pale.

I swear I imagined it, though, because within a second, he's clearing his throat and taking a drink. A long one. After he downs the entire glass of juice, he stands. "That's good. It's a good thing. I'm going to get all this cleaned up. You guys go ahead and start on those blankets.

Don't open that present from Lyric and her husbands until I'm there, Rosie." Josh smiles and grabs some dishes.

"I can help," Dallas says quietly. She starts to gather some empty plates as she stands.

"No. I got it. I do. Go do your thing. I'll be there soon." Josh disappears in the kitchen. Dallas watches him sadly.

I look at Damon and lean into him. "The fuck is happening?" I ask low enough for only him to hear.

Damon clears his throat. "Whatever it is, it's none of our business," he whispers as he turns and kisses my neck.

As Josh cleans up, everyone else makes their way to our living room, which has been turned into party central. All of the baskets are ready to go. They are all with ribbons that match the color of the tulle they are covered in. Each ribbon, made by our own graphic designer, Lyric, has the Crane family crest on one end; the Lucinio family crest on the other.

The gift bags are filled with things for the kids. Matt, DJ, and Lyric all made sure to get coloring books and so many books and crafts to keep the kids busy for weeks. For the parents, we got them all a relaxation package, complete with a masseuse who would be going straight to them so they didn't have to leave the hospital.

We decided a lot of them wouldn't want to leave the hospital, so we brought everything they'd need for a break to them. Including dinner. We got local restaurants to agree to deliver to them if they didn't want to go out. Many of the places we chose for this, the most fancy places in the city, don't usually deliver. When they heard about what we were doing, they were all lining up to make it easier on the families.

"These turned out fucking fantastic," Damon says as he starts tying one of Lyric's ribbons around the neatly rolled blanket Rosie hands him.

"I know. Makes me want one for us." I lean over and kiss his cheek.

"She sent one for all of us. She made huge king sized ones. I'm pretty sure she's bringing them when she flies in tomorrow."

I smile. "She thinks of everything."

Damon looks up when Josh comes into the room. He says nothing, but he's smiling and helping. He follows Rosie's orders with no questions. I don't think he knows how haunted he looks in this very moment. I choose to say nothing because my husband is right. It's really none of our business. Though, I'd be stupid not to see that it has something to do with Dallas. If I didn't already have that feeling, I would when Alec leans over and whispers something to Josh as he's rolling his eyes.

When we finish with everything Rosie wants us to do, we allow her to open her birthday gift from Lyric, Matt, and DJ early. They weren't certain they'd be able to make it to the kids gala because of some training Matt and DJ had, but they managed to make it work at the very last minute.

"Oh my gosh!" Rosie exclaims as she pulls out a king sized blanket.

It's navy blue and has the Crane family crest embroidered on one side and the Lucinio family crest on the other. Like the blankets we're giving to the kids, hers is weighted. It was done that way because weighted blankets bring comfort. Like a hug. I'll never forget the first weighted blanket I was given. It soothed me so much and made me feel like I was wrapped in my adopted parents' embrace.

Rosie pulls out more things. "A gift card to Barnes' &' Noble! Yes!" Her eyes widen. She and Dallas both squeal. She pulls out a framed portrait of herself as an avatar. She's sitting on a throne with a tiara placed on her head. There's a sash that comes down her body that says 'Queen Knight' on it. The avatar is dressed in a beautiful purple gown that reminds me of Cinderella.

I snuggle into Damon as we watch our family enjoying each other's company. As Dallas and Rosie curl into each other under the Lucinio and Crane family blanket while we all start watching a movie, I'm struck at how perfect this all is.

We might always have a threat to us on the horizon, but this family, our family, sticks together. We love hard and protect fiercely. No matter what darkness comes our way, we are one another's light.

I can't be more grateful for them all coming together for a cause so close to my heart. Tomorrow's event is so special to me, but they've all made it special to them as well. Just as important of a cause.

Regardless of any situation we might face, our future's look bright.

Chapter Twenty Four

☙ Damon ❧

"You know that tightening in your stomach that happens when you're so turned on you're about to come?" I ask Lance.

His eyes shoot to me, and he freezes while coming out of the bathroom. His gaze is more than heated. It's scorching. I can feel him burning me from here. He's completely naked. Just that has me tense and ready for him.

I swallow. Hard. Much like he's making my dick. The slow smile that turns his lips upwards as he unabashedly allows his eyes to look me up and down sends shivers all through me. He walks slowly to me and drops the towel he'd been using to dry his hair onto the floor.

"I don't think we have much time before we go, but I'm more than happy to help you out with that hard dick you're sporting." He grips my dick a little roughly, taking me by surprise, and pushes me back towards the bed.

When the backs of my knees hit it, I sit with a groan as Lance drops to his knees, still gripping my dick. "Why don't we just sixty-nine so I can suck you off, too?"

Lance grins and starts stroking me hard and fast as he twists his wrist. My eyes roll back in my head. "Because our shower escapade that made me paint the glass shower door was a powerful enough release that I don't think I'll be able to come again for a week." He lowers his mouth to my cock and starts hoovering as he strokes.

I groan and thrust uncontrollably into his mouth, gripping the sheets underneath me. "We'll see about that. Maybe I'll be a nice guy and let you take my ass later tonight after the kid's gala. See if you can hold off filling me then."

He smiles around my dick and moans. "You know damn well what that will do to me."

He keeps stroking with one hand. With the other, he runs a finger from my balls to my hole and back while he tugs my balls and rolls them in his palm. He sucks my dick hard. His tongue slides up and down the vein on the underside of my dick.

Lance knows exactly what to do to get me off, and he does it well. Efficiently. My dick thickens for him. I shiver as jolt after jolt shoots down my spine. The pleasure settles in my lower back through to my dick. My stomach tightens, and as he swallows around me when I touch the back of his throat.

I fall back on the bed and arch into him as I come. "Oh fuck, Lance!" My hips jerk into his mouth as I unload down his throat. There's something incredible about someone as sexy as he is swallowing my come. I pant as I lay on the bed with my eyes closed, completely spent.

Lance pops off my dick with an audible moan that makes it jerk. "I love when I get dessert before dinner."

I grin and open my eyes as I sit up. Lance is already getting dressed. I raise an eyebrow. "Are you denying me dessert?"

Lance laughs. "No, baby. But we do need to get dressed. If we aren't ready to go on time, I think Rosie might blow a gasket. She's really taken the lead on this. She loves it. If we're late, she'll drag us there naked."

I laugh as I stand. "Okay, I'll give that to you."

I quickly put my suit on. I don't wear them often. I hate them. Rosie, though, insisted that all of the men wear matching suits. Black pants. A white shirt, white vest, white jacket that we're allowed to take off should we get too hot. It is August after all. All of the women, including Rosie, will be wearing black dresses.

A few moments later, I'm leading Lance down the stairs. At the bottom is our very impatient daughter.

I grin when she looks up at us. "You look beautiful," I say, cutting her off before she can start her lecture.

"Thank you," she says with a blush. "We're meeting everyone there, but I'm afraid we're going to be late."

"Not a chance in hell," Lance says. "Not with your dad driving."

I wink at her and guide them both outside.

Hours later, the gala for the kids is in full swing. Everyone has been fed. The parents got a good meal of their choosing. The kids did as well. Hospital staff set everyone's giftbags in their rooms while they were out. Those who weren't able to attend were delighted at the gift. The staff took lots of pictures and have already emailed them to Rosie, as she was the one who really wanted to head this entire thing. Lance and I were only too happy to allow her and guide her along the way. She really has a talent for this.

"Going once. Going twice! Sold to number twelve!" Rosie says with a huge grin from the stage she's been ruling for the last hour.

The kid who won the bid squeals in excitement as his mom takes him up to the stage to claim his prize. Rosie planned the perfect auction for the kids. The adults each got a relaxation prize package, but the kids are all using fake money that looks real but has Josh's face on one side and Ryan's on the other. The kids got a kick out of it.

They were all given a list of the prizes they could bid on. Each kid was given a thousand dollars in play money. The parents helped them pick out the prizes they really wanted. Since we have so many prizes, everyone has managed to get something they've wanted.

"Okay, everyone," Rosie says dramatically. I grin because our girl really can hold a room full of people. "This last prize is seriously coveted. We saved the best one for last because it's so special. But I'm not going to be the one auctioning this one off. This one is going to be auctioned off by none other than the man so many of you have been enthralled with tonight." She pauses for dramatic effect. There are gasps and wide eyes from the kids. "Josh Lucinio!"

I laugh as the room bursts into applause. She gives Josh the microphone and steps off the stage, smiling brightly. She meets Dallas near the edge of the stage. They whisper and giggle together. Their dates turned out to be real duds. They weren't as into this event as they were into trying to get the two girls to kiss them. It took all of me not to take them both by their neck and throw them out. Fortunately for everyone involved, all it took was a look from me, Josh, and Alec. They both left on their own accord.

And on their own two feet. Lance wouldn't allow me to break their legs.

"She's doing incredible up there. She has a real knack for this," Lance whispers to me.

I grin with pride. "That's our girl."

"Okay, everyone," Josh begins. "Before we do the last item, I'd like to give you all a truly heartfelt thank you. Lots of you know how much work my family does with kids. When this opportunity arose, we jumped at it. Thank you all for spending your night with us. We hope that you have been enjoying yourselves. We've already gone through and announced the silent auction winners, but one thing we haven't mentioned is something we've decided to do as a family."

Ryan jumps up on stage after Rosie gives him a microphone and pushes him. "We've all gotten together and asked ourselves what we could do for you. Something more than just dinner and some relaxation. We know lots of you are worried about finances and bills. So, if you allow us to, we'd like to help you all out with a few things." He looks at Josh with a wink.

Josh grins. "Firstly, we'd like to pay off the bills you've incurred now and through the treatment your child will be needing."

"And second," Ryan says over the gasps spreading throughout the room. Lance takes my hand and squeezes with such a huge smile on his face that I can't help but lean over and kiss him. "We'd like to pay off all your past bills, your car payments, mortgages, and anything else you all have over your heads that takes away from your ability to concentrate fully on the treatment going on here."

Josh smiles as sniffles and more gasps flood the room. "Last, we'd really like to offer you our services in fixing up your homes. Some of you may need to make it more accessible for your child and family. Others may have a leaky roof. Maybe others just have a poor living situation. Whatever it is, it would be our pleasure and honor to use our resources to help you. Your focus and attention should be on your family. You don't need extra stress."

"Over the next few days, Josh and I as well as our family will be making our rounds to gather information on all we can do to help you," Ryan continues.

"Off of that, we'd also like to announce that we're starting a fund in the name of one of our brother's who had childhood cancer." Josh meets Lance's eyes. I smile because this is something I knew about. We wanted to surprise Lance. Lance looks between me and Josh a little confused. "This fund will be here and can be used for low income families who may not be able to afford the type of treatment they should be able to get. Whether that be insurance issues or finances. It doesn't matter."

"We're each putting two and a half million dollars into the fund," Ryan says. "So, it will start with five million dollars. We'll be holding a gala each year. The money we raise from the gala will be donated directly to the fund."

"And that fund…" Josh trails off with another grin meant just for Lance. Lance looks at me, questioningly once more. I rub my thumb over the back of his hand. "Is called the Lance Knight Fund."

Lance's hand flies to his mouth. I barely hear anything as I pull Lance into my arms. I hold him close to me as he breaks down in a wave of emotions and tears. Other than his adopted parents, this type of love and support has never been shown to him. He didn't feel like Josh or anyone else in the family would understand him, what he went through, or even support him like this in a cause that he's so passionate about.

The type of support and love that our family shows for each other is something all of us sometimes struggle with. Most of us have fought some battle or another on our own. Having a close-knit group of people to fall back on takes getting used to.

So, as Lance lets all of the overwhelming emotions he feels loose, I hold him close. Everyone in our family comes to us and hugs him, showing their love and support. Once Josh finishes auctioning off the final item, he comes by and hugs Lance, whispering his support in his ear.

By the time the night is over, I can tell my husband is past the point of exhaustion. Feeling all the love and support he has throughout the night has to be overwhelming. Coming to the realization that this is really all being done for him and in his name I'm sure came as a shock.

As I drive home, his hand still in mine and Rosie's on his shoulder, Lance is silent. But I know he's okay because he has a soft smile on his face. The kind of smile a person gets when they are content and realize that everything is perfect.

I grip the wall of the shower as Lance pounds into my ass while grunting and groaning against my neck. I turn and kiss him deeply as I clench around his hard cock. I grip myself and start jerking my dick. Lance rolls his hips against mine, slamming deeper, harder, and faster into me. I push back into him, meeting him thrust for thrust.

"Oh my fuck...," Lance moans. The shower water beats down on us.

I squeeze my dick when I get close and let my head fall back against Lance's shoulder. "If you don't come soon, I'm pretty sure I'm gonna have to make you."

He wraps his arms around me. His fingers on one hand dig into my chest. The others dig into my abs. "You feel so good," he rumbles. He pushes deeper, making me clench tighter around him. "So fucking good." He slams into me one last time and comes so hard, we both collapse against the wall as we catch our breath.

After several moments, Lance slides out of me. I turn and kiss him deeply before we start cleaning up. Once we're finished and dried off, I lead him to our bedroom and collapse onto it in a tangle of limbs. I wrap us both in the blankets and snuggle him into me. He breathes out a content sigh.

I kiss just below his ear as I hold him tightly and close to me. "How do you feel after today? I know that was pretty overwhelming."

He turns his head to me with a smile and kisses my jaw. "I've always known what I had with this family, but I've also always been the kind of person who didn't want to burden anyone with my issues. You know that already. I guess this whole thing, though…" He trails off. I kiss his shoulder and hug him closer. "It just makes me realize that I was foolish to ever do that. I've seen everyone come together and rally around everyone else. I've been a part of that. I guess I just never wanted to be the one who did that."

"Because you're stubborn." I grin into his hair.

"Stubborn. Definitely stubborn. But it really stemmed from a place that I'm a giver. Not a taker. Seeing all of this stuff being done in my name, and watching those faces of everyone as we were helping them, it just made me grateful. Truly grateful. Humbled. No matter what we go through, someone else always has it worse. It's a sobering thought, but being in a position to help is amazing. It's the fact that Josh and Ryan, both sides of our family, stepped up and made all of my dreams come true. I never would have been able to do what they did. And then to have a fund set up in my name? I still can't wrap my mind around being loved like that, but fuck. It fucking feels good."

I gently grip his slightly stubbled jaw and turn his face towards mine. "I love you. We all love you, baby. You're an amazing man, spectacular husband, beautiful human, and most recently, incredible father. You deserve this. You deserve it all. I'm happy I get to be the man to give it to you."

Lance smiles, and I kiss him. I slide my dick into his ass and start thrusting slowly and deeply, pouring my whole heart into my movements.

As I make love to my husband through the night, I can't help but think that whatever life throws at us, whatever shit we have to deal with, we'll do it as a family. We'll stand tall because we have each other.

Because we're not just Knights.

We're *Lucinios*.

The End

Next In The Lucinio Family Series

The devilishly dark and alluring Lucinio Family Series continues with
Fighting My Fate.

I'm Chicago Police Department's problem Lieutenant, and I like it that
way. I lead my own Major Crimes Task Force. My brother is Lucinio
Mafia's fearless King, and my cousin is the leader of the Crane Mafia.

It's only obvious that I'm going to have an authority problem, which I do,
and want to lead things my own way, also what I do. I'm good at my job.
Probably why I still have one.

But that all crashes down when I find out the woman who once possessed
my heart has a dark past that still has its vicious claws in her.

Skyla Winters might just be a friend who became a painful to be around
acquaintance, but I'll never allow her demons to drag her back to the hell
she came from.

Only, Skyla and I have history, and it's not that innocent. I'll do whatever I
need to do to protect her, but I'll be damned if she thinks she'll ever hold
my heart in her hands again.

Order ***Fighting My Fate*** Today!

The Lucinio Family Series

Available Now

Rising From The Ashes
The Player's Rebel
Encrypting My Heart

Other Books By Melony Ann
The Beautiful Dream Series

Available Now

Loving You
My Love, My Heart
Softening Lyric
Undercover Temptations
Captain Charming
Breaking Boundaries
Crashing Into You
Tactical Inferno
Ravishing Our Queen
Cherished By The Texan
Unveiling Our Passions

Box Sets Available

The Beautiful Dream Series: Box Set: Part 1
The Beautiful Dream Series: Box Set: Part 2

The Crane Family Series

Available Now

The Reluctant Mafia King
Sweet Lies
Billion Dollar Love Story
Be Mine
Protecting Her
Dangerously Forbidden Love
His Heart
Love In The Dark

Box Sets Available

The Crane Family Series

The Deimos Trilogy

Available Now

Connor's Legacy
Aryan's Alpha
Kade's Redemption

Box Sets Available

The Deimos Trilogy

The Forbidden Temptation Series

Available Now

The Detective's Forbidden Temptation
The Running Back's Forbidden Temptation

Multi Author Series
Piper Falls: Firehouse 49

Available Now

Ignite My Fire by Melony Ann
Regain My Fire by Kindra White
Playing With My Fire by D.L. Howe
Fight My Fire by Darley Collins
Against My Fire by Anneke Boshoff
Relight My Fire by Louise Murchie
Harness My Fire by Ayana Lisbet
Quench My Fire by Havana Wilder

Let's Be Friends

Follow me on

Bookbub

Facebook

Goodreads

Instagram

Tik Tok

Visit my website
www.melonyannauthor.com

Subscribe to my newsletter and get a FREE never-seen-before NOVELLA
just for subscribers!
https://www.melonyannauthor.com/exclusive-content

Join my Facebook Reader Group!
Jason's and Melony's Sizzling Book Nook

The official Lucinio Family Series Playlist on YouTube
https://youtube.com/playlist?list=PLGEiD5wbQmDdjFYhMKrFsomQOTr
RK7x9Y

Dedication

When life throws curveballs, you help us hit them out of the park.

Acknowledgements

Brad - Loving you is like breathing. It's natural. Beautiful. Necessary. Second nature. I love you always and forever.

Laura - Like the sun rises and sets each and every day, your love and the love of our family is the one constant in my otherwise chaotic life. I love you always and forever.

Jay - When the moon brightens the sky, it's light in an otherwise dark world. Beautiful and full of hope and wonder. Just like you. I love you always and forever.

Ayana - Since the very first moment I started this, you've been there in my corner. All this time later, you still are. I love you.

Anneke - You've inspired me and pushed me to keep going when I really didn't think there was a point. And you still do it to this day. I love you.

Jason - You never let me give up. For that, and so much more, I love you.

To the Bookstagram Community.

To my family.

To all of those who believe in me and support me.

To all of those who don't.

Cover by: Carter Cover Designs

Edited by: Alyssa Skaggs

About Melony Ann

Melony Ann began writing short stories and poetry as a child. She continued honing her craft over the years until she took the plunge and began publishing her work, despite having severe anxiety.

Melony writes contemporary romance stories that are full of suspense and a lot of steam.

When she isn't writing, she is loving her family and working to make her life something she deserves.

Melony believes that if her writing can inspire just one person, then all of her hard work is worth it.

Her hope is that her writing allows each and every one of her readers to escape for a little while. To dive into a different world one book at a time.

www.ingramcontent.com/pod-product-compliance
Lightning Source LLC
Chambersburg PA
CBHW070451260626
47161CB00004B/1273